INFINITE REQUIEM

DOCTOR WHO – THE NEW ADVENTURES

Also available

THE NEW

DOCTOR WHO

ADVENTURES

INFINITE REQUIEM

Daniel Blythe

First published in Great Britain in 1995 by
Doctor Who Books
an imprint of Virgin Publishing Ltd
332 Ladbroke Grove
London W10 5AH

Cover illustration by Barry Jones

ISBN 0 426 20437 9

Typeset by Intype, London

Printed and bound in Great Britain by Cox & Wyman Ltd,
Reading, Berks

for Rachel 'TV' Tilford, who patiently shares me with the world of fiction.

Thanks also to: my ever helpful editors, Rebecca Levene and Peter Darvill-Evans; and to Barry Jones for the cover.

Also to Steve 'n' Julia Goddard for stability vibes.

For some pre-reading of these and other arcane things: Mum & Dad, David Simms and the ursine posse, Julia Thomas, Chenab Mangat, Elliot Smith, Kate Orman, Craig Hinton, Simon Stratton . . . and all who bought *The Dimension Riders*, of course.

Prologue

The Wanderers

We are three.

No, we are one.

No – the She the He the Other. I feel the loss of the He first and then the breaking of the Other.

The splintering, the unimaginable pain, is both now and a distant memory. The same thought is in our Unity, our mind, as it becomes *minds*; something is happening. This is not how it was meant to be. I am conscious of it happening in what might be described as a millisecond, and yet I am allowing these thoughts to carry me through that shaft of time –

To drift, and finally to master our path through this whirl of possibilities, was the choice we took. The choice we made when faced with the unknown, or death, was to become voyagers.

And now it seems we are to die after all.

I feel them slipping away from me.

I am Kelzen.

I am KelzenJirenalShanstra.

Like fragments of flotsam, they are gone and I am alone, and now the reality, the mere three-dimensional, hellish being, is constraining me again.

I am Kelzen.

I am – *falling* –

Part One

A PHOENIX HOUR

The 'Plan' of Nature I detest. Competition, and struggle, the survival of the strongest and of those with the sharpest claws and longest teeth. Life feeding on life with ravenous, merciless hunger – every leaf a battlefield – war everywhere.

Robert Ingersoll (1893)

You cannot step twice into the same river, for other waters, and yet other waters, go ever flowing on.

Heraclitus (6th century BCE)

1

Dreams Burn Down

Gadrell Major Dominion
Common Era 2387

When the final wave of flamers climbed the rise, Captain
Cheynor knew he had to be running or dead.

Silver tanks, like giant woodlice, sparkled in the battle-
fires, living machines lit by the destruction they had
wrought. From across the devastation there was a deep
and animal roar. In the battlefield twilight, a tide of liquid
flame ate up the mud and poured into the city ruins.

They must all have fired at once. He rolled again and
again as the thought kicked in like a stimulant. Monstrous
heat scalded his back and there was a noise – just a
hundred metres from him – of spectacular demolition.

Behind the wall of what had been the government
building, Darius Kieran Cheynor slammed a new cartridge
into his pistol, and faced for the thousandth time his
own bewilderment that he had ever returned to front-line
colonial service.

*And he saw the city, the intact city, laid out before him
to touch, what seemed like an eternity ago.*

*The hologram had glittered in front of Captain Cheynor,
turning on its axis. The general clicked her pointer here
and there on the image, making streets and buildings glint
in relief as if under moonlight.*

The general, her face impassive, had told Cheynor his

Survey Corps experience would be highly valuable in this kind of assignment.

'In any case,' she had said, 'there's talk of harmonizing the Earth-controlled institutions more. Lots of you chaps working with the Office of External Operations. And naturally, the Colonial Office was full of praise for you, Darius.'

Cheynor, who had wondered whether 42 might be late for such a career swerve, had started to feel rather more optimistic. In the six years since taking command of his own ship, the Phoenix, he had come up against ever more situations requiring the logistical skills of a battle commander. In the end, he had realized it was what he was best at, and a transfer to Spacefleet had been forthcoming.

Gadrell Major, a still uncertain colony, had been facing repeated threats due to its uncanny richness in minerals, including especially large deposits of porizium. It seemed the medicinal ore was needed by more than just humans.

And this only got through to the Colonial Office, Cheynor had noted wryly, when the first advance fleet of Phractons had been detected.

'You did a good job,' said the general, 'convincing them we had to go.'

'Yes,' he said. 'I hope it's not too late.'

It was, of course.

'Cheynor to base.'

They had only gone to monitor the situation, having detected vast energy output from the citadel of Banksburgh. Just before all the sensors on board had gone – well, he was still not quite sure what had happened to them. Halfway across the plain, Cheynor's skimmer had encountered the globe of an airborne Phracton unit: shimmering, two metres across, packed with circuitry at the heart of which crouched, like a demon, the cyborg creature itself.

The first blast brought them to a crashing halt on the red dunes, sending up great fountains of sand into the air. Cheynor yelled an order and they scattered.

The Phracton attacker had banked and wheeled before

6

doing the run again. The globe had soared high above them twice, dissecting the skimmer with its fire, and Cheynor glimpsed, within the unit, a blur of the part-organic warrior, shrouded in cables, hunched over its controls.

'Cheynor to base, come in!'

The untranslatable screams of the ether tore themselves out of his radio. On the incline, the flamers thundered onwards, a former apartment block smashing to rubble beneath the combined advance.

And then, at last, salvation. His comlink.

'Darius? What the hell's happening?'

'Horst, I need backup, or I need an immediate vacation. Get me out of here!'

'The importance of Gadrell Major cannot be exaggerated.' Cheynor had heard his own voice echoing in the conference room, and wished he had brought the cooler to pass from one sweaty palm to the other. 'Its mineral wealth is almost as important as its strategic value.' He saw one or two familiar faces exchange knowing glances at that 'almost'. Well, he wasn't going to let Corporation reps get to him.

'The situation is this,' he said, and he folded his hands on the table in front of him. 'That one fleet, two days away from the colony now, is enough to wipe out every settlement.'

'Captain Cheynor?' He nodded respectfully to Veronique Hagen, from the Guild of Adjudicators. Her unblinking eyes, with their glittering points of brightness, met his gaze across the table. 'We are told repeatedly – we were told it just now – that we are free from the tyranny of wars in this period of our expansion.' Hagen raised her voice, and looked around the assembled council. 'And yet one colonial incident after another has reared its ugly head since the Cyberwars – well, since much earlier than that, I don't doubt.' Her voice took on an edge which Cheynor almost tasted, like the coldness of steel. 'You must prove, Trau Cheynor, that this skirmish is any more deserving of attention than the scores of others already under way.'

'Krau Adjudicator,' said Cheynor, raising a hand, 'I have

*seen the holovids of the famine on Tenos Beta. And of the
storms in the Magellani system. All current situations have
been taken into account. We must act to preserve Gadrell
Major, and we must act now.'*

Horst Leibniz scanned the readouts in front of him. He
saw his own face shimmering in the dials, his pale skin
flickering with coloured lights like some alien infection.
His face, although young, was naturally thin and drawn,
as if his skin and bone were made up entirely of crisp
vertical lines. His eyes were red-rimmed and his face was
topped with a brush of spiky white-blond hair.

He manoeuvred the skimmer, a dartlike vehicle with a
strengthened bubble-hatch on top, and brought it in over
the splintered ruins of the citadel.

Leibniz winced. His scans cut through the haze of
smoke below him, revealing the destruction in colour
maps and infrared images. Still standing tall at the centre
of Banksburgh was the library. Its shape was an elongated
pyramid, skewering a globe of black glass at ground level.
Its surface telegraphed the destruction around it. Somehow, this fragile pinnacle of learning had escaped the
bombardments while all around was reduced to rubble.

Any reassurance that Leibniz could gain from this was
shattered by the sight of the rest of the city. The streets,
laid out in the Wheel of Life pattern typical of many
colonial outposts, were burning. The Wheel, Leibniz
thought wildly, the Wheel itself was ablaze.

One of the scans tracked over the ruins of the governor's home, which he understood had been bombed to a
ruin early in the conflict. Now, even the ruins were being
destroyed. A gaping fascia, like a chessboard of soot-black
and hellish red, was all that remained.

He flicked a few controls as he came in over the fringe
zone, and traced Cheynor immediately. The captain had
a clear run towards safety.

The hatch of the skimmer folded behind Darius Cheynor as the Phractons' flamers ate their way into the
chequered Londinium Plaza. Horst Leibniz turned and

8

grinned like a ghoul. Cheynor collapsed into the seat, a man at the end of his strength.

'This is madness,' Leibniz said, the grin intact. 'Nobody will blame us if we don't act sane in dealing with the Phracs.'

Cheynor felt his body aching with exhaustion, with the sudden release of latent terror. He closed his eyes against the rushing landscape. 'They will,' he said. 'That's the problem.'

Rivulets of dust trickled from the roof of the reading hall. Disks lay scattered like dead fish in a polluted river, and consoles were cracked or overturned.

A young woman with quicksilver-glossy hair and a round, intelligent face was stuffing as many of the disks as she could find into a denim haversack, occasionally glancing at her wristwatch. Now and then the building would be rocked by more nearby explosions and more unwanted patterns would etch themselves into the floor and ceiling.

She snapped the haversack shut, looking around with nervous, sharp eyes. They were green and had pupils ringed with a haze of yellowish orange. After satisfying herself with her owlish scan that the coast was as clear as it could be, she swung open the hatch leading down to the stacks, and lowered her athletic body on to the ladder.

She got halfway down before she had a mental picture of those vast underground vaults of information being sealed off forever – with her body slumped and rotting between Ichthyology and Iconography.

Suzi Palsson, Chief Archivist and Librarian of Gadrell Major, bit her lip, weighed the preservation of history against the preservation of her life, and, opting for the latter, ascended the shaft again rapidly.

She hefted the rucksack, zipped her tunic and slipped the protectors over her eyes. At the gallery, Suzi paused, leaning on the rail. As she looked out again at the devastation of what had been Banksburgh, she wondered – and doubted – if the Phractons had ever heard of Alexandria.

9

2

Some Days Are Better Than Others

Bernice Summerfield sometimes wondered how soon it
would be before she became history.

Sometimes, wandering the corridors of the Doctor's
complex, still almost magical TARDIS, she would think
she sensed the ghosts of long-departed friends there in
the dim light of the roundels, transient souls who fluttered
like mayflies through the Doctor's near endless days. She
shuddered at those times, a future echo of what she might
become. And she sometimes wanted to speak to them, to
reach out, and to ask: have you felt what I have felt, have
you seen the same unresolved anguish of the years ahead
and behind?

On such occasions she had the strongest yearnings to
leave the TARDIS, to get the Doctor to open his box of
tricks and places and times once more. For it occasionally
called to Bernice Summerfield, that sense of empty loneli-
ness. It called to her like the vastness between worlds, like
the calm on Heaven before the deaths, like the sound of
distant oceans. It was a kind of subconscious chill that
made her wonder if she had now, inescapably, become a
part of something too great for one human being from
one world. It called her like the sense of an ending.

The lights were dim and Benny was running her hand
along the rows of assorted clothes in the TARDIS wardrobe. In the less-than-perfect mirror, she saw herself, and
sighed heavily.

It was just her now. Alone with the Doctor. With Ace's departure had come an onerous feeling of responsibility.

'What if something goes wrong now?' she said out loud. 'After all we've been through?'

Her fingertips pressed against those of her image. Dark eyes looked into dark eyes. She was stylish but not conspicuous today, in a hand-dyed velvet waistcoat over an aquamarine shirt of raw silk, and ultra-white pleated trousers tucked into high, black buccaneer boots.

'Don't ask me,' said her reflection.

Benny jumped. She stood there aghast, looking at herself. The mirror-Bernice had her hands on her hips and wore a stern expression.

The mirror warped. Her image fell like a cascade of water, and in a second she was looking at the small, white-suited figure of the Doctor. He smiled, beneath the lines of suffering on his impish, alert face. 'I thought I'd surprise you,' he said.

She shook her head, drew breath. 'Maybe I should count myself lucky. You don't normally think first.'

'Oh, really, Benny, you say the kindest things. It's a simple interactive hologram, nothing more.' The rectangular outline of the mirror wobbled, turned into smooth globules like mercury, and became a tiny silver pyramid in the hologram Doctor's hand. 'I've been meaning to give you this for some time, actually,' he said, gazing at the small prism. 'Ace would have had it, but . . .'

'But I'll do.' Bernice folded her arms. 'Do I really need another one of you?'

'Didn't you ever watch broadcasts, and wish you could talk back to them so that they would hear you?'

She shrugged. It was perhaps not the question she had been expecting. 'Well, yes, I suppose so.'

'Now's your chance,' said the Doctor, and coalesced.

Light rushed into the pyramid, giving it a golden aura for a second before it clunked to the floor, leaving no trace of the image. She picked it up. It appeared to be seamless, was cool to the touch like marble, and sat neatly in the palm of her hand.

11

'Something for a rainy day,' said Professor Bernice Summerfield.

That sardonic inner self – the person, perhaps, to whom she addressed her diary in times of stress – was heard to mutter, *What if it snows?*

Sometimes the TARDIS, too, rested. In the dimness of the console room, only the time rotor moved like the breath of sleep, and surprisingly frictionless, unhindered . . .

There are dreams in sleep. If the TARDIS, linked to its owner by symbiotic nuclei, reacted, it was maybe like a flash of knowledge in such a dream. There could have been nothing of significance in the tiniest flicker on one of the console screens. It meant that a signal had come to the attention of the half-slumbering TARDIS.

It might have told the Doctor something, if he had been there. Told him of . . . not danger, exactly; not an intruder, for sure, as he had tightened up on those precautions.

But it might have told him something.

It was gone after an instant, and the TARDIS, silently breathing, travelled on.

A few years ago, when a twenty-three-year-old Suzi Palsson had been appointed assistant archivist on Lightbase, life was good. She was earning a comfortable salary, she had her own apartment, and above all she had met Colm Oswyn.

When the disintegration of her life began, it happened so slowly that she did not notice it at first. One by one, Suzi's assumptions were undermined. Getting away with being five minutes late, and using the office vidphone for her personal calls – these were things which she was sure everyone did, and which she tried tentatively at first, then with more brazen aplomb. But she was being watched. She was being monitored.

Furthermore, she had always been slightly paranoid that Colm, who had been going out with a hypermodel who had thrown him over, still secretly hankered after the goddess's company and was using Suzi as a stop-gap relationship. Her questioning became more persistent. 'If she wanted you back, would you go?' she would demand to know. 'She wouldn't come near me again,' was his stock answer, which effectively avoided the question. The tension became arguments, became violence, even.

Colm left her in the same week that her director of resources called her in for the 'little talk'.

From there, it was downhill all the way.

She shuddered now as the shells bombarded Banksburgh. She clutched her haversack to her chest and relived the subsequent events, almost torturing herself with the bittersweet memory.

First, she had refused to accept it. She had gone to Colm's apartment, high on pills and extreme hunger and lack of sleep –

'Help me!'

– and when he had come to the door she had relished the sight that she must have presented, half dead through his lack of affection, dying because of him. The guilt, the guilt would bring him back to the arms of Suzi Palsson, and once he was back it would be a simple matter of telling him he was right whenever they disagreed, of doing everything to please him, so as to keep him, to keep him at all costs, because –

'Please! Please help me!'

It was a woman's voice, and it jerked Suzi back into the reality of the shattered city.

Crouched in the library foyer, she weighed up her chances. A Phracton flamer was trundling down the middle of the street, its turret sweeping in a full circle. A pile of rags and rubble – she did not like to think what else might be in it – burned with high and strangely beautiful fire in the gutted doorway of a trader's store. The orange rippled in the mirrored surface of the Phracton machine as it soundlessly advanced.

That memory, like a pungent smell. She could have chosen to dive in and save him, but instead she put her sunglasses on and walked away.

13

The cry seemed to be coming from the other side of the street, where a walkway led to Londinium Plaza and the fountain. She checked everything. Her gun, a Raz-33, was taped to the inside of her jacket. The haversack was there, with everything else she'd need, all that had meant anything to her on this backwater planet, all except the disks she could not save. She'd had to leave Solzhenitsyn, Wilkie Collins, and others.

Suzi took a breath, and as an afterthought, tied back her shiny hair with a bootlace. The giant machine was heading into the next block now, and she had a clear run across the shattered street.

She put her head down and slipped out into the chaos of what had been her birthplace.

From a distance, it could have been a giant spar of glassy rock, rising from the plain in a glittering cone, catching the dregs of the light like water. As one approached, the crevices and shadows became portals and docking bays, upthrust spires resolved themselves into weapons and sensors of extraordinary complexity.

The *Phoenix*, a cathedral of inert technology, dominated the plain at the heart of Gadrell Major's paltry stretch of land. It welcomed a tiny skimmer into one of its niches.

Seconds later, Cheynor and Leibniz emerged into the vast auditorium of the docking bay, hurried into the nearest elevator-tube, and were carried down.

Darius Cheynor closed his eyes. He knew it was not really having any beneficial effect, but it always helped him to imagine. Cheynor had done a lot of imagining in the years since becoming a captain. Imagining what might have happened at each point in his life, had he chosen to take a different route.

After various attempts at beards, Cheynor had settled for a raw-looking growth that was little more than black stubble. Behind it, his tanned face, which had once exuded strength, wore lines of tiredness, more than his forty Earth years should have given him. Time, and life, had not been gentle with Darius Cheynor.

In the six years since transferring from the *Icarus* – shortly after that business with the Time Soldiers and the death of his commander – Cheynor had not been able to shake off the idea that he was no great success. True, he had his own ship now, and his own crew, but that had been his first and only tangible achievement.

He came back to reality as the elevator deposited them on the command deck. The ship was bustling with more than its usual level of activity. There was a good reason for this, Cheynor knew.

He left the bridge in the capable hands of Leibniz and headed straight for the briefing room. As expected, the general's head was waiting on the table.

Cheynor nodded respectfully at the stern features which bobbed above the conference table. The holo blow-up was lifelike down to the last pixel – in fact, it was probably rather more accurate than the general would have liked herself, as it picked out in crisp electronic detail the grey-ish mole just above her mouth, and the glistening, taut skin of a dozen wrinkle-jobs.

'Reporting, ma'am.'

'Just get on with it, Cheynor.'

'There is very little of Banksburgh left. Before the sensors went down, we detected from orbit that Kaneston and all the McNab Gorge settlements have been reduced to radioactive ashes. The ground Phractons are using hylerium-plated intrusion vehicles, probably hymetusite-powered, with average 0.34-second reactions. Airborne units are – '

'Cheynor, I didn't ask for a technical lecture. Can we smash the little blobs to hell of not?'

'With respect, Krau General – ' Cheynor took a deep breath. His shoulder was still throbbing from the impact of that fall, although there was no way the general could have known that – 'I don't feel that's quite the question we should be asking,' he ventured.

'Oh?' The general's enormous brow furrowed. 'And what, in your wisdom, Trau Cheynor, is the question we should be asking?'

'There are several. Whether we can locate survivors without any sensor equipment. If we can organize a concerted rescue without endangering further life. That sort of thing. Humanitarian stuff. Boring, I know, but I happen to consider it essential, Ma'am.'

The general had closed her eyes briefly during his speech, and her glittering face had grown a little larger, neither of which was a particularly good sign as far as Captain Cheynor was concerned. 'I assume you have your TechnOps working flat out to repair the damaged sensors?' she asked eventually.

'That's the other problem.' Cheynor's legs were aching and he was longing to sit down. Occasionally, when he had met the general face to face, she had invited him to do so. At the moment, it seemed to rank alongside getting a decent meal in the next three weeks as being one of the things he would be least likely to do. 'We lost most of the instrumentation shortly after landing. The Phracs' virus somehow manages to mimic the structure of our own artificial intelligences, and furthermore it seems to be rigged to embed itself deeper in the systems the more we attempt to extricate it. We're becoming almost totally reliant on manual and analogue operations.'

The general raised her eyebrows. Cheynor got the idea that she had been trying to raise only one. 'It should be good test of your initiative, then, Captain.'

Cheynor had to restrain himself from becoming very irked at that comment. He did so by curling up the toes of his right foot very tightly inside the combat boot. 'Even the drones are not responding,' he told the general acidly. 'We're having to send skimmers out just for information. We can still communicate across land with conventional radio, but it may not be long before they latch on to that, too.'

'All these external channels are still open. You could intercept sub-ether transmissions monitoring the situation.'

Who the hell from? thought Cheynor. We're the ones who are meant to be sending them.

16

'We've thought of that, ma'am. There are no comsats within range of Gadrell Major. I think the Phracs must have taken them all out on initial approach. But Leibniz is looking into launching one.'

What a way to fight, Cheynor thought bitterly. They might as well have been back in the trenches. One of the most advanced warships that Spacefleet could hope to send, and just about every circuit that could tell them anything about what was happening in Banksburgh was dead, or transmitting rubbish, or re-routed to the games room. All thanks to a nice little bit of intrusive electronics from the devious globes of pulp in their attack vehicles.

'Then I hope you will be able to give me a comprehensive report very soon,' said the general.

Cheynor sighed. 'So do I, ma'am,' he answered. 'So do I.'

Livewire was in the kitchen of the shelter, sharpening a piece of flint. She had been sharpening it ever since they had seen that Spacefleet ship land out on the plains, and that was making Trinket very uneasy indeed.

The shelter was full of shadows. It seemed to have been built out of shadows, the little underground apartment with its kitchen and living-room and tiny sleeping-spaces not much bigger than coffins. Occasionally, though, a spark would fly up, a yellow flash in the redness of the shelter's emergency lighting, and Trinket would shiver as he caught sight of Livewire's sharp, sixteen-summer face under its halo of golden hair. He reminded himself at times like this that he had never seen anything so frighteningly beautiful. And then he would turn back to the comfort of his own glitter in the darkness, the multi-level version of ShockWave that he'd salvaged from the wreck of their home. Manipulating his little fighter across the screen with the two thumb buttons. Trying to think about beating his hi-score. Trying to think about anything but the devastation above. Or the girl in the kitchen.

Something came clattering down into the shelter.

17

Trinket jumped, dropping the game on to his foot. But it was only Polymer, coming back from watch.

'You're supposed to call out,' he reprimanded her.

Polymer spat in his general direction. At fourteen, she was a year younger than the boy, but she had the air of knowing more than he possibly ever could, when it was just the two of them around. When Livewire was talking – Livewire, who was older and wiser than the pair of them – then Poly's deference made Trinket sick and angry. But Livewire was not talking. She was, as Trinket had been observing over the past hour, sharpening flint on the kitchen sideboard.

Polymer, the new arrival, was a fat girl with spirals of greasy black hair hanging across her eyes, which tapered at the back to a crew cut and then to nothing. Two chins wobbled beneath a thin and disparaging mouth, but the arms and legs under her stolen fatigues were remarkably muscular and blubber-free, so she always seemed like a square of compacted energy to the boy Trinket. She took a swig from a flask, and dropped, with a wobble of flesh, on to the couch.

Trinket watched with nervous eyes. For a few seconds, the only sounds in the room were satisfied, deep breaths of a thirst sated, and the regular clicking sound that might be produced by, say, a qualified murderer honing her newest weapon. On the kitchen sideboard.

Poly wiped her mouth. 'All hell,' she said simply. Her eyes were dead and bleak behind the forest of fringe.

'The Phracs,' said Trinket. It wasn't a question.

'I saw something else.' Polymer was getting her breath back now.

'Yeah?'

'Someone alive in the library. Think it's the one with the mirror on her head.'

Trinket did not frequent the archives, and frowned as he tried to picture who Polymer could possibly mean.

The truth was that, with the odd gap, he knew the town and pretty much most of the people in it. From a certain perspective. He knew the timing of the governor's meals

18

and what time the scraps came out into the processing bins. He knew the trading stalls that were set up with the dawn, a light still hazy enough to hide a scrawny youth liberating a few gara fruit. Or rather, he had known these things. Trinket had wondered briefly if it were actually possible to forget knowledge, to erase it like a disk file, because now he needed a new world-view. He was just getting used to the new, phantom topography, to the piles of flaming cloth and flesh on most of the streets, to the fact that the governor's residence had been hit in the first air strike and that there was no such thing as order in Banksburgh or anywhere else on Gadrell Major any more.

It should have made things easier. It made them terrifying. They had got anarchy overnight and Trinket had realized it wasn't so great after all. Anarchy, despite the claims of protest songs throughout the ages, had turned out not to be big or clever, but nasty and ugly. (And Trinket understood the singers of those songs well enough to know why they didn't really want to smash the system, because it was the system that provided their holovid royalties, marketed their 'subversive' T-shirts.) No, anarchy shook society like earth in a bowl, so that the big lumps floated naturally on top and the crumbs settled underneath.

The shelter was in the basement of Livewire's family house, and Livewire was a sort of half-sister of his, although it rarely showed. The oldsters had it built during the nukeophobia of ten winters ago, when the continent, in Trinket's eyes, had gone crazy for a year or so, with the Council muttering about limited strikes and mutual deterrents and acceptable casualties. (Trinket reckoned that was what most people saw him as, in general. One of life's acceptable casualties.) And then it had been gradually forgotten. Sealed off with a pneumilock, to which Livewire had appropriated the key. And it had been their unofficial home for months. Now, the Phracs had come. And now, there was nowhere but the shelter to go.

He returned his thoughts to the woman from the library. 'So why are we worried about her?' Trinket tried to sound unconcerned, as if he were above anything that could worry Polymer. As was often the case, the answer made him feel stupid and hotly angry.

'She's got a gun,' said Polymer, and lifted the bottle to her thick-lipped mouth again.

'A gun.' Trinket couldn't think of a clever answer.

Something landed on the table in front of him. It took him a couple of seconds to register the whistling noise and the chunky thud, and then he looked down and saw the sharp piece of flint that was embedded in the table about three centimetres from his hand.

Trinket turned, very slowly, and was conscious of Poly's jowls doing the same.

Livewire uncurled herself from the kitchen doorway, stretching her taut body. Her face – tall and hard, a Grecian statue's visage – wore shadows down one side, like a mask of warpaint.

'The point being,' said her splintered-glass voice, 'that there are three of us, and there's only one of her.'

Suzi, coughing, scrabbled furiously at the wreckage. There were things she could salvage here, cans and flasks that she could use. Automatically, the young archivist rammed a couple of them into her backpack, but her mind was concentrating on the job of clearing the piled rubble and plexiglass. Clearing the pile from under which she had heard a woman's voice.

The hand was the first part of the body to become visible. It was then that Suzi wondered whether there was any point in continuing. It was a cold hand, empty of life, like part of the stone itself. And yet something drove her on, forced her to clear the rest of the rubble.

From outside came the drone of a Phracton air module.

Suzi worked frantically, hurling stone and plaster across the room, and chunk after chunk shattered in the remains of the shelves. An arm became visible, then the whole of the upper body, lightly sprinkled with dust. It was a woman, her face and limbs unnaturally long and thin. Beneath the layer of dust, a pool of rich dark hair, longer

20

and blacker than any hair Suzi had ever seen, spilled like blood across the floor.

She could hear the Phracton module advancing down the street. It had to be homing in on the heat-trace.

Suzi Palsson stood up, dusty and sweaty, and told herself that she was stupid. That she had expended the last energies of her life in uncovering a corpse.

And then the whine of the alien reached its highest pitch, and she turned, confronted it. She saw the translucent ball flickering with unimaginable circuitry, with the shrivelled, indistinct form crouching spider-like at the heart of the machinery. A laser-tube snicked out and pointed at Suzi Palsson.

And the eyes of the dust-coated woman on the floor snapped open wide, burning with a jade-green fire.

Suzi knew it then. They both had to live.

'I imagine,' she said, facing the Phracton directly, 'that your orders are to eliminate me?'

Several frequencies of sound presented themselves in the room. Every second or so they would coalesce into recognizable speech from the translator grille mounted on the front of the Phracton's globe.

'We – des-troy – when threatened. You – will – leave.'

'This woman has been injured. I can't move her alone, but I know a place, a safe place I can take her. Please – we are civilians.' Suzi mentally kicked herself for begging, even in front of this monstrosity, and hardened her voice. 'All I want to do is get off this lousy planet. You can keep it, as far as I'm concerned.'

Deep within the globe, the Phracton communed with its Swarm.

+++Hum-fem-unarm loc 8–7–5–7 param 4+++Stat varies
+++Weap scan +ve Weap primed-ve>>PROP ELIMIN??
+++Centr advise +++Centr advises warn

21

+++Ifno activ aggress>>NO ELIMIN
+++++++
CONSERVE ENERG+++++++NOKILL
UNAGGR

The Phracton seemed agitated. Lights flickered on its surface. Again the grille commanded. 'You – will – leave.' The laser-tube retracted into the globe.

Slowly, unbelievably, the Phracton bobbed backwards, starting to move out of the shattered building.

Suzi wondered whether to let out the breath she had been holding. And then, with the Phracton's shadow still receding, something moved at her feet.

She thought it might be a rat. She jumped. There was a movement of grey and black, a cascade of dust. Faster than Suzi could move or even think, the woman beneath the ruins had sat up, dust streaming from her like water as if repelled by an inner energy. It was only now that Suzi noticed with horrified fascination that the woman's body was naked. And those eyes, those eyes of green, were burning like beacons across the shattered land.

Inside its casing, the Phracton convulsed.

Suzi heard the unnatural, tortured screech from the translation grille an instant before she realized what was happening. The alien's globe-shaped module wobbled, sank like a deflating balloon, the creature within thrashing in agony as if impaled. The module crashed to the dust with a crackle of sparks and a scream. Suzi watched in mounting horror as the globe began to fill with blue droplets which spattered like glutinous rain against its interior. Suddenly it was all over. The globe rolled once with a slight squelching noise, and lay still. The only sound was, once more, the distant gunfire of some small pocket of resistance.

Somehow Suzi tore her eyes away from the wreck and back to the being she had saved. The woman was glistening as if wet. Suzi saw her put her spindly fingers to her temples once, which seemed to make the emerald glow recede from her eyes.

She slumped, as if a terrible weakness had seized her, but still the eyes in the bony face met Suzi's with a level gaze.

The eyes in the almost alien face.

Suzi swallowed once. 'It wasn't going to do us any harm,' she ventured.

The woman did not answer. Her long face seemed to wear an expression of intense agony for a second, like a mere shadow of pain, and then it passed and a smile of serenity settled there.

'You killed it,' Suzi said in horror, pushing her silver fringe from her eyes. The aftermath of terror was rushing through her limbs, searing them with cramp.

I merely induced a conflict. I sent a message persuading the organic cells they were being attacked by the technology with which they harmonized.

The voice, to Suzi Palsson's creeping unease, was inside her head. It soothed, like an ambient lullaby.

This produced a mental breakdown. The creature was dangerous. It had to die.

Somehow, it resolved itself, like one of those pictures of a young woman which is simultaneously an old crone. The thought settled in Suzi's mind and she recalled the Phracton's laser-tube pointing at her. It had been going to kill her. This was a war, surely? No amount of pleading would have dissuaded a hostile from eliminating its prey. The woman had saved them both.

The green eyes smiled at Suzi.

They said: *My name is Shanstra. Take me to your place of safety.*

Bernice found the console room dim and empty. The Doctor's hat and umbrella were hanging on the hatstand. She sighed, pivoted on one heel and wondered where to go and look for him next. As she slipped her hands into the pockets of her waistcoat, her fingers came into contact with the smooth little pyramid again. She took it out, stared at herself in its shiny surface.

How did one activate this kind of thing? There were

no visible switches, not even flaws in the surface that might have been touch-pads. Maybe it had to be rubbed like a magic lantern, and out would pop the enigmatic little genie. Absently, Benny stroked her thumb along the edge of the pyramid.

It lost its form in her hand, sparkling like fireflies, and before she knew what she was doing she had let go of the little pyramid and it was floating on a cloud of light. The cloud resolved itself into the shape of the Doctor. It was immediately obvious that the hologram, although inter-active, did not correspond exactly to the Doctor's current physical being, as the image was leaning on his umbrella and wearing a hat and the Doctor's old, chocolate-brown coat. The realism was perfect, though – were it not for a slight haziness around the edges, it could easily have been the Doctor himself. He was looking around as if puzzled about something.

Bernice cleared her throat, and, although she had expected it, she was still surprised when the hologram's eyes alighted on her as if seeing her for the first time.

'Ah, Benny. Still here, are you?'

'Yes. And it might help matters if I knew where *you* were, don't you think?'

'Mmm.' The Doctor nodded gravely.

'There doesn't seem to be much going on in the console room. I just thought you should know.'

'That's all right. Everything's perfectly in order.' The holo-Doctor – Benny decided mentally she had better start calling it the h-Doctor if they were going to get acquainted – smiled absently at her and began to examine the floor with an expression of intense curiosity, eyes flicking back and forth in that owlish way she knew so well. The mannerisms had been meticulously pro-grammed. 'Tertiary console room,' he said to her. 'Come and find me.' The image started to dissolve.

Benny spread her hands. 'I can't remember – '

'How to get there? No, of course, you weren't there when I last used it.' A neat map of blue lines floated out of the h-Doctor's mouth. 'Think you can memorize that?'

'Well, I suppose so – '

'Good.'

The map became a funnel of light, which rushed downwards towards one single point. The pyramid sat on the floor of the console room, looking as if it were waiting for Bernice to pick it up.

She pocketed it. She closed her eyes and allowed the map to float in front of them again. 'All right, Doctor,' she said to herself, 'let's see what you're playing at.'

25

3

Memory Lane Ahead

England, Earth, 1997

In the grey city, it was drizzling, and Nita was beginning
to wish they had brought an umbrella.

The sky above the city was like stained steel, and the
tower blocks were standing out as if someone had painted
them black. Traffic and people scuttled. Nita, adjusting
her sari, hurried to keep pace with her mother, and
thought now of the City Hall and the colours and sounds
that would be awaiting her. There, too, if she was lucky,
she might meet her future husband.

Parked at a meter in the street outside the City Hall
was a white Volkswagen Polo which Nita recognized. She
knew the occupant, too, but could not acknowledge her.
Nita had sensed her mother's tight-lipped expression without even needing to see it, and lowered her eyes in shame
while they went by the car.

They ascended the steps, passing a large advertising
pillar on their right and an archaic blue police box on
their left.

Deep within the TARDIS, the tertiary console room cast
its bluish light on the Doctor's face.

He was deep in thought, standing at the stone console
with his fingers pressed together in an arch in front of his
closed eyes. His face was even more deeply lined now,

his tousled brown hair was tinged with grey, and despite several weeks of quiet meditation he still felt drained from his last adventure. The TARDIS clicked and hummed quietly as the Doctor remembered.

Ace had gone. That much was certain. It was unlikely that he would ever see her again. It was too soon for him to say exactly what feelings that aroused in him – the last few weeks had been spent in a kind of spiritual and emotional limbo. The Doctor had deliberately cut himself off from most activity, communicating with Bernice only in scribbled notes pinned to roundels. He assumed she would think he was sad, mourning Ace's departure; or maybe she understood him fully, knew that he had been trying to pass through a kind of gateway and make a fresh start? This time, even after all his suffering, the refuge and comfort of regeneration had not been afforded him, and he was beginning to wonder if that natural process would ever happen again. Just how much did his body and mind have to be punished before it could be renewed? The recent wound in his shoulder had not entirely healed, and every time it twinged he was reminded of his past, and all that had built up to this moment. The cycle of events that had brought him into conflict with the Monk again, the subsequent return to exuberant adventuring – the three of them, a fine team – and then . . .

There was no more Ace. There was Bernice Summer-field, a thirtysomething professor of archaeology and life, who would carry the torch of his travelling companions. They trusted each other implicitly; that was good. Perhaps she would leave him soon too.

Or maybe she knew. Maybe she had come closer than any of them to working it out, the sad and haunting truth that the Time Lord had worn ever since Susan left: that he was afraid of dying alone.

His eyes flicked open. He was trying to recall something.

The Doctor had not been idle in his weeks of seclusion, and when he had not been meditating he had been scanning the TARDIS databanks to refresh the gaps in his knowledge. If he was going to begin adventuring again,

27

he wanted to do so with a full complement of useful facts, and even a few useless ones. But had he not come across something that had rung a bell? A name?

His hands came down to rest on the cool blue-grey surface. There had been a sound.

He smiled. They were ready to start again.

A scraping, rumbling noise echoed through the tertiary console room and yellow light tumbled in, almost reluctantly, as if slowed by some special relationship to time in that sepulchral chamber.

A tall silhouette, hands on hips, she stood on the threshold and sniffed. 'H'mm. Early Baroque, with late Gothic hints. I'd hoped for something less obvious.'

It had taken Bernice longer than she had expected to locate the Doctor, and she made a mental note to brush up on her map-reading – which used to be second nature to her – one of these days.

Her first words sounded nonchalant, but could not hide the fact that she was impressed. The tertiary console room looked like a church of technology. Crumbling stone walls were adorned with alternating pilasters on which wisteria had made its home, while above, where the blue-greyness became dark and indistinct, she could make out a ribbed vault with pointed arches, supported by stone squinches at the corners. The elevation was also bound together by a series of clustered colonnettes reaching up into the darkness. The room was cold. At the centre, there was a stone-coloured version of the hexagonal console, behind which stood the Doctor.

He opened his mouth to greet her, but words would not come out. Bernice took this for surprise at first, but then she realized that he had probably not uttered a sound for several weeks.

'There's no need to look quite so shocked,' she said, descending the steps with a smile. 'I live here too, you know.' She shivered, looking around at the strangely time-less carvings and shadows in the room. 'I always thought there might be a cellar. Needs a lick of paint, but we could probably let it out to someone who wasn't too fussy.'

'Hello, Benny,' said the Doctor, and raised his eyebrows. 'Good grief, my throat feels dry.'

Bernice, her superficial flippancy as usual masking deep concern, was watching him intently from the other side of the console. 'You went through a lot back there. How is it? Your shoulder, and everything?'

The Doctor seemed to spring into life, his hands moving over the panels, lighting up coloured displays, revealing hidden monitors. Concealed lights of orange spilled warmth into the chamber, and the feeble illumination revealed the lingering hint of a bruise on the Doctor's face.

He looked up triumphantly. 'I'm perfectly fine,' he said, and he sounded it. 'The TARDIS has just landed.' He peered at a screen. 'I don't think it's a random landing, but I didn't programme any coordinates.' He looked up sharply. 'Did you?'

'Me? Heavens, no. Do anything for a quiet life, me.'

'Hmm.' The Doctor swallowed slightly. The unaccustomed act of speaking was still proving a challenge, Bernice supposed. 'I wonder if she's been trying to tell me something?'

Bernice frowned. 'Like what?'

'I don't know. First I was looking through those log records . . .' He stabbed decisively at a control. 'No use hanging around here. Let's see where we are.'

He hurried up the steps, and Bernice, after a last glance around the unfamiliar room, followed him.

Tilusha Meswani looked in her rear-view mirror.

She saw the pillars of the City Hall façade. She saw multi-coloured and filigreed cholis and saris glittering through the rain as the revellers hastened inside for the Navaratri celebrations. She saw a box, like a dark-blue workman's hut or a strange telephone kiosk, which she was sure had not been there the day before. And she saw her own deep-brown left eye, and the thick fringe that

29

fell across her deep-brown right eye, and a wide, strong mouth which she knew to be hers. A sad mouth.

Sitting inside Tilusha Meswani was a growing life which had no business being there. The life had been made by her and Philip Tarrant. Now she no longer wanted it and she was pretty much indifferent to what Philip Tarrant wanted, but at the same time fearful with the knowledge that he would get his way, again. At the moment, though, she thought, he was probably too far out of his skull to care.

Tilusha's family in effect no longer knew her. Her parents did not much care for Philip Tarrant, and with good reason. He tended to enforce his opinions with well-aimed blows, and to get what he wanted by keeping Tilusha in a more or less constant state of terror. Of course, she wanted to leave him now, but she lived in his flat and had been disowned by her own family, so there was nowhere really for her to go. Furthermore, she had been guarded so protectively by her family for the first eighteen years of her life that now, at twenty-one, she was certain that no one else would want her if she allowed herself to break free from Philip Tarrant. This was an unfortunate conviction, for if Tilusha had only known it, her trim figure and big dark eyes and glossy hair often caught the attention of young men as she walked down the street. Secondly, and more sadly, she had decided that all white boys were probably like Philip Tarrant, and that no Asian boy would want her now that she was so disgraced.

Her only friend was her cousin Nita, who usually met her in secret. When they saw each other out in the city, they usually avoided each other's gaze, as they had done just now. Nita was respected, cherished, in the bosom of her family and off to dance the new year in and see if the stick she held would click with that of an eligible bachelor. It was a life Tilusha had lost.

As if that were not enough, the baby was talking to her.

It had been only a hint, not even a whisper at the back of her mind – more an impression, a conviction that she should do a particular thing. One day she had decided not to go out to the shops, a decision which surprised her, as it did not seem logical, until the heavens opened five minutes later and hail came clattering on to the earth. And she felt that the child had known this, and had somehow conveyed it to her.

The second time, which had convinced her, was when, one Saturday night with the video on, she had been seized with an urge to go into the bedroom and bolt herself in. Tilusha had sat in the dark with her heart thumping for several minutes, and then it happened. Phil. The worst he had ever been. She heard him kick over the table, she heard the splintering of glass and his shouted obscenities, and she sat there shivering in terror as he thumped again and again at the door, calling her bitch and cow and other names. After half an hour it seemed as if the rage had subsided, but Tilusha sat awake till dawn, listening to the city breathe. At first light she opened the door a crack and saw the inert figure on the sofa, his force expended, the chaos of a drunken rage around him. Had she been the first object he encountered on coming in, she would doubtless have served as that night's punchbag. She, and the child within her.

Tilusha sat now at the wheel of Phil's car and thought about what she had to do. She had come to talk to Nita and her family, to see if there was any possibility of refuge, or even just a number she could call. But would Nita thank her for breaching the unspoken protocol, for bringing their friendship into the open at the most public event of the year?

There was no choice. It had to be now, for Phil Tarrant was a man at breaking-point, and Tilusha knew that each day could be the one to bring the fatal blow. He was there now, she knew, down at the Four Pennants, drinking snakebite. There would be no stopping him when he came back, and there was no guarantee that the child was going to help her this time.

Tilusha Meswani took the keys out of the ignition and opened the car door. She stepped out, neat and precise

31

in the kind of clothes she wore to work behind the desk at the Department of Employment – black suit with broad, white lapels and a belt with a gold clasp. She locked the door. Taking a breath of the wet air, she let the fine raindrops needle her skin.

The baby kicked.

Tilusha, shocked, stood rooted to the spot for a full minute, allowing the rain to soak her jacket. Inside her. It was there inside her, this thing that was half Phil, and it was watching her.

She shuddered. There were no more signs of movement. She took another deep breath and stepped towards the City Hall.

The Doctor, standing by the TARDIS, sniffed the air. Fossil fuels: always one of the first smells he noticed on late twentieth-century Earth. Shops and high grey buildings faced him on the other side of the street – the bustling front of a Mothercare, a loudly throbbing Our Price, the gaudy blue and yellow of an Employment Service. Cars came and went constantly. Most of the people hurrying by did not pay him any attention, and he was not over-concerned with them, either – except for the tall, beautiful and sad-looking Indian woman who was getting out of a white car about fifty yards from the TARDIS.

The Doctor checked his temporal disruption monitor. It had come in useful in London in 1976, and he occasionally used it now.

There were some very odd readings on the dial.

The Doctor looked up. He frowned at the figure of the woman as she ascended the steps of the City Hall. Maybe the TARDIS had brought him here for a purpose.

'You are going to regret that, son. You're going to regret it a great deal.'

When a table and chair crashed to the floor of the Four Pennants, several people were already grabbing their coats and leaving.

Barry was indeed beginning to regret what he'd just

32

said to Phil Tarrant. He forgot how it had begun – the usual round of disparaging remarks about choice of partners, he supposed. And now, he was pinned up against the trivia machine with Phil Tarrant's rancid breath in his face and Phil Tarrant's sinewy hands round his collar as a result of having made a little joke. A little comment about Tilusha having a bit of fun when Phil wasn't around.

'Have you ever had your nose broken?' Phil's square, thuggish face was distorted, like squashed plasticine. 'I kind of believe in giving people new experiences, like.'

Only, of course, Barry realized as his alcohol-addled brain worked overtime and his bowels slowly loosened, it hadn't just been that little joke; he'd gone a bit too far and suggested that Tilusha might have achieved her condition from another source. And that had been rather too much for Phil Tarrant. Barry cursed his stupidity. His adversary was a renowned one. Nervy, squat and muscular Phil, with his firm white teeth, cropped hair and black eyebrows that met in the middle, had vented his spleen on others before, in ways that had required extra cleaning staff to be called in the next day.

'Hey. None of that here.' The landlord's hand was strong and firm on Phil's shoulder.

He dropped Barry, who slid gratefully against the wall. Phil squared up to the burly landlord, before relaxing his gritted-teeth expression.

'Why don't you go home, Phil?' the landlord suggested.

'Yeah,' Phil muttered, casting a spiteful glance in Barry's direction once more. 'Reckon I just might. Don't really care for the company round here any more.'

He turned on his heel and slammed out of the pub. The door swung to and fro several times after his departure, and several audible breaths were released.

Barry got to his feet, rubbing his neck. He didn't like to think what the poor bint had coming to her now. Still, he thought with considerable relief, at least it wasn't him.

The Doctor strode into the main console room of the TARDIS, put his hat down on the time rotor and plugged the temporal disruption monitor into its socket on the console.

Bernice watched, intrigued. 'Any more thoughts?' she asked tentatively.

'Plenty.' The Doctor nodded, and pointed to the monitor screen, where the view outside was clearly displayed. 'That white car there, it's a Polo. I want you to get the number.' He put his hat back on, nodded to himself and headed for the door again. He stopped, just before the door, and gave Benny a reassuring smile. 'If you wouldn't mind, that is.'

She spread her hands. 'It'll pass the time, I suppose. Are you turning into some kind of intergalactic traffic warden now?'

'No, I leave that to the Time Lords. Meet you in the park in ten minutes.' And he was gone.

'The park,' she said. 'Right.'

Benny hoped that the Doctor wasn't in one of those moods where he left all the explaining until after the event. She liked to know whom she was fighting and why, especially these days.

She took her notebook and a pencil from her waistcoat pocket. 'Car numbers,' she said despairingly, addressing her remarks to the TARDIS roundels. 'He'll be asking me to go train-spotting with him next.'

It was difficult for Nita Bedi to persuade her mother, who was after all her chaperone and guardian, to let her have five minutes to talk to Tilusha Meswani. As far as Mrs Bedi was concerned, the girl had disgraced the entire family and should never be seen again. Nita, though, was a kindlier soul and more inclined to believe in redemption.

She had to look twice around the marble lobby, not realizing at first that the smart young woman sitting by the potted plants was her cousin. They exchanged smiles, squeezed hands, but then an unspoken sadness passed between them and Nita let her grip weaken, awkwardly.

'You won't be able to come to the dance. They won't welcome you, Tilusha.'

The older girl was visibly angry. 'You think I don't know that?' Her voice echoed around the vast lobby, and she lowered it slightly. 'Nita, I know everyone's against me. But the only way I can get myself free of him is if someone will help me.'

'No,' Nita said quietly. 'First you need to help yourself. First you need to *want* to be free of him. Not to keep going back like you have done before.'

Tilusha raised her eyes. 'Are you going to help me?'

Nita looked away awkwardly. She paced up and down, a brilliant splash of blue and yellow silk against the white-ness. When she looked back at her older cousin it was with a coolness that belied her youth. 'Your parents did the right thing. He's not a good man for you. You should know that – '

'You're just prejudiced. You just don't like him because he's from a different background.'

'No!' Nita's voice surprised them both. 'I don't know how you can dare to say that. I – yes, all right, I can't stand Phil, and you know why? Because he enjoys hurting you, Tilusha. He treats you like a little plaything. And I can't bear to see that happening!' There was silence in the lobby for a moment. 'I've got to go,' Nita said quietly, and turned back towards the staircase.

'Hope you find someone there.' Tilusha's voice was resigned, hoarse, the voice of bitter experience.

The irony – the mockery, even – was not lost on Nita. She hurried up the stairs without looking back.

The sounds of Indian music and laughter rippled down the stairs towards Tilusha. She did not need to go in. She knew what she would see: shy young men, eager and colourfully dressed young women, all from a life she had left behind. And for what?

She turned around, headed back towards the exit.

There was a little man in a crumpled cream-coloured suit reading the notice-board. He raised his hat to her as she went past.

35

Tilusha Meswani frowned, wondering if she should know the man, and where she had met him before.

She stopped in her tracks.

She felt a tingling in her spine.

She let go of her handbag and it hit the floor, scattering the contents: coins, lipstick, a bus timetable.

She dropped to her knees, with her mouth wrenched open and her hands across her stomach.

Mouth open. Hands across stomach.

Dimly aware of the little man turning, as if in slow motion, and running to her side. And she screamed.

And screamed and screamed.

Bernice looked at her watch.

She sighed, shifted position on the wooden park bench. At least it had stopped raining, but that didn't make the city any more attractive. The park was a hopeful sign, but it still looked as if its visitors were not familiar with the concept of the litter bin, and seemed somehow to be an afterthought. A lake, little more than a large pond, was home to a few optimistic ducks. The trees' leaves were green, but they sat in the shadow of two huge blocks of flats.

Bernice allowed her eye to wander over the buildings. She saw balconies brimming with washing, the occasional satellite dish thrusting up into the sky, looking for bright fantasies to colour the dreary world, to break out from the neighbours above and the neighbours below and the neighbours to every side. Looking for the stars, where there were no dogs and no acrimonious disputes and no corners smelling of urine. Bernice knew her twentieth-century social history, and there were many colonial buildings of her own time which were not too dissimilar.

'Sorry to keep you waiting.'

He seemed to have appeared on the bench with no sound or warning. The Doctor, still looking vaguely absent, unsettled. Benny knew that look.

'I got the number,' she said. 'Is everything all right?'

'No,' said the Doctor. 'Things are very bad.'

'Nothing new. Why are we here?' No answer. 'Doctor, I'll give you your car number in exchange for an explanation about why exactly you want it and what we're doing here.'

Solemnly, the Doctor produced a paper bag full of stale fragments of bread. 'Feeding the ducks,' he said, and passed the bag to Benny.

4

Don't Need No Thought Control

Far across time and space, dusk was falling in the citadel
of Banksburgh on Gadrell Major.

The sky was patterned by searchlights, whirling as if on
an infernal dance floor. Buildings burned. The silver tanks
of the Phracton flamers coursed the alleyways through
the destruction.

Suzi Palsson had worked something out about the
flamers, something pretty important. Anything that got in
their way was destroyed. Everything else was ignored.
And so getting the woman who called herself Shanstra to
somewhere safe had not proved that arduous.

They moved swiftly in the gathering darkness, Shanstra
swathed in a fake velvet cloak which Suzi had looted from
the nearest boutique. The woman seemed to understand
and accept the need for haste and silence. Suzi had taken
them through the backstreets, into Corporation Boulevard
with its stagnant fountains.

Suzi, a former member of the Banksburgh Women's
gravball team, was equipped with a pass key for the sports
centre, and so getting into the foyer had not been a problem. Inside, the key let them move around with surprising
freedom. One glass door had not yielded, and so Suzi had
kicked it in with unaccustomed verve. They had found
themselves a plush, abandoned office for refuge.

Suzi, settling herself on the mahogany desk, saw only
now how impressive Shanstra was. She had to be two

metres tall, possibly more. Her mane of hair was so dark it seemed to repel light, and the face it framed was somehow beautiful and hideous at the same time. It was high-boned and oval, but too long to be comfortably attractive, while the nose was little more than a fold of skin with two holes in it. The most beautiful thing about Shanstra was her mouth. It looked as if it could encompass every language, every action a mouth was required for. The lips were full and shone like the skins of nectarines, unblemished. It was like a clownish stripe of red across the bottom of her face, a larger-than-life advert for some wonder product. Suzi could not take her eyes from Shanstra's mouth.

The woman was looking around like a blind person who had just regained the power of sight, stroking the air with her hands and looking unblinkingly at every detail.

'This is your . . . residence?'

She had spoken. Not inside Suzi's head this time, but in the real world. It was a voice like burgundy, deep and rich and satisfying.

Suzi could not help laughing. 'My what?' She pointed to the window behind the desk. 'I had an apartment in the third precinct, on Argolis Avenue. It's a pile of dust now, I expect. I tell you something, I'm not going back there to find out.'

She untaped the gun from inside her jacket, then dumped both gun and jacket on the desk with her backpack. All she had in the world. She scowled.

Suzi approached Shanstra carefully, afraid of finding some electrical aura around her. She remembered how the dust and rubble had slid from that nakedness, leaving not a trace behind.

Shanstra loomed over her. She looked down, as if inviting Suzi to speak.

Suzi said, 'You used your voice.' It sounded feeble. There were a hundred and one things she was dying to ask this woman and –

You would prefer mental communion?

It was a surprise, and made Suzi take a step backwards. 'No,' she said. 'I mean, yes, but – ' She was sweating.

She decided that she would very much like a drink, and sidled over to the wall lockers to see if she could find anything.

There is no need to be frightened of me, Suzi. I am grateful. You are my friend. I found myself in a strange land, weak, my powers latent. And you helped me.

Suzi had found an unopened bottle of whisky that looked like the real stuff from Earth. She looked at the label, and saw that it was fifty-year-old Laphroaig. She smiled. 'Yes. You see, I think I'm still pretty shell-shocked. That's my world out there, Shanstra. And I don't know where you come from, but I don't think it's this world, is it?'

Shanstra's mouth performed a grimace – or was it a beautiful smile? – that made Suzi blush. *Think it, child. I'll hear you.*

Suzi unscrewed the top of the bottle and drank a much-needed gulp. She slammed the bottle down. 'You mean – I'm telepathic too?'

If that is what you choose to call it. The term is not one I use, but there are latent forces in all the early races, yes.

What did she mean 'the early races'? Without realizing it, she had done as Shanstra bade her. A thought, lobbed between the beautiful-ugly woman's eyes. And it had hit home.

You, said Shanstra, caressing her mind. *I am talking about you.*

Suzi swallowed, and the physical world seemed to drift, to take on a secondary importance. It was as if she had always known it to be a palimpsest, a perception.

Fascinating to find a highly developed sensitivity in such a primitive race. Shanstra's hand was against her cheek, she could feel that much. *Oh, you are a myriad. A myriad, child! There are race memories, thoughts of violence, of a strong, all-pervading emotion that calls itself –*

For the first time, Shanstra frowned visibly, the pleats of skin like knife-cuts on her giant forehead. Then her brow brightened, and her eyes were burning with green again as they met Suzi's. *It calls itself guilt.*

The mental exploration ceased. Suzi felt her body shot through with weakness, as if she had been retching with nausea. The room blurred. She tried to focus on Shanstra, and was rewarded with a pounding headache.

Shanstra spoke. 'A very human trait, this guilt, so far as I can perceive. Attaching moral tags to actions, and then regretting them later.'

'Nothing can be that simple. I don't think you know what you mean. You don't understand humans.' Suzi, wary now, staggered to the desk and slumped into the padded chair. Her mercury-coloured hair was clustered in damp strands in front of her eyes. She pushed it out of the way. She saw the gun on the desk, and Shanstra beyond it.

Thoughts crowded Suzi's tired mind. She had not forgotten the way Shanstra had dealt with the Phracton unit. The Phracton unit which had been going to . . . attack her?

There was something very unsettling about the way Shanstra ignored the gun – no, was *indifferent* to it, as one would be to a cup or a waste-bin.

Suzi tried to adjust to the strange events that had overtaken her. Outside, darkness had fallen. Banksburgh flickered with flame below them, and an uncertain future awaited it. She could not shake the eerie conviction that its future had something to do with Shanstra.

'Have you ever felt any guilt yourself?' asked Suzi softly.

'No, child.' Shanstra smiled. Her face glowed with the orange light of destruction from outside. 'Let me feel it now.'

And Suzi, who understood, almost without thinking, what she had to do, opened up her mind.

Shanstra's thoughts reached into her.

Trinket was beginning to have doubts again.

It had all been very well in the bunker, and Livewire had a persuasive attitude, to say the least. But surely there had to be easier ways of getting a gun?

The tube-cars were still operational; that had surprised even Livewire. Poly had done something to the electrics and they'd got one of the sleek, bullet-shaped carriages

41

back on line. The stations were all eerily still, so quiet they could hear the lights buzzing. Trinket's mouth was dry and tasted foul to him as they hopped off the line at Corporation Plaza.

They saw no one as they rode the escalators, silent and watchful. Trinket was hot, but shivering too.

As they reached the top, Livewire's boot took out the sensor-pads of the computerized barriers in a shower of black glass. There was no need. Everything was inert. They vaulted over the barriers into the ticket hall. A couple of scavengers were there, rooting in the food stores, but they turned and ran when they saw Livewire. Trinket wasn't surprised. Her hard, cold face was bad enough at the best of times, but now that she was dressed in her father's old combat gear, with her crossbow at the ready, she looked ready to take on anyone and anything. Trinket didn't want to know what was going on in Livewire's mind.

Their booted feet echoed in the ticket office, shadows bouncing off the concrete.

Livewire turned sharply at the station entrance, making Trinket and Poly stop in their tracks. 'If this woman won't give us what we want,' she said quietly, 'what do we do?' Her eyes, behind green-tinted goggles, flicked back and forth.

Trinket wondered if this was to be one of those clever questions Livewire asked, where only she knew the answer and she enjoyed watching the others hopelessly trying to get it. Trinket glanced at his other companion. He saw Polymer's chins wobbling, and as he watched she picked a spot absently from behind her ear, leaving a green trail of pus down her neck.

Livewire smiled. 'She's dead meat. Right?'

'Right,' said Trinket a little too quickly, and went pale as he felt his legs shaking beneath him.

'Right,' Poly attested. She sounded bored.

Trinket saw Livewire, his loved and hated half-sister, lower her goggled eyes till they were on a level with his. 'Listen. Trust me. The streets are full of Phracs. Everything's ruined, there's hardly any people here now. Those that could get away did. The only ones left are the total losers, and those who've stayed around to get the benefits. Us.'

'Benefits?' Polymer asked.

'Yes!' The older girl turned sharply to her. 'There aren't any rules any more. No one to say you have to be back by a certain time. No one to tell you that you can't steal and you can't kill. We are exploring the possibilities of being human.' She looked from one to the other. Trinket tried not to look as dubious as he felt. He was thinking about lumps and crumbs in a bowl. 'Just what is it that you want to do?' Livewire said quietly.

It was an incantation, its origins lost in time, and they knew the correct response. 'We want to be free,' Trinket and Polymer answered in unison. 'We want to be free to do what we want to do.'

'All the way, babies. Let's go.' Livewire primed her crossbow and led the way up the stairs.

The lights were dim in the observation gallery of the *Phoenix*. On the walkway, a lone figure stood, his head slightly raised, his hands clasped behind his back. The guards stationed at either end of the spindly metal walkway had their backs respectfully turned to him. This was a regular occurrence. The captain was here, and he was thinking.

Cheynor knew he had not been sent here to Gadrell Major expressly to fight the Phractons. But he was here to protect the interests of Earth's off-world citizens. Although the major evacuation had already been effected – with hundreds of thousands of civilians now transferred to the orbital platform and awaiting the arrival of the relief ship *Darwin* – Cheynor knew there were still isolated groups hiding out in Banksburgh and the other, smaller settlements, existing on looted goods, some without water or electricity.

He felt responsible. But what could he do? Three units had tried and failed to break the Phractons' hold on the city. He had the idea that the general already saw Banks-burgh and its remaining inhabitants as acceptable casualties.

The *Phoenix* was safe for the moment, up here in the wastelands, but despite everything they knew about the Phractons, there was still no way of monitoring them, no way of telling what they might choose to do next.

He knew they existed as separate entities, and each had a conscience and a will like a human soldier. Phractons, as hard as it was for some humans to understand, formed attachments and loyalties. If you shot a Phracton, it wasn't like killing a Dalek or a Cyberman. Phractons screamed. They suffered. They were mourned by their Swarm-brothers.

He knew as much as any human about the Swarm, which was not all that much. A Phracton brain, as well as being linked to its own personal computer, formed a cell of a greater entity, constantly absorbing and assessing information, acting on that information and sending new instructions. They worked faster than any interactive software devices so far developed by the human race. Cheynor felt angered and depressed that the Phractons were their enemies. He had often contemplated the possibility that the two races could teach one another a great deal.

But for now, they were the hostiles. Because they wanted the porizium from a desolate rock with a few paltry settlements. A mineral supply which, in truth, was probably almost exhausted anyway.

He was keeping in the back of his mind the thought that the *Phoenix* was not invulnerable. And if the Phractons had not attacked yet, the reason was quite likely to be that they had not yet chosen to.

How much did they want Gadrell Major? They wanted it more than Darius Cheynor did, that much was certain.

He lowered his eyes from the night sky. He had realized again that he was fighting a battle he didn't really believe in. Cheynor, whose own personal tragedies still weighed heavily on his heart, had known this for a long time. He

44

wanted to save human lives, not count bodies in the name of colonialism. But it was colonialism that paid his salary.

Cheynor sighed deeply, realizing again that, however well he did, it probably wouldn't be good enough for the Earth authorities.

He turned abruptly and strode along the walkway.

'Call Leibniz,' he snapped at the guard. 'Tell him I'm on my way.'

The web shimmered against a blue-blackness, each of its luminous strands carrying more information than any human could process in a lifetime. At its heart, coloured sparks crackled and chased each other's tails like playful dragons, forming a constantly shifting enclosure around a translucent globe. And in the globe sat the enormous Phracton Commandant.

He had a name, but sixteen of its required inflexions used communicative means and organs undeveloped by any other race. Commandant, therefore, was the title he always used in dealings with other races; the translation machines had no trouble with that.

He was the nerve-centre of the Phracton base. From outside, one would have seen the stars and spindles of data being diffused at his globe, unscrambled in the interface, absorbed. It would have been difficult to make out the Commandant's actual form; it was indistinct as that of any Phracton. There was a hint perhaps of a flat, wedge-shaped cranium, moving back and forth, and several extrusions that could have been twitching limbs. They could also just as easily have been electrical cables.

The Commandant had arrived to take personal charge of the situation on Gadrell Major, which up until now had been controlled by his Secondary, catalogued as Phracton 4Z-88*. The Commandant was appalled at the unnecessary destruction that had been wrought upon the planet. His experience told him that the citadels of the humans could have been taken and held much more cleanly, and in much less time, too.

He had immediately given instructions that no human

was to be harmed unless it directly threatened the life of a member of the Swarm. The Secondary had chosen to interpret these orders very liberally indeed, and the Commandant, in accordance with his rank and powers, had been forced to place inhibitors in the Secondary's neural software. He sensed them now, straining at the borders of the communal mind, gnawing at him. The Secondary was begging again and again to be given a free hand to wipe the humans from what was rightfully Phracton soil.

The Commandant's responding impulses were stern. The soil of Gadrell Major did not belong to the Phractons, he reminded the Secondary; they merely needed the porizium for the ailing members of their race. The same substance had once been needed by humans, to render them immune to a plague, but now they were merely protecting their colony.

Secondly, he enforced the reminder that the Phracton Swarm was not a butchering horde. The race had a long and noble history of fighting according to a code of conduct, and only a life-form which actively threatened the Phracton Swarm was an enemy. Anything else was to be treated with clemency.

The Secondary sent a vituperative, spitting retort through the web. It was felt by Phractons at the extremes of Banksburgh, and one or two flamers swerved from their true course as a result of it.

Bristling with indignant frustration, the Commandant considered his position. He was wondering if humans fought amongst one another with anything like such virulence.

The Doctor contemplated his latest puzzle, watching the water ripple as Bernice idly tossed bread to the ducks.

Overhead, black clouds were gathering.

He had not immediately gone to the aid of the woman when she had fallen to her knees and screamed in the lobby of the City Hall. Her belongings had scattered over the space between the two of them, and a diary with a name on it had skidded almost to his foot. It was not

46

a name he knew, but he had made a mental note of it. Obviously. And he had looked around, whirling a full circle, holding his umbrella up like some protective talisman. The Doctor did not always think of the immediate problem. He saw deeper, and further.

Nevertheless, he had been at her side in just a couple of seconds. She was breathing with difficulty and clutching her chest, but she was able to look up at him and meet his gaze.

'You're troubled,' whispered the Doctor. He had one hand on her perspiring brow while the other held his temporal disruption monitor, which, as he expected, was having something approaching an overload.

'The baby,' the girl had said. 'Talking to me.'

'Of course it is. I understand.' The Doctor put an arm round the girl's shoulders as she rocked back and forth. Slowly, the effect of the trauma, or whatever it had been, seemed to wear off. He helped the girl to her feet, made sure she could walk.

'Remember me,' the Doctor had said, sternly, and had left for his next appointment. With Bernice and some ducks.

And now, he was wishing he had not let the girl disappear so quickly.

'I want you to find someone for me, Benny,' said the Doctor. 'A girl cast out by her own people – she's our key. She's why the TARDIS brought us here.'

Bernice turned around. Her fringe was over her eyes, but she looked worried. 'What are you going to do?'

'I'm going to find out who owns that car. You go to the City Hall and make inquiries about a girl called Tilusha.'

She nodded, then crumpled the empty bag and threw it into the nearby bin. 'Doctor,' she said, placing one booted foot on the bench, 'is this going to be something important?'

'Yes,' he answered. 'Very.'

'Ah.' There was another silence between them. Behind and to all sides, distantly, the city purred. Nearer, the ducks squabbled and splashed. 'Just us again,' said Bernice eventually. 'Kind of funny, isn't it?'

'Not really,' said the Doctor.

'I mean, now she's gone, who do we send in first when things look nasty?' Bernice leaned down, waved a hand in front of the Doctor's face. She shrugged apologetically to the ducks. 'Hmmm. Not a smile. Not a flicker.'

The Doctor stood up, hooked his umbrella into the crook of his arm and straightened his hat. 'It's not a question I'd considered until now,' he said, and his face was creased with concern. 'Back here,' he added as he strolled away, 'in an hour.'

Tilusha was not going to take Phil's car back.

It was irrational, she knew, but if she was going to break from him then that first act of defiance had to be something irrational. She would take the bus back, pack up what she needed and get out.

She hurried along the street, with an even pace, caring not for the puddles she walked in, nor for the people who had to dodge out of her way. She was confused by that pain, and that strange little man, and . . .

Once again, it seemed that she was propelled by something independent of her, yet part of her, a force simultaneously external and internal.

Deep in the back of her mind, where the unfathomable grasped and danced with the forgotten, laughter was echoing.

Laughter was echoing.

Suzi Palsson swallowed. Her mouth tasted of salt and old sleep and its own flesh. She opened her eyes into near-darkness, and saw Shanstra poised, catlike, watching her. Or rather, she saw the silhouette of Shanstra in the dimness of the office, and a pair of burning green lights that could perhaps, in one of her worst nightmares, have been humanoid eyes.

Suzi tried to move her head, and realized she felt strangely lethargic.

48

Laughter.

In her head.

Don't worry, child, said the voice of Shanstra from somewhere amidst the flotsam of Suzi's memories. *This is only the beginning.*

5

Damaged

'Here we are,' said the Doctor with satisfaction. 'That's what I was looking for.'

The technician stroked his beard rather worriedly. 'Are you . . . quite sure you should be accessing that particular gateway?'

'No,' said the Doctor with a brief smile. 'But I've done it now, so it's best not to make a fuss.'

Terry, the technician on duty in the computing centre of the university, was beginning to have second thoughts about the little man he had allowed to log on to the network. He was sure that the chap had shown him some kind of identification, but he could not actually remember what it had been – that part of the last ten minutes was worryingly hazy. Terry, pretending to be busy fixing the jammed printer, had observed the guest: there he had been, sitting calmly among the students at his terminal, occasionally muttering to himself, and swivelling on his chair. And now it looked as if he had managed, from guest protocol only, to enter something that looked worryingly like police motoring records.

The man scribbled down a name and address on a piece of paper and tucked the paper into the top pocket of his jacket. Then his fingers stabbed at a few keys, he clicked twice on the mouse and the screen was back to the usual prompt, with no evidence of the illicit activity.

Terry moved to his shoulder. 'Listen, um – '

'You have a problem?'

Terry tried to meet the strange little man's gaze, but it proved tricky. His eyes were always darting this way and that, and at least one of his expressions seemed designed to make you feel as if there were something big and nasty creeping up behind you. 'No,' Terry said. He spread his hands and smiled. 'No problem at all.'

'Good,' said the little man, and he managed, somehow to make that one word sound threatening and reassuring at the same time.

Terry blinked as if something very bright had been shone into his face. When he opened his eyes, the man had gone.

Outside, it was still raining, and the town was sheened with a cold and slippery layer. The Doctor opened his umbrella and set off, stony-faced, for his destination.

He hoped, as he often did in circumstances such as these, that he was not going to be too late.

Nita was not sure what to make of the chic, dark-haired woman who had collared her in the ladies' room and asked about Tilusha. Nita, though, was perceptive, and somehow she managed to grasp that something very bad was going to happen to Tilusha if they did not get to her soon.

'Do you have a car?' asked the woman, who had introduced herself as Bernice.

Nita, rummaging in her clutch-bag, grimaced. 'I should be so lucky. Listen, what do you know about Tilusha?'

Bernice shrugged. 'Someone I travel with seems to know something's up with her. That's all.'

Nita faced Bernice. The younger woman's brown eyes opened wide, looking at, or even through, her new acquaintance.

'All right,' she said. 'I believe you. It's something to do with that baby, isn't it?'

The odour of people was disagreeable to Tilusha Meswani. As she clutched the slippery strap that was holding her in

51

place on the bus, she closed her eyes, swallowed and wondered how much longer she could hang on without fainting. There was something particularly offensive about sweat, even more so than other bodily odours. She supposed it was the pungency of it, the way it stabbed her olfactory system in a way that could not be ignored, awakening all the unwashed and unhygienic images she could think of in her mind.

The bus was long and had a concertina section in the middle, which, as far as Tilusha was concerned, made it worse going round corners. She clutched her strap and winced as another sharp turn pulled at her arm.

There was an old man on the seat next to where Tilusha stood, and he was nodding feverishly. She would have been just about able to cope with it if he had been nodding in harmony with the juddering bus. He looked up at her. She saw his eyes like shiny egg-whites, his shrivelled, prunelike skin, and the smile that telegraphed despair hidden behind its showcased gold tooth. Tilusha flinched. The bus chose that moment to jolt, and she came closer than was comfortable to the leather-jacketed youth behind her. He gave her a hard stare. She took a breath of the stale air and longed for release.

The bus was ascending to the edge of the city. It slowed to pass a parked lorry, and just before it started up again, Tilusha happened to look through the tiny portion of smeared and spattered window that she could see. Hurrying along the pavement was the little man in the white suit and the paisley scarf. Tilusha felt her heartbeat quickening, and then, before she could even see it coming this time, the nausea again, the feeling that there was something taking over her body and she did not have the power to prevent it.

Tilusha closed her eyes and hung on grimly.

Where was he hurrying to, the little stranger who had said, 'Remember me'? And why did she suddenly have an overpowering urge to grab the toothless old man by the throat and demand to be told all of his secrets?

Tilusha lurched forward. The bus was approaching her

block of flats. Somehow, her thumb came firmly into contact with the request stop button.

Suzi Palsson shivered as she stood among the orange seats of a huge ice auditorium. It was still and abandoned, like the rest of the Banksburgh sports centre where she and Shanstra had taken refuge, and its vastness, together with the biting chill of the air, made it seem like a vault of ghosts. High above her, girders meshed around a plexiglass circle revealing the night sky. Inert vidscreens, dull and black, were clustered around the edges of the rink like watchful sentries.

Shanstra, wearing nothing on her feet, had walked out on to the ice and now stood at the centre, marvelling at its construction. She turned, her dark cloak rippling, and smiled at Suzi across the whiteness. 'All this is ours,' she said in her intoxicating voice. 'It seems to be no one else's home.'

The alien woman's tones echoed through the auditorium. Suzi shivered, zipped her jacket up a little further, and decided that she felt even more horribly alone.

Shanstra threw back her head and laughed. The peals of rich, dark laughter ascended to the girders of the roof, whispered around the seats of the auditorium. She strode forward on the ice, her hair unnaturally black, her eyes the green of gemstones from a spectral mine. *You have no fears*, said her internal voice to Suzi. *Do you not know yet what I can give you?*

Suzi, uncertain, sat down.

Shanstra seemed to glide to the edge of the ice, and the night, with all of its beauty and horror, was in her hair and voice. She reached out a spindly hand and plucked the locket from Suzi Palsson's neck. Suzi, reacting quickly, reached for it, but she was pacified by the kindness and warmth in Shanstra's eyes.

Calm, child. Let me tell you what I see. And I will share it with you.

The memories contained in the locket, the history it had floated through: Suzi now knew that all of this was rushing into Shanstra by some sort of induction. Slowly the wounds opened once more, and scenes from Suzi Palsson's life were splashed across her conscious mind in the most vivid 3-D colour.

She closed her eyes, and saw what Shanstra was seeing.

Every vidscreen in the arena sprang into flickering life. Colours slowly resolved themselves, and Suzi saw the screens growing, pictures billowing out of their frames and into her mind.

Centre stage was the locket. It was held in the hand of a tall young man with ruffled dark hair and a slightly concerned expression. Despite his relative youth he had a greying fringe, and his eyes smiled from creased hollows. He was talking to Suzi.

'Colm,' she whispered.

It was as if the ice-rink had darkened and become a blue-lit auditorium where her life was to be re-enacted.

'I can't change anything, Suzi.'

The image spoke. It *spoke* to her. Shanstra was there, watching, although her eyes were closed. Suzi felt their minds touch.

The image of Colm Oswyn, whom Suzi had loved, moved closer to her, shaking his head. 'I can't change the way I feel. It's not something I have any control over.'

Suzi wanted to scream at him, to tell him that she had managed to convince herself that she loved him, to trick her feelings, simply by not analysing them. It seemed unfair, when they split, that he chose to apply logic. It had never mattered before.

So, this is guilt.

The voice was Shanstra's, lulling and intoxicating as before, but to Suzi's horror it issued from the mouth of Colm Oswyn. The mirage – illusion, memory, she did not know what to call it – grew in size.

You might be able to have him back, after a fashion. If I find you cooperative.

Mad thoughts were coursing through Suzi like the whisky she had drunk earlier. It couldn't happen. Colm was dead. She knew, because she had seen him die, and furthermore –

Like cold water hitting her subconscious, the clarity of the everyday world slammed back in, jolting Suzi upright. It was as if her reflexes had been stimulated with a hit of caffedeine or adrenalin, and she saw everything brightly, clearly. The crisp white of the rink, contrasting with the darkness of Shanstra. The vivid orange of the spectators' seats.

'That will do,' said Shanstra. 'For now.'

Tilusha was sure the kick inside had redoubled its force now. And she felt very nauseous indeed.

One by one, she ascended the steps to the perilous blue door of the flat. She was uncomfortably aware that, once she got in, it would be difficult standing her ground. She just had to hope that Phil was not in too violent a mood.

She approached the door and turned the handle. The door was ajar. Decisively, she shoved and the door, propelled by her force, flew inwards and slammed against the paintwork of the hall, scattering shards across the threadbare carpet.

Tilusha's body was shaking, but this time she had told herself that there was no going back. And so she had to keep that promise. She kicked out with one sensibly shod foot and hooked the door back, slipping into the narrowing crack as it closed, then pressed herself hard against the wall of the hallway. She stood there in the dimness for a few seconds, breathing in the odours of beer, cigarettes and stale cooking.

She heard a movement in the living room.

She braced herself, ready to kick out again.

And then, with a terrifying, totally unexpected wrench, the child seemed to grab her from inside and claw at her stomach.

A taxi driver who was later questioned by the police about an incident at Westbrook House Flats was to report that he had, at about five-thirty p.m. on the day in question, deposited two rather agitated young ladies at that very building.

He estimated that they were in something of a hurry, and he noticed that they only just had the correct change between them. He remembered them very well. One was in her early thirties, with short dark hair that fell over her eyes, and she wore an expensive-looking waistcoat and leather boots. The other was younger, twenty maybe – Indian, with a sharp face, large eyes, and decked out in all her regalia as if, the taxi driver speculated, off to one of those big weddings or something. After paying they hurried across the forecourt of the building at such a pace that he thought they must be running to prevent some terrible crime or tragedy. But, well, it wasn't really for him to say, and you got all sorts in the back of a cab. There was one time he'd had that Harold Chorley bloke from the BBC ...

Phil Tarrant lurched out of the lounge and looked down at Tilusha Meswani. He saw that Tilusha was doubled up, apparently in pain. He smiled. He was going to enjoy putting her in her place this time.

'Someone told me,' Phil said hoarsely, supporting himself on the banisters, 'that they knew things about you. About what you do when I'm not around.'

Tilusha did not respond.

He snorted with laughter. 'It wouldn't surprise me. You probably think you need other men. God knows, half the time the only way I can enjoy myself is by imagining you're someone else.'

Tilusha was breathing heavily. She started to raise her head, her dark hair glossy but dishevelled in the evening light.

Phil blinked, and struggled to get a hold on what he was saying. He seemed to have lost the thread, which annoyed him, and so Phil Tarrant did what he normally did when faced with frustration. He lashed out.

He grabbed Tilusha Meswani, who shared his bed and carried his child, by the lapels, and hauled her up to face him. His teeth were like a dam, glittering, ready to burst and unleash torrents of anger and hatred.

'Where have you been, bitch? Where have you *been*?'

Tilusha lifted her head. Her eyes, as they looked up to meet his, were bright, clear, and filled with the light of pure emeralds. 'Many places,' said a voice which was not that of Tilusha Meswani.

For a moment, Phil Tarrant stared with bloodshot eyes at the woman before him, his face registering incredulity, rage, horror. Then he pushed her away, swung back his fist and hit her as hard as he could across the face.

Tilusha reeled.

A pair of hands slipped under her arms, caught her.

The Doctor, supporting a half-falling, half-standing Tilusha, looked beyond her into the hallway at her attacker, and his face was suffused with a dark and timeless fury.

Seconds later, the whole place seemed to shatter.

Bernice could feel a tingling in her head. She wondered if it was tinnitus from the loud pneumatic drill of the roadworks outside in the street, but she did not have much time to stop and contemplate the matter, because she was leaping up the stairs of a fire-escape three at a time.

Bernice got to the top of the clanging stairway just before Nita and hit the corridor beyond at a run. She was not really sure what she was doing, but Bernice Summerfield had never been one to stand by when she knew someone was suffering, no matter how irresponsible it might seem.

She was aware of the younger woman keeping pace behind her. Benny found two fire doors at the end of the corridor, and heard Nita shout at her to head right.

She emerged on to a communal landing, stone-floored and featureless. Her footsteps echoed down a large, ugly stairwell, and in front of her was the door, gaping wide, of number 22, the flat they were looking for. Nita hurried up behind her.

'So,' Benny said, 'do we go in or what?'

57

Nita opened her mouth to answer, just as a whirlwind seemed to erupt from the flat.

They were blasted backwards by an incredible shock wave and a burst of glittering radiance from the open door

And then there was a terrible, dense silence.

6

Mind over Matter

In the Library and Archives of Banksburgh, Polymer, standing on an old-fashioned trestle table, rifled through box after box of diskettes. Trinket was picking rather less than half-heartedly through the rubble, and Livewire stood with her hands on her hips and watched them.

The library did not appear to have been subjected to direct shelling, but it looked as if it had received more than its fair share of secondary damage. The mural of the original colony ship, which dominated the west wall of the reading room, was shattered and crumbling, while shelves lay like the fallen dead, their sacred disks scattered across the dusty floor. The pillars that held the vaulted roof were still intact, but Trinket was alarmed at the creaking sounds which every so often would ripple through the structure of the library. Of their quarry there was no sign.

'She's not here,' Poly snarled, jumping off her table and crunching across the rubble.

'I know that,' Livewire said with her self-assured arrogance, her voice sounding out clear and strong, as if she was addressing her confidence to the library itself. 'I thought you might use some initiative to deduce where she had gone.'

Polymer squared up to Livewire, her fat jowls wobbling and her mouth drooping with petulance and frustration. Trinket, uncertain, squatted in the background and carried on moving the odd chunk of rubble. He did not want to get involved. He saw Poly shrug, which he knew was not a good move.

Livewire snorted with contempt and kicked the table from under one of the computer terminals. The screen wobbled and then crashed to the floor with a shower of dust and plastic that made Poly take a worried step backwards.

'Think!' Livewire ordered.

She had taken charge, Trinket remembered, when the oldsters had gone, because she believed that to be the natural state of things. She was the inventor, the innovator, the natural leader. She liked to take action, and she had an intellectual advantage over the other two, bolstering the validity of her plans by citing writers and revolutionaries whom neither of them knew. 'Better to come together,' she had once said, 'in one, single, decisive act of violence, then to sit by and be passive while violence takes over around you.'

Trinket knew her style. Whenever there was a hitch, Livewire, through practice, was most adept at making that seem the fault of one of the others, while claiming any successes as the fruits of her own resourcefulness and strong leadership.

Trinket considered himself intelligent, shrewd even, but he was easily intimidated, and that was what Livewire appreciated both in a half-brother and in a subordinate. Polymer was more belligerent and challenging than Trinket, and hence more of a threat to Livewire, he fancied. Poly needed delicate handling, and to be given a false sense of her own importance. This usually satisfied her, partly because she enjoyed pushing Trinket around, but mostly because she was stupid. He kept such thoughts to himself.

'Are any of these working?' Trinket gestured vaguely at the computer terminals.

Livewire folded her arms. 'You won't find out by speculating.'

Trinket looked down at his shoes. 'Action, boy, action!'

'How do we get to find out her log-in and pass code?' he asked despondently.

Livewire strode up to Trinket and took his chin in her gloved hand. She patted it, an affectionate gesture that neatly counterpointed the edge to her voice. 'You're supposed to be the hacker. You override them.'

Trinket, who was perspiring with fear, nodded.

Polymer had been watching the exchange with smug amusement, and now she let out an involuntary snort of laughter at the boy's discomfort.

'And you,' Livewire snapped at her, 'do something productive.'

Poly shrugged, and took one of the chunkiest paper volumes from the dusty floor. 'All right,' she said. 'I was just gonna sit here and devour a good book.'

She tore out the frontispiece of the tome, bit off half the page, and sat there on her pile of rubble, her broad jaw clunking ruminatively as she chewed the paper.

Bernice could hear the sound of her own breathing inside her head, echoing as if recorded and played back to her through headphones.

She was crawling on her hands and knees. The entrance to the flat was bouncing in front of her eyes – or rather, four different versions of it were, so she hoped she was heading for the correct one.

She reached the door. Tentatively, she stood, using the door-frame for support, but her vision was still wobbly and tinged with red. 'Doctor?' she called.

She slipped inside the flat. There were various smells in there which she thought she ought to recognize. At least one of them was the odour of stale beer, which brought several memories of the twentieth century back, and nearly did the same for her last meal.

There was a door leading off the hallway. She tried it.

A dish exploded against the wall by her head.

Inside the lounge, a whirlwind raged. She had a brief impression of a tall, beautiful woman standing at its heart and smiling, and at the edge of the tableau, hanging grimly

61

on to his hat, the Doctor. Across the room flew papers like demented birds, crockery (flying saucers, said Benny's confused mind), a few ornaments. Videotapes rode the channels, unravelling themselves, and festooned the furniture.

A squat, ugly body which Benny assumed to be that of Philip Tarrant was hanging by its fingertips on to the fake leather sofa. With a rip of animal hide and a gush of foam, his mooring gave way and the force smashed him against the wall. Bernice could feel the wind blowing her hair, and at the back of her mind something was trying to tell her about unexplored possibilities. The Doctor's hand was huge in her field of vision, like that of a celebrity grasping for a press photographer's lens. She realized, in a dream-like haze, that he was trying to keep her out of the room.

There was a gasp, an all too human sound. And then the chaos ceased.

The room could have been the lounge of any suburban flat after a particularly nasty row. Benny registered a girl kneeling in pain at its centre, and the Doctor rising swiftly from concealment to take command.

To Benny's surprise, he came to her first. His palms were warm against her cheeks. She realized her heart was pounding.

'Everything all right? Nothing broken?'

'No – Doctor, I – '

'Save it for later.' He flashed her a brief smile, and dropped to squat beside the groaning specimen of humanity at Bernice's feet, who was still clutching a chunk of sofa in his white-knuckled hand, and who smelt most strongly of Skippington's Old County Brew and smoke.

'He'll live,' muttered the Doctor, and with a sudden burst of energy he tossed his umbrella to Bernice. She caught it, to her astonishment. When she blinked again, the mercurial Time Lord was at the side of the gently swaying girl. Benny knew this had to be Tilusha.

There was a rustle of silk at Bernice's shoulder. She jumped, but it was only a very dishevelled Nita Bedi. Benny, guiltily, realized she had forgotten all about her.

'I don't believe this,' said the girl. 'Tilusha! What happened here?'

Nita was about to rush over to her cousin, but Benny placed a restraining hand on her arm. 'Leave it to him. He's a doctor.'

The Doctor finished shining a pencil-torch into Tilusha Meswani's staring eyes. 'Catatonic trance,' he said curtly, with a dismissiveness that, even after all this time, shocked Bernice slightly. 'Help me get her on to the – the – ' He waved almost absently at the sofa, with its unorthodox garlands of magnetic tape.

The three of them laid Tilusha down and made her as comfortable as they could. The Doctor put his hat on the floor beside the sofa.

'Can I get her some water, or anything?' Nita was desperate to do something useful.

'No,' said the Doctor, his eyes barely flicking in Nita's direction. Bernice raised her eyebrows in apology, but Nita just shrugged.

The Doctor was giving his whole attention to Tilusha Meswani, smoothing her hair, peering at her face. After a moment he took a small, conical device out of his capacious pockets and placed it against Tilusha's belly, where he listened intently. 'Almost time,' he said, with a dazzling and unexpected smile. Then, the object was gone, the Doctor's head was lifted upwards again and he somehow flicked his hat up from the floor to his head. 'Do either of you,' he asked carefully, 'feel anything remotely unusual?'

Nita shook her head, with a jangle of jewellery.

'Baffled,' said Benny, folding her arms, 'but that doesn't qualify.' She rubbed her eyes, suddenly aware of how heavy they were. Then she began remembering. 'I did feel a kind of tingling, like a shiver, but as if it was inside my head.' She looked up, and saw the Doctor nodding, gesturing with both hands in that way of his which showed that he wanted to hear more. 'It was just as we were coming up the stairs. And just now, as . . .' Benny gestured

63

vaguely around the wreck of the sitting-room. 'All this happened.'

'Excellent,' said the Doctor. 'You're slightly sensitive to telepathy. I'd suspected as much.' A grim smile adorned his lined face for a second. 'But Tilusha's child has greater powers. Especially when defending itself and its mother from a potential aggressor.' The Doctor spared a brief glance for Phil Tarrant, who was still lying on the floor, breathing drunkenly, with his hand over his eyes.

'I suppose you're going to explain to me,' Nita ventured, trying to keep her voice level and rational, 'why it is that my cousin looks nine months pregnant, given that when I last saw her she was barely showing a bump?' Her face was taut and angry, her blink rate unnatural.

The Doctor perched himself on the nearest chair. 'Yes,' he said, 'that is rather interesting.'

Benny felt an involuntary shiver. She looked in horror at the rounded flesh under Tilusha's loosened blouse, and then back to the Doctor again. 'So what's growing in there?' she asked, steeling herself.

Rain spattered gently against the window-panes. The Doctor rested his chin in his hands and scowled. 'If I'm right,' he said, 'a Sensopath.'

'Excuse me?' Nita stared in incomprehension.

'A highly telepathic humanoid, for whom mental images and communication supersede all the conventional senses of experience. Linked to another, similar being. Possibly others. I'd imagine being shut in there, helpless in amniotic fluid, is only marginally worse than the mental distance from its fellow.'

'Fellow?' Bernice gaped at him.

'Yes. I'd suspected something like this for a while. The TARDIS picked up on one of the traces and it's been trying to warn me. There were a couple of hitches. First of all, I've had so much on my mind that I didn't immediately notice.' The Doctor smiled briefly at Bernice. She knew he was thinking of their recent experiences, and of the still unsettling absence of Ace. 'And secondly, as a result

64

of that, I'd imagine the trace it latched on to was recorded and followed, but maybe not consistently.'

'Which means?' said Benny.

'That the Sensopath in the other time zone – or others, if there are more than one – may have caused the TARDIS to be diverted. The TARDIS attached itself to the wrong part of a splitting signal.' The Doctor returned to face the window and stood for a few moments looking at the grey, rain-lashed city. 'The question is,' he murmured, 'does the other want to be found?'

Bernice realized that this all had to be rather incredible for Nita, but there was no escaping the fact that her cousin was now in an advanced state of pregnancy.

And softly talking to herself.

Bernice and Nita realized – and turned – in unison. They saw Tilusha's mouth moving, glossy and wet, forming sounds that were as beautiful as they were alien.

It seemed to Benny that the sound was in perfect harmony with the whispering of the rain.

'Got it,' said Trinket.

The others crowded round the terminal, and he used the blip-pointer to show them what he had found.

'Librarian and archivist Suzi Palsson,' said Trinket, clicking on an icon to bring up a hi-res image of the person they were looking for. Her pixelled hair gleamed, sparkling at them from the screen. 'Apartment in Zephaniah House, Argolis Avenue.'

Poly was chewing page six of an old book called *A Suitable Boy*. Her breath was hot and rank on Trinket's face and it was making him feel sick. 'Argolis Avenue's a bomb site,' she objected.

'He knows that,' said Livewire.

Trinket brought up three frames of information. 'Not hard to get into Government records from that protocol. Listed all her connections. See this? She was a member of the gravball team.'

Livewire was, naturally, keeping up. 'She'd have a pass key for practice access. And it's in one of the intact areas.'

She nodded, smiled. 'Where do you go when your home is bombed?'

'Somewhere you can get into, of course,' said Trinket. 'Somewhere you'd have a pass key to.' He thought his services were still being required to explain the obvious. He had not seen Livewire straightening up, the sleek hunter, beside him.

There was the slicing sound of a crossbow being expertly reloaded. 'Corp Boulevard,' said Livewire. 'Come on.'

When Cheynor got his update from Leibniz, it was not quite what he had been wanting to hear. The relief ship *Darwin* had sent communication: it was still 48 hours away from Gadrell Major, and the evacuees on the orbital station would just have to sit things out until then.

On the communications front, things were not much better. TechnOps were still working round the clock, valiantly trying to delouse the computer systems – Cheynor had just not realized how much work would be necessary to create a whole new batch of antivirus programs.

He looked around the sleek, reflective table in his briefing room. To his left, Horst Leibniz, unmistakable with his spiky ash-blond hair and hangdog face. To his right, Major Jocassta Hogarth, the communications officer, dark hair cut so close to her pale skull that it was almost invisible, her long, translucent fingers tapping on a pile of info-cards. Her good right eye was flicking its focus back and forth between her captain and Leibniz, while the sensor-pad over her left eye pulsed gently. Cheynor knew that she and Leibniz did not really get on, but their working together was essential if the *Phoenix* was to become operational again.

'How close is the comsat to launching, Horst?' Cheynor asked.

Leibniz exchanged a glance with Hogarth. A tiny image of him was reflected in the square over her left eye.

'It's ready for final testing,' Leibniz confirmed.

Major Hogarth made a disgruntled sound. 'It's been tested,' she objected tersely, folding her arms.

'Not under the kind of conditions I want, Major,' Leibniz answered. This argument had a stale air, as if it were being aired for performance in front of the captain after endless and dull rehearsal.

'It's imperative,' said Cheynor sternly. 'You both realize,' he added, leaning forward with his hands folded under his dark beard, 'that if the Phractons were to launch a full-scale attack upon this base, we would have little chance of repelling them?'

'I suggest that the Phracs know that too,' said Hogarth lazily, leaning back in her chair with an assumed ease.

'What do you mean?' Leibniz asked crossly.

Cassie Hogarth smiled. Her mouth was thin and pink and the smile caused her face to crease from chin to temple – a couple of face-jobs showing there, Cheynor thought with grim satisfaction, and wondered for a moment if she were older than the 35 or so that she looked.

'Simply that if they wanted to attack us, they had the perfect opportunity as soon as our systems went down. And they didn't. The logical surmise from that is that they don't want to attack us. Yet. Wouldn't you say, Captain?'

Cheynor spread his hands, nodded slowly. 'Cassie does have a point, Horst,' he said apologetically. 'For the moment I suggest that we step up security as high as it will go, try and get some force-field capacity back on line, and get that comsat launched within the hour.' He stood up, and the two officers followed suit. 'And keep plotting the *Darwin* from its scan bolts. I want to know if it slows down or speeds up.'

He departed for the bridge, leaving Cassie Hogarth and Horst Leibniz glowering at each other across the briefing table.

'Come on, big boy,' Hogarth said, and threw Leibniz an info card. 'Let's go and fix our thrusters together.' She forced a grin, but her face was taut with tension.

'My lucky day,' muttered Leibniz through gritted teeth, and followed Hogarth out of the room.

His officers' bickering was not as high on Cheynor's agenda of problems as it should have been. For one thing, it was happening all over the ship. It might have had something to do with all these months in the colonial outposts, but he was hard pressed to remember working with such a jaded, tiresome and generally lax crew as this one. Many ships in Spacefleet ended up being run on similar lines, but he never thought his would be one of them.

All the same, there was something more than stubbornness and conviction about the way Horst Leibniz's eyes shone when he was putting his views. Leibniz was new for the Gadrell Major mission – he hadn't been part of the crew before. Cheynor wondered whether his first officer was the kind of person who took some getting used to.

Something else was bothering him, too.

He thought about it in the elevator as he ascended to the bridge. He kept thinking back to that briefing, and the faces that were present there: the general, Adjudicator Hagen. He had wondered at the time why he, of all people, should have been chosen for such a mission. Cheynor did not flatter himself that the general's words of praise had actually been meant in all sincerity. No. It was something very obvious, he decided, but he was going to have to reflect on it.

7

Splintering Heart

Phil Tarrant had been getting in the way. He was eventually moved to the kitchen, which was as chaotic as the lounge. He sat slumped by the sideboard, amidst the broken crockery.

In the lounge, Nita channel-surfed through Sky (the television had remained undamaged). The Doctor brought everyone some tea which he had managed to make before the kitchen was Phil-filled. Bernice monitored Tilusha Meswani's pulse with one of the Doctor's portable instruments, a small black rectangle with an LCD readout. Both breathing and pulse were quite normal.

'I should really be getting back to my family,' Nita murmured. 'They won't thank me for being here at all, let alone getting mixed up in this.'

The Doctor sipped his tea as he watched Benny attending to Tilusha. He waved his free hand absently at Nita. 'Don't worry, no one's going to get you mixed up in anything.'

Nita sighed loudly.

Benny knew the girl found him patronizing and she wished she could explain about the Doctor, tell her that he could be perfectly charming sometimes. That he operated according to a different set of rules from humans, and that she shouldn't take any of it personally.

'What I want to know is,' muttered the Doctor, 'why

the TARDIS brought me here instead of the 24th century.'
He took a brief, angry sip of his tea.

'The 24th century?' Benny looked up in surprise. 'I
thought you didn't know the location of the original
trace?'

'I was in the tertiary control room, remember. Some
things didn't pass me by.'

Once again, the Doctor was a couple of steps in front,
but this did not unnerve Bernice Summerfield as it used
to. When someone's ahead of you, her friend Clive on
Heaven used to say, at least you can see which way to go.

The Doctor swung around and squatted by Nita. 'Tell
me about Tilusha. Tell me what kind of life she has.'

The girl was sulky and petulant in her answer, punctuat-
ing every sentence with a flick of the remote-control. 'Her
family hate her because of the way she's led her life. She
went to university, lost touch with her loyalties. She's a
good person, but fiercely independent, she loves our
sacred texts but she doesn't believe in ritual. I don't know,
Doctor. Where do you begin to describe someone you've
known all your life? I seem to be the only person who
cares what happens to her.'

The Doctor had been hanging on every fragmented
word. 'Don't stop. I was just getting a fascinating picture.'
His voice was coaxing, kind, almost desperate, and he
looked up at Nita with the pleading air of a lost puppy.
She met his gaze, shrugged, and continued giving her
attention to the remote-control. 'I can help her,' said the
Doctor urgently. 'I understand what's going on here, and
it's got something to do with time, Nita. "Time ripens the
creatures, time rots them".'

Nita spared him a brief glance which was slightly less
hostile – she did not meet many non-Hindus who could
quote the Mahabharata.

'Trust me,' said the Doctor gently. 'What's happening
to Tilusha is only part of a very dangerous problem I
have to solve. And until I've put the second phase in
motion, I can't do very much at all.'

There was a clattering noise from the kitchen. Bernice

shot a worried look at the Doctor and he motioned her to go and investigate. It was the sort of thing he did these days. There was a time, Bernice knew, when the Doctor had been overly protective of his companions, but the two of them had become so close by now that she knew he would never send her into real danger.

She crossed the hall and flung open the kitchen door. Phil was struggling to get up from the tiles, clutching his bruised head. Benny instinctively went for the nearest defensive weapon to hand on the wall behind her. It happened to be a large and heavy non-stick frying pan. She looked uncertainly at it for a second, her hand wavering, an unpleasant memory coming back, before letting it clatter to the floor.

'Just sit there and do nothing, will you?' she snapped at Phil. 'It's better that way.'

He had levered himself up, clutching at the cooker. 'Who the hell are you sodding people? What are you doing here?'

'We're your uninvited guests. Want to call the cops? I'm sure they'd be delighted to hear from you.' Benny folded her arms, and looked down in contempt at the ugly man, who was slowly sinking to the floor again. 'Do you know, I've done a lot of reading about domestic violence in the twentieth century. About men who enjoy having someone to push around. Well, it's gone beyond that now. Beyond anything your puny mind could comprehend, even when sober. So just do us all a favour and go back to sleep.'

Bernice, somewhat surprised at the force of her own tirade, slammed the kitchen door behind her. She noted the sound of splattery chunks of vomit hitting earthenware, and shook her head wearily.

As she crossed the hall, there was a tingling in the back of her mind again. And this time, it was more eerily perceptible. She got the distinct impression that someone or something was chuckling quietly just behind her ear.

She looked over her shoulder into the shadows by the stairs.

71

There was nothing there. Of course. And yet something in the flat was making her very uneasy. It had to be, she decided, the thought of what might be growing inside Tilusha's womb. It was bad enough that it should have been put there by that belching animal in the kitchen, without something . . . *else*. Bernice shuddered, and turned round to enter the lounge again.

She saw a pair of dark eyes.

She jumped, before realizing that the Doctor had slipped out into the hallway without her seeing him. His hair was tousled, his face grim. 'You startled me,' she said.

'I know.' He smiled, but it was not a real one, she could sense that much. 'I'm sorry. I want to talk to you.'

'Is this capital-T Talk?' Benny stuck her hands in her pockets and swivelled on one heel.

'It's time to get the second phase going. Ever since the TARDIS brought us here I've had the feeling that one of us should be somewhere else. Benny, I'm going to try something very dangerous and I need your help. I'd ask – ' The Doctor paused, shook his head, looking at an invisible globe of space just a few centimetres below his eyes. 'No. I'm asking *you*.'

He looked up again, and with a shock she recognized something that she did not often see. It was an expression on the Doctor's face, something so unusual that it seemed to transform that lined, wise countenance into the lost face of a much younger man, someone more uncertain of the ways of the universe than he ever liked to reveal.

The Doctor was frightened.

He said: 'I want you to go to the planet Gadrell Major, in UCD 2387.'

Bernice swallowed and did not answer for a moment. 'You're sending me in the TARDIS?' she asked eventually.

He nodded.

'Alone?'

He nodded, then paused. A half-smile, and a sideways glance. 'Not totally,' he said. 'See you back in there.'

She did not fully realize what the Doctor had meant

72

until she thought to slip a hand into the pocket of her velvet waistcoat, where it encountered the smoothness of a small pyramid. And then she remembered the Doctor who was not the Doctor, the uncannily responsive hologram which walked and talked and was, if anything, more enigmatic and frustrating than the genuine article.

And she began to wonder exactly how long the Doctor had known that she would be needing it.

In the fiery shadows of the sports centre's observation dome, Suzi was on her knees, gazing at Shanstra.

Above them, the plexiglass dome glittered, and below them the city flickered and burned. The occasional cry or distant explosion could be heard. Out there, somewhere, fights and lives were being won and lost.

Kneeling on the blue carpet of the dome's huge floor, Suzi Palsson felt more calm and peaceful than she had done for many years. Shanstra's dark gaze held love. It held the love of Colm Oswyn and the love of her parents and the love of a new and trusted friend.

The alien woman had found herself something new to wear: a close-fitting black suit taken from the gravball lockers at the ice-rink. Over it, the stolen fake velvet cloak was draped. Both somehow looked tailor-made for Shanstra's giant body.

Suzi felt Shanstra's gloved palm descend on her head. *Many will assail us, Suzi. There are those who don't understand the love of the soul. The beauty in the way creation harmonizes with destruction, into one. Do you know that?*

Suzi nodded.

On the wall by the curve of the lift doors, the indicator was climbing slowly up its column of lights.

Shanstra saw it, and was pleased. 'Now,' she said, using her voice, her lips moving in exquisite undulation. 'I want you to take out your gun, and to place it on the floor beside you.'

Suzi felt a twinge of panic above her calmness, like a wasp buzzing round her face on a soft summer's day.

'Don't worry,' said Shanstra. 'I knew you had it with

73

you. I realize you are not a fool. And luckily, my dear, neither am I.'

Suzi pulled the Raz-33 out from concealment with a quiet swish of metal against material. It felt heavy in her hand, and she thought she could smell its angry heat; for the first time, it no longer felt like a friend. She placed the gun on the carpet beside her.

The lift was five floors down.

In the cylindrical lift, three faces. Three very different faces.

Livewire, set and chiselled, as if every emotion had been programmed, every response mapped out and followed to the letter. It was not calmness – more a kind of channelled tension.

Trinket, whose eyes could not keep still, whose tongue ran over too-dry lips, making them drier.

Polymer, with lazy, hooded eyes above a cruel and blubbery face, not really anticipating what was to come.

Going up.

Coming down, there would only be one of them.

Shanstra's head turned at the sound of the lift doors. She smiled.

'Welcome,' she said.

Trinket was to remember that it had happened like this.

He had just a couple of seconds to register the contents of the room: the plush carpet, the smooth, padded furniture, the observation panels. At the centre, there were two women, one kneeling and the other, dark-clad and impossibly tall, standing.

The woman in black gave them a smile like running blood, and she said something which he did not hear.

He saw the gun glinting on the floor, in the thickness of the carpet, and he supposed Livewire must have spotted it at the same time.

It was Livewire who shouted at Polymer to get the gun,

74

and to Trinket's surprise, Poly obeyed, making a lunge across the floor at Suzi Palsson.

In that same instant, or so it seemed, there was a flash of the brightest green, like the very heart of a coppery flame. Trinket was bowled off his feet by a force that lifted him from underneath and threw him back, luckily for him, into the nearest of the padded seats. Livewire's arrow, which had been fired an instant earlier, curled up in mid-air like a dying slug. It fizzed green sparks and thrashed in currents of invisible power before shattering. Livewire, angered, was knocked aside as further radiance streamed from the woman's eyes and hands.

Polymer actually got quite near to the gun. Her fingers closed over the butt. Unfortunately, they remained attached to the rest of her body for only a further half-second.

Trinket blinked as he saw Polymer apparently hit by a wall of streaming green flame. There was a sound like petrol igniting and she was hurled back minus her right hand. Copious flesh was stripped from her body, and it sizzled on the carpet in fatty pools. The carbonized skeleton, all that remained of Poly, twisted once and crumbled as it hit the wall by the lift doors. Slithering to the burnt carpet, it left a smeary trail of charcoal.

Green sparks buzzed like hungry flies between the body and Shanstra's hand. Trinket realized then that the woman's smiling face was turning round towards him.

He threw himself towards the lift, his heart pounding, thinking that at any moment he might be turned to ash.

The doors swished open.

Trinket's memory would forever be burned with the memory of the woman smiling, her head cocked slightly to one side as in reproof, her black hair streaming out behind her like an executioner's cloak, standing amid the green swirl of light and chaos and the ashes of Polymer's body. With Livewire struggling to her feet against the far wall.

And then the door clamped shut and the image was gone, and the lift began to descend.

75

Trinket was shaking. He felt himself sliding to the floor, and was not inclined to stop himself because his legs could not support him any longer.

Livewire. Still up there.

The thought did not deter him from running as fast as he could when the lift reached the bottom floor. He ran out across the foyer, through the plexiglass door they had smashed on their way in.

There was something happening out on the street. Whatever else might be going on, there was still a war in progress. This occurred to Trinket with sudden clarity when he saw two low-life scavengers running across the rubble, momentarily picked out in a beam of light.

A Phracton search beam. So now, he was safe nowhere. And unarmed. Although, Trinket thought in frustration, it wasn't as if he'd have much ability with a gun even if he did possess one.

He ducked behind a cluster of metal bins. Something squealed and thumped like a firework, and then he saw a fountain of incinerated rubbish spewing out in a flash of light. The Phracs were on to his hiding-place.

If Trinket had been in a more thoughtful frame of mind, he might have stopped to wonder why the Phractons should be bothered with him, when according to the bulletins they had made clear their policy of not attacking civilians. But Trinket accepted his role as prey now, and saw every shadow as a hunter. He was not in the mood to question.

He saw the glint of their hovering globes as he made a dash across Corporation Boulevard. The Phractons were right behind, the droning of their travel units shrill and clear in the night.

He made it behind a vid-booth in one of the central islands of the boulevard. He flattened himself against its smoothness and risked a glance.

He heard the multi-frequency crackles that always seemed to accompany the Phractons, and knew they had to be close behind him – twenty metres at the most.

Well, he would give them a good run. Trinket clenched

76

his fists, told himself again and again that he was not an acceptable casualty. And then he broke cover, and ran for the nearest alleyway.

It tingled inside Benny's head now, and it was beginning to annoy her. Just on the edge of hearing the sound lurked, and she wondered how it sounded to Tilusha, stretched out on the sofa. If she had understood the Doctor correctly, Tilusha was hearing an amplified version of the same signal.

She rubbed the back of her neck, and tried to concentrate on what the Doctor had said to her in the dimness of the hall.

He had held up a flat, round device with a single red control on it.

'Stattenheim remote-control for the TARDIS,' he explained. 'Been broken for a long while, but I repaired it recently.' He grinned rather sheepishly at her. 'After that time I had to get back to you in San Francisco, I thought I could do with a quicker method of recalling her.'

'Very tidy. And so?'

'It's programmed,' the Doctor said, 'to give you six Earth hours. That's how long you'll have to find the source of the Sensopathic emissions. After six hours precisely, the TARDIS will return to its starting point here in England.'

'Why? Why can't I just come back?'

The Doctor had appeared agitated, looking over his shoulder as if he ought to be getting back to the situation in the lounge. 'We're moving on, Benny. I want you to start something for me, and then I'll join you as soon as I can.'

Bernice nodded, drawing breath. 'I suppose there's no point asking why I can't stay here with you?'

'It might not be safe.'

'Really? Wonders will never cease.'

'I don't know why the Sensopathic distress signal should have been split into segments. If my hunch is right, the

77

whole structure of the cosmos could be at stake – and the focus of the danger is here on Earth.'

'Charity begins at home,' Benny sighed.

And now, Bernice Summerfield, with the holo-pyramid and TARDIS key in her pocket, stood in the thickening rain outside the City Hall and contemplated the TARDIS. She could refuse, of course, she thought as she pushed strands of damp hair out of her eyes. She could slip away from the grey city in the TARDIS and leave the Doctor to sort it all out. Escape from it for good.

But there were several problems, naturally, with that approach. What would be the cost of non-intervention? When the Doctor had interfered in the past, it had usually been for the best. He had told her all the stories about his people, the Time Lords, and how they pretended to despise the thought of stepping in to change history. They had even put the Doctor on trial for it twice, but were not averse to using him as an intergalactic troubleshooter whenever they did not want to get their hands dirty.

And now, as she kicked a puddle and looked up again at the dark blue police box which was waiting for her, she knew that she could not let the Doctor down.

She slipped the key into the lock, noting, as she had before, the way that it seemed to become part of the door, to guide her hand to open it. She took one last look at the city: the cars swishing through puddles, the bobbing multi-coloured umbrellas, the workmen shovelling furiously in a coned-off hole on the other side of the road.

Bernice frowned. She had visited twentieth-century Earth several times now, but this was the first time that the sheer ordinariness of it all had unsettled her. It was almost as if she was wondering, momentarily, if this slightly melancholy view would be the last she would ever see of this planet in this time.

The TARDIS door closed behind her.

The doors hummed as they admitted Bernice to the main console room, and folded to behind her. There was a series of clicks from the console as the pre-programmed settings activated themselves.

She kicked her shoes off, slumped into the basket-chair and let out a long sigh. The time rotor clicked into action and began to move up and down, indicating that the ship was in flight.

Just like old times, Bernice told herself wryly.

Except, of course, for the fact that she didn't have the Doctor with her.

Part Two

BROKEN LAND

The one who bewitches you with sleep or darkness and lies with you – we will drive him away from here.

from a prayer for the safety of the embryo, in the
Rig Veda

Medusa was once renowned for her beauty, and roused jealous hopes in the hearts of many suitors. Of all the beauties she possessed, none was more striking than her lovely hair.

Ovid, *Metamorphoses*

8

Chances Are We Are Mad

Pridka Dream Centre, in orbit around Taprid
Beyond Common Era of Earth calendar

'It all seems very interesting,' said the visitor. 'Very interesting indeed.'

The Director's crest of fins bristled slightly, betraying the fact that he – the Director was of mostly masculine gender – felt his visitor was being a little icy. His face flushed a slightly darker blue, and his forehead wrinkled. The tall, dark visitor remained, as before, impassive.

The Director's personal tourdisc floated up through a helix-shaped gallery of light in the vast technological paradise known as the Dream Centre. The Director, when he thought he detected an undercurrent in the tones of the visitor, turned slightly and tried to read something in that long face, but there was nothing but the former inscrutability to be seen.

This Jirenal was a strange customer, the Director had decided. Asking for a tour of the greatest dream therapy centre ever constructed was not unusual, but the distinct lack of awe shown by the visitor was at odds with his apparent eagerness to see everything. And there was something else nagging at the Director's thoughts, too –

When the visitor had first arrived, escorted by drones, he had been wearing the simple black suit of a middle-grade worker. The Director had been informed by the drone's report that the stranger had been naked upon his arrival at the quarantine bay, and although the Pridka set little store by the appearance of the flesh in any form, an order had been given by a senior Pridka to have him covered. There were currently members of over seven hundred cultures residing in the centre, fifty-two of which had a history of finding the unclad body offensive.

The features of Jirenal which had struck the Director then had been those which he noticed again now, as they ascended the helix on their touring disc. A proud, long face, with cheekbones so pronounced they seemed to have been cut with a knife and, indeed, to define the angular shape of the face overall. The skin colour, the Director decided, was that of an exceptionally pale humanoid – it looked a rather sickly hue, especially to a healthily blue-cheeked Pridka like him (but his many cycles as Director had taught him never to respond with disgust to the physical features of another race; the minds of his visitors tended to concern the Director much more). Exceptionally black hair, glossy with fluid light, fell over the man's black-clad shoulders. The Director noticed also that the hands, although like those of a humanoid, were especially long and flat, with spindly, pale fingers which Jirenal kept pressed together as if in meditation.

'How many minds are there here?' Jirenal asked, as space and light spiralled past them. His voice was resonant, and rang with an authority that would probably have intimidated a weaker spirit than the Director.

The way that the query was phrased only threw the Director slightly for a moment.

'You mean, our current rota of visitors? At the moment, approximately fifteen thousand. More are expected this week. It is . . .' The Director blinked slowly. 'It is a popular therapy and, moreover, totally safe.'

'Fifteen thousand minds,' said Jirenal. 'Thank you.'

They floated up still further, past long galleries full of couches, some connected by flux-beams to pulsing globes of thought, others communicating merely with each other. They passed recreational lounges, including one where a group of Monoids was playing a complex three-dimensional strategy game. Another was a spherical tank, filled with thrashing reptilian creatures.

'The Rakkhins need to be constantly immersed in an ammonia supersaturated solution,' explained the Director, and Jirenal gave an almost imperceptible nod. 'It maintains the chemical balance of their bodies and, hence, their minds. They breathe ammonia, and are exceptionally keen on competitive sport. They wanted to organize a tournament for all the visitors, as – ah – recreation. Unfortunately, no one except the Rills could play against them. I think they have an ongoing contest.'

'Is "recreation" an important part of the therapy?' asked Jirenal with the same icy politeness, as the disc merged with the floor of the Director's office.

'It can be,' said the Director with a brief rippling of his fins. He gathered his white robes around him and gestured to Jirenal to step off the disc into the office – a globe-shaped space of textured light, rather than a room in the technical sense. They settled themselves into levitation couches around the desk, and the Director ordered drinks to be brought by a drone, before resuming his conversation with his visitor.

'We like to encourage free expression in conjunction with all the facilities available here at the centre. Many, many races come to take advantage of what we offer. We are at the edge of a conflux, you know, and so quite a few of them are hyper-travellers, like yourself.'

Jirenal nodded, almost mockingly.

'It would seem inappropriate,' the Director went on, 'for the ethical codes of any one culture to apply here, so nothing is expressly forbidden except, of course, harm to another life-form. We pride ourselves on being a cosmopolitan institution.' The Director remembered that humanoids often appreciated a movement of the mouth called a smile – they found it friendly, he had been told, and a mark of trust. The Director, like most other Pridka, preferred the etiquette of the cranial fins, but he had been practising his smiles in deference to his many visitors from

85

the human and Morestran cultures. He tried one now. It was reasonably successful.

'And,' Jirenal enquired, leaning forward, his dark, alert eyes watching the Director carefully, 'are they *all* telepaths?'

'I would not apply that term to all our visitors, no, not by any means.' A drone arrived with the drinks, and Jirenal took his with exaggerated politeness. 'Those people, sir, who use our facilities are those who have chosen Pridka therapy because, obviously, it employs elements of telepathic communication. We are, after all, the dominant species in this galaxy to have mastered the disciplines of the mind, and we pride ourselves on applying them in a healing context.'

'And making yourself a few credits,' said Jirenal. He sipped from his glass.

The Director was beginning to find his visitor more and more difficult. 'Telepathic dream therapy has never been a cheap science,' said the Director haughtily, 'in any sense of the word. No, many of our visitors are normal sensers, but who feel, maybe, distressed, or disturbed, or in need of rebuilding confidence. Our therapy can do that for them. It can repair self-esteem. It can help visitors to come to terms with unfortunate incidents in their pasts, and to return to their lives refreshed and invigorated. It helps, naturally, if they are of a telepathic inclination, but it is by no means necessary. In fact, sir' – the Director was on a hobby-horse now, and was becoming very animated, his face flushing aquamarine and his fins bristling with excitement – 'it is often here, in the centre, that many visitors develop their latent telepathic abilities. We are able to offer them a full course of training and counselling to make it a positive, exciting experience.'

'Which it is,' said Jirenal with a nod. He took another sip of his drink and placed the glass on the levitation beam to his right. 'I am sure of this.'

A pillar of light misted into view in the corner of the Director's office, revealing the call-image of a young Pridka of mostly female gender. Her bald, smooth skull was adorned only with the tiniest crest of fins, and her delicate features were offset by a glittering green robe.

'With your permission, Director.' Her voice was quiet, but confident.

'Yes, Amarill?'

'You are due to address the psycho-opterands' conference in two microcycles. You requested this reminder.'

'Yes, yes, I did.' The Director made apologetic signs to his visitor. 'Please, feel free to take a further look around the centre. In fact . . .' The Director turned back towards the image of his assistant. 'Amarill, how is your schedule for the rest of today?'

'I have only priority seven duties, Director.'

'Excellent! Would you mind looking after my visitor here and showing him anything else he wants to see?'

'I shall do my best, Director.'

'Good, good. I'll tell him to meet you in the grove.' The Director waved a hand, and a 3-D map of the centre flickered into being on his desk. 'I trust that will be satisfactory? I'm sorry, but you'll have to excuse me.'

No, he thought as he said it, not sorry at all. Rather relieved.

Jirenal was already on his feet, reaching out a hand to the Director. 'Most kind,' he said, with only the briefest glance at the map.

The Director saw his visitor out.

As he returned to his desk, he could not shake off the idea that there was something very unsettling about those burning black eyes. He blinked once, shaking his head. No, he thought, and chastened himself for such a physically prejudiced opinion. All the same . . . The Director wished he had asked more about where the newcomer was actually from, for one thing, and who had authorized his visitor's pass. These questions seemed obvious now, and yet, for some reason, there had seemed no need for them while in the presence of Jirenal.

The Director set about collecting his information together. Just a little later, when he was standing in the central lecture area, speaking clearly and confidently to

87

psycho-opterands from a dozen solar systems, he had forgotten all about the mysterious Jirenal.

The Director could not possibly have known that this would be a fatal mistake.

I came through the tunnel of light and time. I came naked, drifting like a lost spirit across the wastelands of the universe. I saw time eaten up behind me and my own civilization left far behind, turning into phantom ruins as it retreated into nothingness, into mere thought, then into the absence of thought, as I hurtled backwards to a time when it had never existed. When I – we – had never existed.

I felt the wrench as time shattered. I felt the screams as our bonds were stretched and cut. The splitting of the One into Three.

Alone, I came first to a battlefield, littered with broken bodies in which blood stiffened the land, in which footprints had been made in rotting flesh, where metal and limbs decayed together under two relentless suns.

I was rescued, put into a ship with the dead and the dying. I allowed this to happen to myself because I wanted them to think I was harmless. I was waiting for my powers to return, thinking at every moment that if they discovered my true nature, they would kill me.

I was carried away from the war to a space station of the humanoids known as Morestrans, where I was treated kindly. Soon, I felt my powers returning. It was not long before I found myself on a passenger ship to this place, famed throughout the galaxy. It is a centre for research and healing involving dreams and telepathy. Dreams! Telepathy! These primitive beings think they understand the meaning!

We are in orbit around a frontier world, called Taprid. Its indigenous population, the Pridka, control the centre.

There are fifteen thousand minds here. Fifteen thousand souls. Fifteen thousand voices with their thoughts babbling to me. I do not know where to start. Soon, I shall have regained the strength to become One with myselves. Soon.

They have not banished us. They have underestimated

us. They do not know how powerful we are, still. They do not know how we have planned, arranged to wait for the optimum point in all three of our closeted existences.

I am Jirenal.

I shall be JirenalKelzenSHANSTRA –
Once more.

9

From out of Nowhere

Light was dawning over Gadrell Major. And Bernice Summerfield was beginning to think it would have been better left in darkness.

The TARDIS had materialized on one of the highest floors of a skyscraper. The bare stone indicated a swift evacuation, possibly followed by some efficient looting. Pillars supported the ceiling. Through the shattered wall, Bernice could see the ruins of the city in the orange-grey light. It had obviously once been an impressive sight, and there still remained some of the glittering, simplistic buildings, like pieces of a giant child's puzzle: silver pyramids, gold and white towers, domes and obelisks. But they were few and far between. Mostly stumps of buildings jutted up from gashed streets, and clouds of smoke, like giant pointers to destruction, billowed into the air at intervals.

Benny, shaking her head, ventured as near the edge as she dared, her footsteps sounding old and hollow, like those of a spectre. She saw a large square at the centre of the town paved like a giant chessboard; and what seemed to be the tallest building left, a giant, reflective sphere that sprouted a central column like a skewer.

She stood with her hands in her pockets; she had changed into the more practical attire of a denim coverall with a leather jacket and laced-up boots. A ghost visitor in a ghost city. But no, it was not dead. There was the

sound of gunfire, echoing up towards her from somewhere
down in the city – and there! At the edge of her vision,
something . . . A fresh cloud of smoke was issuing from
one of the buildings, over on what she decided to call the
western edge of the city.

She saw something else, now – along the shattered
streets, and through the mud where other streets had
been, shiny silver vehicles were patrolling. There were
other, smaller vehicles too, like globes, only from where
she was it was difficult to see them in any kind of detail.
She decided to pop back into the TARDIS and get her
image intensifier, for which there was a small space in the
canvas satchel she wore on her shoulder.

As she turned, the ceiling tore open in front of her.

The remains of plaster and plastic cascaded down
between Benny and the TARDIS. Following them, a
skinny man in standard-issue overalls hit the floor, rolling
on to his shoulder as he did so. He was clutching a black
bag, and only noticed Bernice as he scrambled to his feet.
His eyes were staring, terrified.

'It's all right,' she said, 'I'm not going to hurt you.' At
the same time, she knew that there was no proof of this,
and to a frightened and dangerous man, she could be seen
automatically as an enemy.

At the edge of her hearing, an electrical whining sound
grew. It appeared to be coming from somewhere beyond
the TARDIS.

Benny saw the man trying to edge away from her.
Confused, she looked from him to the hole he had made,
and then over at the comforting sight of the TARDIS.
The man was clutching the bag tightly as if it were a child.
'It's mine,' he said in a surprisingly lucid voice. 'You find
your own.'

'All right.' Benny's heart was thumping, but she
reckoned she had found a logical pivot on which to reason.
'I'll find my own.' Scavenging, she thought. Everyone for
themselves, then. What the hell have you sent me into,
Doctor?

The man nodded furiously. He scrambled along,

91

keeping his distance from her, still hugging the bag, as the whining sound increased. 'Get away from here,' he muttered. 'Like the others. Get away. You should have gone with the evacuations. When the ships came!'

He was edging away, but Benny was desperate for information, and right now he was her only source. 'Why didn't you go?'

'Killed a man,' he said briefly, licking his lips and scuttling for the doors on the far wall of the shattered room. 'Rather take my chances here, mm?'

As Benny watched, he disappeared through the doors to the staircase.

The noise was growing. Benny whirled around, and after fumbling in her satchel, found the small hand-held motion detector which had sometimes come in useful for her. She gripped it tightly and read off the display, which showed distance and direction. The approaching life-form was at a linear distance of forty metres behind the TARDIS, and closing in on her.

Bernice suddenly became aware that her mouth was very dry. The readout now said thirty metres, and the whining sound was echoing off the walls. She began to back up.

Twenty metres. The numbers counted down. Ten.

Linear distance. Linear distance. The thought hit her like a sudden physical slap, and she looked up to the ceiling above the TARDIS, where the man had burst through in such a spectacular manner.

Ten metres. Five. The sound was all around her. Bernice braced herself.

The readout said two, one. And yet nothing emerged from the hole in the ceiling.

Now it was counting back up again. The display on the motion detector was reading one metre distant, two, three. What? Bernice, confused, swung around in a full circle, seeing no signs of any approaching –

Four metres to her left, the floor fountained up as if punched from beneath, chips of concrete flying in all directions.

A translucent globe, about two metres across, rose up from the hole and blocked her path.

It was made up of two halves separated by a band of black material, and she had an impression of something organic hunched inside it, surrounded by – tentacles, or cables? It was difficult to tell. Lights flickered on the black, disclike base of the sphere. From the band around its circumference, there was something emerging that looked rather like a big gun.

'Sorry,' Benny said, 'whatever I did, I won't do it again. Honest!'

Inside the creature's sphere, the lights glowed brighter. A very organic-sounding hiss emerged from the grille on the central band, and the sphere began gracefully to float through the air towards her.

The Phracton Secondary twitched inside his casing. The Commandant, who had requested this personal meeting, had no reason to doubt that his subordinate was, as intended, squirming in terror. In actual fact, he was writhing in impotent anger.

Through the web of light, furious exchanges bounced between the two Phractons. The Secondary, trying to appear calm and subservient, sent out pulses containing the relevant information he wished to pass on – that all bipeds were enemies of the Phracton Swarm, and that every one left alive represented a mortal threat.

The Commandant transmitted reprimands at the highest level following these dangerous sentiments, denouncing them as counter-productive and in breach of Phracton honour. The purpose of the Gadrell Major mission, he reminded the Secondary, was to achieve their right to the porizium supplies with the minimum bloodshed. Orders to keep the humans at bay had been given before the Commandant himself had arrived on the planet to take charge of operations, by which stage the Secondary had interpreted the orders as a licence to carpet-bomb the city, taking out civilian buildings including the residence of the governor. In that first attack wave (as the Phracton

93

Commandant now knew), the human governor of the dominion, his family and his retinue had all been eliminated. This was not necessary. This was not desirable. The Secondary had already been punished for his error.

If the leaders are eliminated (came the lashing response from the Secondary, who would not be silenced) the enemy is weak. What better way was there to show that they truly meant to re-establish their ancient rights to the territories of Gadrell Major?

The Commandant sent impulses of sharp anger to his subordinate, and took a grim satisfaction in the shards of pain-response that glittered back along the web. It had already been made clear that negotiation was to be used, he reminded the Secondary. Instructions had been sent that the governor should be brought to the command ship to negotiate. Of course, somehow that transmission had been intercepted for security clearance and delayed, allowing just enough time for the executions to be carried out. An unavoidable mistake, the Secondary had called this; a flagrant deception, the Commandant called it now.

The Secondary insinuated, by the contemptuous inflexion of his electrical pulses, that the Commandant lacked the necessary resolve to be in charge of such an important mission.

The Commandant fizzed with anger. He had sent a request for the Secondary's replacement, he told him now. They were awaiting confirmation from Phracton High Command. Of course, under the regulations – which the Commandant always followed – he could not relieve his Secondary of duty until that confirmation came, but he intended to watch him very carefully from now on.

The connection was closed. The web refolded around the Commandant as his visitor was dispatched to his duties.

The Commandant was left alone with his thoughts and his guilt. What should the next move be? The war had already taken far too many civilian casualties, and the Commandant felt himself responsible for each and every one. What, after all, was an acceptable casualty?

He tried to picture his opposing number. He did not know his name or his face.

The Phracton Commandant found it hard, in any case, to tell the difference between humanoids – despite the variations in hair, skin tone and weight, they all basically followed the same four-limbed, binocular model, which in his opinion made them too similar to tell apart. Obviously humans felt the differences more profoundly, as the Phracton Commandant had just discovered.

Following his earlier speculations about human hatred, he had accessed, out of curiosity, all the details of Earth history held in the High Command archives. He had read of the humans' former internecine struggles on Earth and its colonies, some of which had been based on seemingly trivial qualities: gender, or subtle variations in skin colour, or belief, or customs.

He had been fascinated to see how impassioned, and often violent, humans could become about that which they had no way of proving – their supernatural beliefs. Far from unifying them over their centuries of existence, the humans' worship of deities had become so disparate and extremized that it led to the most horrendous conflicts. The Phracton had found, by checking footnotes and elaboration globes, that one popular sect emerged again and again as a group of humans practising tolerance and love, while in truth unable to accept elements of any doctrine other than their self-proclaimed, ancient interpretation.

He had also read with interest and some disgust of the tensions between white humans and black humans which had erupted into violence in the conurbations known as Los Angeles, London and Johannesburg. The Phracton liked to pretend that he found this kind of hatred hard to understand. In truth, he did not.

He was not keen on meeting the humans' leader. Given their history, he would not be surprised if, employing subterfuge, the bipeds lured him to a place of negotiation and then –

The Commandant checked himself. How easy it was to start thinking like the Secondary.

So he did not want to speak to the humans. But he wondered if it might be the only way.

The globe surveyed Bernice.

She shrugged, trying to suppress the urge to turn and run as fast as she could. 'Look,' she said, 'I'd really love to talk to you all day, but I have to be somewhere terribly boring right now. I hope you don't mind.'

She smiled and started to back away.

To her surprise, the floating globe did not appear to move with her. She thought she saw the creature inside move slightly.

'You will – remove your-self from this – sec-tor.' It was a voice, which seemed to ride on a wave of squeals and static interference from the grille next to the weaponry panel.

'Right, right,' Bernice said hastily. She nodded, and began to move towards the exit.

'Over here!'

It could have been a worse moment, but not much. A stone was lobbed straight between Bernice and the giant globe at the same time as the voice echoed through the building.

The creature's weapon swivelled with alarming speed and blasted the stone to dust.

It gave Benny just enough time to see a boy, dressed in what looked like old-fashioned coveralls, beckoning to her from behind a pile of rubble.

Benny thought she had better warn him that negotiations worthy of a conciliation agency had been entered into, and that intervention at this stage by a well-meaning third party could well prove disruptive. This flashed through her mind in about half a second, as she considered the best way to put it into words. What would the Doctor say?

'Don't do anything stupid!' she shouted.

96

The boy grabbed what looked like a half-brick from his pile of rubble and sent it spinning towards the giant globe.

Bernice dropped to the floor. The dust had a hot and pungent smell, she noticed, as the half-brick was blown to smithereens with an echoing report. Now they would be in trouble.

At the edge of her vision, she could see the boy ducking uncertainly up and down. And she herself was right in the middle of an open space.

The alien fired again. Brightness cut the air and shattered what remained of the windows looking out over the city. Plexiglass blossomed in the sky and she imagined it falling outside.

Bernice scrambled across the floor, grazing her hands and knees. Her breath seemed to tear her apart. Was she safe? Some instinct had taken her towards the nearest cover. She realized she was behind a pillar, about two metres away from the boy.

'What the hell did you do that for?' she hissed at him, flattening herself against the cold stone. 'We were just becoming chums.'

The boy rubbed his bloodshot eyes. 'The Phractons are killing again,' he said, in a voice that carried an edge of desperation. 'Would have had you.'

'Can we make it to the door?' Benny asked.

The boy judged the distance. 'Yeah,' he said.

'Go, then. I'll follow.'

The Phracton reacted quickly to the flash of movement, but its beam blew out chunks of stone and plastic, and no more.

Though Bernice had not been able to get her hands on her image-intensifier, others were better equipped. Pale fingers held the handgrip, and large eyes surveyed the scene from the top of the sports centre.

One finger performed a simple action and the image zoomed, providing the watcher with a close-up view of two figures scurrying from a shattered building. One was recognizable to the watcher: it was the scrawny, hunted-

97

looking boy who had come with the others and escaped in the elevator. The other was unknown: a tall woman with short, dark hair who moved with a kind of professional litheness.

The watcher smiled grimly as a Phracton flamer swivelled around from the junction the pair had been heading for, shining in the dawn light. They were forced to duck into a shop doorway.

Shanstra lowered the viewer and her glittering eyes became opaque once more. Her night-black hair streamed out behind her, making her an impressive, dark silhouette against the morning sky.

She turned. She looked down at the huntress and the archivist, who were perched on the raised skylight by which they had accessed the roof. The archivist was looking at Shanstra in her anticipatory, slightly puzzled way. The huntress had her crossbow still in her hands, but sat with her hair lank over her eyes, her gaze downcast, sullen. As if waiting for an order.

Shanstra smiled. 'I think we have the potential for a fine day,' she said.

She rested her hand gently on the forehead of the huntress.

And drew strength.

The morning sun showed up the tiny segments of the comsat like the scales of a marine creature. It rose into the sky, an elegant, fragile curve mounted on a cylinder, thrusters burning gently as they lifted it on a pillar of smoke.

From the lip of the crater where they had launched the comsat, Horst Leibniz and Cassie Hogarth watched, monitoring the progress of the first non-computerized piece of machinery they had dealt with for quite some time.

'Supposing they shoot it down?' Leibniz muttered, chewing at a fingernail.

Hogarth monitored the readouts on her portable oscilloscope. 'You'd like that, wouldn't you? Then you'd have an excuse to tell everyone what a waste of time it was launching it.' She nodded, apparently satisfied, and directed a smile towards him.

'Without having innumerable, endless tests carried out in artificial conditions.' Leibniz's white-blond hair was waving in the breeze like a flag of surrender. He pushed it back with an angry gesture. 'I just think that when you're forced to downgrade your technology, your standards don't have to come down with it. You obviously don't agree.' He looked up at her for a second, met her one-eyed, mocking gaze. After a second he slammed his equipment case shut and set off down the slope back towards the valley where the *Phoenix* lay. Clouds of dust followed him like a vapour trail.

Cassie Hogarth nodded ruefully and allowed herself a moment's grudging respect for Leibniz. If she had to be honest, she didn't ever like to meet his stare like that, though – there was something very probing about it.

She looked up at the receding dot of the comsat, rising to the stars on its pillar of smoke.

'*Bon voyage*,' she said to herself.

Cheynor was on the bridge when he got the message. Given the apathetic state his crew was in these days, he was surprised that someone managed to relay it to him.

'Radio message coming through from the lieutenant, sir,' reported a young TechnOp. 'They've launched the comsat.'

Cheynor nodded. 'Right,' he said. 'As soon as ground communications can be opened again I want a channel to the Phracton command vessel.' There were murmurings around the bridge. 'Yes, all right!' Cheynor raised his voice and began to make his usual walk around the upper gallery of the bridge, where he could survey the tracking, weaponry and communications podiums. 'You may well think this has been an easy ride so far, but this is where the holiday fun stops. This is where we do our job.'

If only I believed it, he thought bitterly to himself. And if only I actually cared about this lump of rock.

One of the maintenance crew, who had wandered on to the bridge in search of something to do and now had his feet up on someone's console, cracked open a can very loudly, inviting attention.

Cheynor leaned over the upper balcony of the bridge and gave the man a hard stare. 'Are you quite comfortable down there, Tzidirov?' he asked sarcastically.

The man nodded, wiping his mouth and passing the can to the girl in maintenance uniform next to him. 'Yeah,' he said, taking the question seriously, 'I'll manage, Captain.'

'Have you anything to contribute?'

Tzidirov shrugged. He looked at the girl next to him, who shook her head.

'Well?' Cheynor raised his voice and gripped the rail as he surveyed the motley collection, who had learned over the years precisely what they could get away with. 'Anyone feel they've got the situation so well taped that they could offer something not too inane?' There was an uncomfortable silence. Cheynor nodded. 'As we were then,' he said. 'I want to know the moment I can talk to the Phracton leader.'

'So we are jacking it in?' someone asked, not quite softly enough. Whoever it was, they sounded almost hopeful, and elicited groans of derision from around the bridge.

'Not exactly,' Captain Cheynor informed the crew. 'We're going to invite the Phracton leader here, and we're going to talk to him. By the time he leaves, we'll have convinced him and his Swarm to leave us alone for a very long time.' He looked around the suddenly silent podiums of the bridge. 'Any questions?'

Apparently, there were none.

Well, Cheynor thought with grim satisfaction. That seems to have given them something to think about, at least.

Tzidirov belched.

10

Womb Service

The Doctor watched solemnly as Tilusha Meswani was carried on a stretcher into the waiting ambulance. Beside him in the forecourt of the flats, Nita Bedi pulled her woollen coat tightly around her thin, colourful costume and shivered, grateful for the shelter of the Doctor's umbrella.

'So much depends on the body, doesn't it?' said the Doctor thoughtfully, as the rain pattered above and around them.

She only half heard him, as she was peering anxiously into the ambulance.

'Don't worry,' said the Doctor, 'it'll be fine. All the signs are that it'll be a natural, comfortable birth.'

He raised his hat at the two ambulance men, who stood aside to let him and Nita aboard. Nita didn't know what he had said to them when they arrived, but it had certainly satisfied them. He had even managed to persuade them of the necessity of having Phil Tarrant taken to a different hospital. That, thought Nita, must have taken some doing, and she was grateful for it. But it still didn't mean she trusted this shifty little man. Not at all.

'I was just thinking,' he said, when they were settled into the seats, facing each other, 'that for human beings, the concerns of the body sometimes override all else. Determine their state of mind. If you're rushed, you feel hot and bothered, you get more flustered. If you're hungry, you get impatient.'

The ambulance doors were closed. The nurse who was monitoring Tilusha's blood pressure smiled reassuringly at the Doctor and Nita. The girl scowled back. She'd had enough of reassuring smiles, and, she was beginning to think, about enough of the Doctor's philosophy too.

'I'd imagine that's what the Sensopath has locked on to. The strongest emotion in Tilusha was – is – the bond between mother and child. That physical-mental link. Ideal.' He frowned, and lapsed into introspective broodiness again. 'Ideal for it. And I don't even know if I should be letting it happen.'

Moments later, the ambulance was gripping the wet road, cutting through the city traffic.

A breath away from tragedy.

'This city is steeped in blood. New and ancient blood.'

Shanstra was marvelling at the fresh strength and information which she had drawn from the young minds of her two newest acolytes.

She sat at the centre of the ice-rink, in a huge, raised chair which had been borrowed from one of the offices. Its purpose was to make Shanstra feel important.

'This place,' she murmured. 'It cannot have been chance that brought me here.'

Shanstra –

She closed her eyes and decided to summon her powers. She would see what she was strong enough to do now. The ice began to hiss. *Shanstra, my sister, my self.*

She gripped the chair with her enormous hands, sending out crackles of rogue energy that fizzed around the auditorium like fireworks. Some of them melted the spectators' chairs into fantastic shapes.

The ice was lifting in great, irrepressible clouds from the rink. The layer of steam curved in a bowl-shape towards the dominating figure of Shanstra.

Shanstra, do you hear me?

* * *

I hear you, Kelzen.

Tilusha was murmuring as if delirious. The nurse, efficient and calm, watched her closely.

Nita could see an expression of intense concentration on the lined face of the Doctor. The ambulance rounded a corner, and his umbrella clattered to the floor. He looked up at Nita, and his expression was almost pleading.

'Talk to me,' he said.

'What?'

'Talk to me, Nita! Tell me the stories of the gods, of Vishnu and Siva. Or if you like, tell me about yourself, about the desk you had on your first day at school and the first boy you kissed.'

Nita's mouth moved, but she could not think of anything to say. The ambulance moved on, inexorably. Tilusha breathed. The rain hissed. Harmony.

'Rain,' the Doctor said softly, watching it lash like angry monsters against the ambulance. Almost as if it were trying to impede their journey. 'In your mythology, the soul can come back from the spirits to earth in the rain, can't it? Clinging to raindrops.'

'If it goes the Way of the Spirits.' Nita nodded eagerly. 'If it alights on a plant, and the man eats the plant, he can then impregnate a woman with the reborn soul. That's what we are taught, anyway.'

'And some,' said the Doctor broodingly, 'go the Way of the Gods. To Brahma.' He sighed, and leaned back in his seat. 'The Greek philosopher Epicurus, on the other hand, claimed that if there were gods, there was no reason at all why they should be the least bit interested in mere mortals.' The Doctor smiled sadly, as if at some private joke. 'Intriguing, don't you think? The idea that we invoke greater powers because we just can't face the idea that we might all be alone.'

'I don't feel alone,' Nita said. 'Tilusha, she believes in the gods. But not in rituals, she never saw the point.'

'I make a point of studying cultures,' said the Doctor. 'Religious faith ceased to have any meaning for me, long ago, after seeing so much conflict. But I still respect those for whom it's important.' He made that urgent, gesturing motion again. 'Tell me, Nita. Keep talking.'

In her own way, Nita was beginning to understand. She cast a horrified look at Tilusha, then back at the Doctor, her heart increasing its pace, as the ambulance continued to judder through the city, rain clattering on its windscreen.

'You want me to help you block that – that thing, don't you?' she said, fearfully.

'I'm too strongly telepathic. It's latching on to me as a kind of booster.' The Doctor was almost gabbling, his hands twitching in his lap. 'Talk to me.'

Nita took a deep breath. 'I didn't know what to do when Tilusha started seeing Phil. I had to see her in secret. Her family no longer knew her, to all intents and purposes. Her father, he's a good man, I still see him . . .'

Livewire's head hurt. She could not remember why she had come to this place, but she knew that she had to survive, that was what life in Banksburgh was about, that was what it had always been about. It was dog-eat-cat, dog-eat-vomit.

One of her phrases. Or was it? No, it was someone else's. The name, no the nickname – what was a nickname? Polymer. Poly. Where was Poly? She had gone under, obviously. And Trinket. He would go under, too.

Of course. She remembered now. There was Shanstra, who had spared her and saved her and who was going to take her to a better place than this, because Livewire was strong, and a leader, and a survivor, and deserved it. And Trinket and the ship from Earth and anyone else who wasn't needed, they would go under because they hadn't made the grade and it was all their fault.

She found her new friend in the rink. In the midst of a whirlwind of vapour, from which tendrils of light streamed out, sometimes fizzing with sparks against the vidscreens or the stalls. The ice was lifting from the surface, all turning to steam with a hiss like a million angry snakes. Or was it rain?

Shanstra was at the centre, glowing triumphantly.
Kelzen.
Livewire heard the name buzzing in her head.
KelzenShanstra.
'I hear you!' Shanstra screamed.

'She was going to have an abortion when she found out she was pregnant by Phil. I told her not to. Can you believe that? I had this crazy notion that he might grow up to be a great scientist or politician.' Nita licked her lips. 'How am I doing?' she asked anxiously, sparing a glance at Tilusha. Her cousin, bathed in perspiration, was moaning, her head lolling from side to side. The nurse looked up, but this time her reassuring smile seemed more fake.

'Don't stop!' The Doctor's voice was furious. His screwed-up face and unmasked anger caused the nurse to gasp out loud.

And then the window of the ambulance cracked right across.

Nita was jolted from her seat, with the sound of skidding tyres in her head.

The TR7 had been driven by an inconsequential driver whose car stereo was on at full blast, and who did not hear the ambulance until it was too late. In trying to get out of its way, he did not realize that the skilled ambulance driver had already compensated and was coming in for a safe pass on the wet city ring road.

Effectively, he swung his car right into the path of the ambulance, just too late to be avoided. The ambulance sheared across the soaking road and slammed into the set of traffic-lights which it was permitted to ignore. The slim pole gave way before the onslaught of the vehicle, allowing the jammed wheels to skid further still, across the right-hand junction. Then, carried by the wind and its own weight, the ambulance crashed over on to its side.

'No!' Shanstra leapt from her seat.

105

Livewire blinked in confusion as she saw the chaos all around her beginning to subside. There was the gentle cracking sound of a huge film of water refreezing at an incredible rate.

Shanstra's long-boned fingers covered her oval face for a moment, and when she looked up again, her expression was dark and terrible with anger.

'The connection has been broken,' she said in menacingly quiet tones.

Livewire frowned. 'So what's that mean?'

'It means our enemies have won another reprieve!' snarled Shanstra angrily, and she strode through the resublimating vapour, frost settling on her velvet hair. Energy rustled like a train behind her, and then split off into hundreds of tiny pieces like yapping dogs at the hem of her cloak. 'It means,' she said, gazing past the girl and into nothingness, 'that we need a stronger unity of minds.' Talking more to herself than to Livewire, she raised a long finger. 'I need to know more about this place. About the blood. There are – ' she frowned, and her lips pressed together in redness ' – whispers here, like a conversation in the next room of my mind. All one voice, and yet – ' a pause ' – more. I need to find them.'

It was an unsettling experience for Livewire, but for once she thought she knew what Shanstra was talking about. It was something to do with the life she had just left behind, after all.

'The Phracs,' said Livewire.

'Phracs?' Shanstra turned her head very slightly, as if listening to something beyond what Livewire was saying. The vapour, swirling white, cooled around them. 'Of course,' she said slowly, realizing. 'Those aliens.'

'The Phracton Swarm. They invaded the colony weeks ago,' said Livewire. 'Decimated the population and destroyed most of the city before something stopped them. Now, they just kind of patrol, looking menacing.' She frowned, as if she should not really have been remembering any of this. 'I've come close to taking out one or two. But it's hard, you're fighting your own kind too.

106

Fighting them for a few looted cans of food.' Livewire's face was taut with strain.

'How very entertaining,' said Shanstra. 'Show me.'

She touched Livewire's forehead, as she had done before, and the screens around the ice-rink leapt into startling action. The stentorian voice of a newscaster, projected from Livewire's subconscious memory, filled the arena.

Shanstra was not very concerned with what the voice was saying, as she found the pictures evocative enough – images of Gadrell Major taken from space, and stock footage of Phracton vehicles rolling through creamy mud, blasting down all in their path. Human beings running across ridges of mud, some trampling one another, one or two stopping to grab rings and purses and bangles from the fallen bodies.

Shanstra removed her hand from Livewire's forehead, and the images slammed back into darkness once more.

'Very interesting,' said the Sensopath. 'I think we should go to the battlefield.'

Suzi watched them from the glass-fronted restaurant above the rink. Her headache was coming back, and she needed Colm. Shanstra had promised her Colm, and she intended to make sure that Shanstra kept her promise.

The girl Livewire had regarded Suzi with slight contempt ever since she had arrived. Ever since – no. Nothing had happened. Suzi reminded herself that nothing had happened and that there was no need to go up into the observation dome, no need to see the charred skeleton, because if she told herself for long enough that it didn't exist, then it didn't exist. That was what was so good about Shanstra. She took all the things which life had told Suzi she could never have, and promised them.

So, how to react to Livewire? She was a huntress, one of a kind with Shanstra. There was something about the girl, an edginess, a sharpness that made her look as if she could kill. As if she had killed. Suzi did not know who the boy had been, or where he had escaped to now. It did not matter. Shanstra was going to unite them all in her love and her great scheme, and there was no need for worries or responsibilities.

A gap had been filled. Suzi felt the contentment, almost physically. She realized that what she had been needing all this time was the desire to worship. To be abject – for she had always suspected that she was, essentially, worthless and sinful – and to adore something greater and more beautiful than herself.

She closed her eyes and filled her heart with love: for creation, for destruction, for the will of Shanstra.

11

No Escape from Reality

I know you can hear me.

Many voices had called to the Doctor in his dreams before, but none had been quite like this one. He was not entirely sure, for one thing, that this was a dream. He remembered the impact, the ambulance turning slowly, so slowly, and then –

There was a reddish blackness just at the edge of his vision, and an almost electrical tingling between his ears.

I am Kelzen. Help me.

The Doctor blinked. His eyes appeared to be open, but he could not feel or see his body. There was nothing but the blood-blackness, and beyond it this insistent voice that was a mixture of sound and feeling. It was, he decided, a female voice, tinged with nervousness and, maybe, kindness.

The Doctor licked his lips. 'So, you're the Sensopath who's been causing all the trouble.' He frowned, not sure that the words had actually come out of his mouth.

I am Kelzen. I am lost and alone. I came unwanted to this world and I took refuge in the mind of the half-formed. It seemed appropriate, as I was in need of recuperation myself.

'What happened? Why are you here?'

We floated, bodiless. I attempted to . . . experiment with my developing powers, and I found the child . . . receptive.

109

There was no need to find another host. But now the mother and child are in danger.

Tilusha, thought the Doctor. 'Can you do anything?'

I shall try. But there are others who may try to stop me. I cannot fully control myself alone. It is . . . difficult to explain. There was a pause, as if the Sensopath were deliberating. Then the question bounced into the Doctor's head and fizzed there like an aspirin dissolving in water. *Your mind is richer than that of these beings. Who are you? Where are you from?*

'I'm not prepared to tell you that, yet. But I'm the one who intercepted the distress call. The same signal from two sources at once – fascinating. I had to follow it up.' The Doctor swallowed. 'Who exactly did you take with you in the vortex and drop off in the twenty-fourth century?'

There was a rippling of the strange environment, a pulsing in the Doctor's head, and the Sensopath's voice struggled to maintain its level tone. It was almost as if something were trying to break through.

You are mistaken. It was I who was abandoned in this barren place. Shanstra's powers were the greatest, and she was able to direct Jirenal and myself according to her will. To scatter us where she pleased.

'Shanstra? Jirenal? There are three of you?' The Doctor's hearts were racing. He could feel reality surging in and had the strangest feeling that he was about to wake up. It was imperative, then, to get information while the link was still strong.

Yes. We are three.

'Kelzen – is Shanstra dangerous? Is it her, in the twenty-fourth century?'

The answer began, like the sound of rain rustling against a sheet of glass. It ended in the helpless, breath-giving screech of a new-born child.

The Doctor's last thought before he awoke was of Bernice, and of how he had been stupid enough to send her into the greatest of danger.

* * *

Cheynor sat alone in his briefing room. His beard had grown slightly thicker over the past 48 hours, and it gave his face an even more intensely brooding aspect than before. Leibniz and Hogarth, arguing about something as usual, had reported back within the last hour. All they had to do now was wait for the comsat to attain its optimum position. In the meantime, Cheynor was following up a hunch. It was the kind of analysis – looking beyond the obvious – that his old captain, Terrin, had taught him.

'Computer,' he said.

'Internal systems only on-line,' the computer reminded him, in the soothing, adrogynous voice he had selected for his terminal.

'I know, I know. Access history files: Gadrell Major.'

'Information processing. Information accessed.'

'Cross-check with Dalek war, Cyberwars, porizium deposits. And give me a hard copy of all the major conflicts centring around, or related to, the mineral porizium.'

'Processing.'

Cheynor drummed his fingers on the table while he waited for his hard copy. He had a feeling it was going to be a very decisive document indeed.

It was like a great, thundering tide of metal pursuing them down the street.

Bernice had seen tanks before, but this one seemed to be almost alive, to slither over rough terrain like a hunting animal. She and the boy Trinket ran through the back streets of the near deserted city, their feet pounding the muddy ground, gunfire echoing distantly, and the rumble of the great metal tank growing behind them with every second.

Bernice's lungs were burning. Mud splashed up on either side of her, great fountains of it. She kept running, and hoped that Trinket knew where he was going.

'Here!' The boy grabbed her arm and pulled her into the rickety entrance of a warehouse.

Darkness descended in front of Benny's eyes. She moved forward, confused. There was the sound of a metal covering of some sort being opened, and then a light briefly smudged the darkness. She saw the shadowy form of Trinket, lit dimly from beneath, which confused her further still for a moment, until she realized he had opened a metal hatchway and she was expected to climb in after him.

'Service tunnels,' Trinket said briefly from beneath her.

Benny made the briefest of sounds to show that she understood. She could smell metal and oil as she lowered herself on to the ladder, and pulled the hatchway down behind her. It clanged shut.

She heard the rumble of the Phracton machine as it hurtled past on ground level, and felt the vibration in her fingertips.

After a climb down of about twenty metres, she found herself in a space large enough to stand up. She rubbed her rust-smeared hands on her trousers, thankful that she'd been practical enough to change.

Trinket was leaning against a curved metal wall, under one of the dim panels that illuminated the passageway. 'It could have got us, you know,' he said, looking at Bernice through his tangled fringe.

'I'd gathered that much. I presume you don't call them flamers for their sparkling conversation.'

'They fire a combustible gas and ignite it. It can trash anything up to about fifty metres.' Trinket took a deep breath and shook his head. 'The Phracs are playing with us. It's as if they only want us dead in certain parts of the city, and at certain times.'

Bernice squatted down, rummaging in her satchel. 'That sounds like the beginnings of a theory, Trinket.'

The boy shook his head, again with an almost twitchy response. Even in the dimness, Bernice could tell there was something not quite right with his eyes – as if he were suffering from some kind of delayed shock, maybe.

She found her chocolate, broke it, offered half to Trinket. At first he backed off. Not used to being offered something for nothing, Benny reasoned. She bit off a

112

chunk of her own half, offered again. This time he took it, with a brief smile of gratitude.

'You see,' Trinket said, 'I dunno what's going on here any more. Not since that woman. I think I've seen someone else more dangerous than the Phracs.'

Bernice stopped chewing. Her eyes widened and she swallowed hastily. 'Trinket,' she said, 'tell me everything you know about this woman.'

Darius Cheynor believed in clutching at straws. Whether this was brave or stupid he didn't really care as, for once, it had worked. Minimal communications and monitoring facilities had returned to the *Phoenix*.

He stood at the table of his briefing room, with Jocassta Hogarth and Horst Leibniz once more at his side.

He nodded. Hogarth operated a sequence of controls on the panel in front of her, and a crackling holovid began to form on the table in front of them. Within about five seconds, they were looking into the glittering web of the Phracton communications network.

Cheynor stared into the heart of the web.

'This is Captain Darius Cheynor of the Spacefleet vessel *Phoenix*. I request an audience with the Phracton Commandant.' The network of glittering blue whirled and crackled. Fractal images formed into a giant, pulsing eye which could have been that of a Phracton itself, or simply the computer's representation of an interface portal.

'What message do you wish to convey?'

Cheynor took a deep breath. Leibniz raised his eyebrows.

'I wish,' Cheynor said slowly, 'to meet your representatives in one hour at a venue to be arranged. I wish to make arrangements, as the advocate of Earth Council and the Colonial Office, for the surrender of the Earth forces on Gadrell Major, as represented by the *Phoenix*. With the Commandant's consent, I wish to accede to the Phracton claim to Gadrell Major, and to arrange for the dominion to be handed over to Phracton control as soon as possible.'

There was a brief silence. Understandable, Cheynor thought, in the circumstances. Blue light played over his darkly handsome face, as if searching it for any betrayal of irony, mockery.

Then came the reply. 'The Commandant sends thanks for your decision. You and your senior officers will assemble, unarmed, in Londinium Plaza in one hour. Your ship's weaponry and communications systems are to be deactivated during the meeting. You will not bring extraneous personnel. You will listen to our arrangements, after which you and all remaining human civilians will leave Gadrell Major immediately.'

'Agreed,' said Cheynor.

The link snapped off.

'Smart,' said Cassie Hogarth from the shadows, her arms folded. 'Remind me never to play you at poker, sir.'

'Poker?' said Cheynor, straightening up. He wore a hint of an exhausted smile. 'I'm playing snap, Cassie.' He looked at her calm, stern face, then over at the more edgy Leibniz, who had been about to say something. 'I'm perfectly serious. I meant what I said. In one hour, I intend to hand Gadrell Major over to the Phractons.'

For the first time since being appointed Cheynor's advisors, Horst Leibniz and Cassie Hogarth were united in stunned, silent disbelief.

Trinket lifted the hatchway very slightly and peered up through the crack. There was only the desolate, empty street to be seen in either direction. He braced himself, pushed the cover off and climbed up, then reached down and helped Benny up.

She slotted the cover back into place and shivered slightly in the early morning wind. 'Where now?'

'My folks had a house off Londinium Plaza. We've got a sort of base there. It's like a bunker. If Livewire got away, she'd make for there.'

'You think Livewire did get away?' Bernice did not want to hurt the boy, but she wondered at his optimism, after what he'd told her.

114

'I have to keep thinking that, don't I?' he answered, and his voice was dull and blank, like unpolished metal.

'With your new resident in town, I'd keep an open mind.' Benny knew that didn't sound reassuring. 'Come on, then.'

They scurried along, keeping close in to the shattered shop-fronts. Bernice saw Trinket scoop up two cans and stuff them into a pocket without even breaking his stride. She wondered how long it would take her to relearn the art of scavenging.

They stopped at a corner. Broken glass crunched under Bernice's feet. She could see that, beyond the stumpy remains of what had probably been commemorative trees, the street gave out into a broad square with chequered paving. Four statues with broad, conical pedestals stood at the corners – portraying famous governors, she guessed from looking at the braided uniform of the one nearest to them. The statues looked rather like larger-than-life chess pieces awaiting their move. At the centre of the square, Benny could just make out the inert, curved nozzles of a fountain display, pointing in silent dryness towards a central metal pillar in the shape of a hand. The fountain-sculpture had probably been quite beautiful when it was in action, but now it just looked sad and abandoned.

'Just a minute.' Bernice put a hand on Trinket's shoulder to stop the boy from making a run. 'Let's do this sensibly.'

She took out her motion detector and scanned the read-outs. After a moment, she whistled softly to herself. Over such a broad space it was hard to get an exact fix of direction, but still . . .

Oh, Doctor, Bernice thought. On a scale of great ideas, this ranks right up there with doing baked Alaska in a microwave.

'Right,' she said, 'we need better cover. What about over there?'

Shanstra, pausing in the desolate street, stepped on a fragment of something brittle. It broke like fine china

115

beneath her booted foot. When she looked down, the Sensopath was mildly interested to see that she had crushed the remnants of a human skull.

A few metres to her right and in front, Livewire walked, slowly and carefully. She was Shanstra's hunting dog. She moved like a warrior, her pale hair fluttering in the breeze, her crossbow in front of her like a part of her body. To either side of them both, high, shattered buildings cast their shadow.

Shanstra could feel the minds growing stronger. The unified minds which threatened to crowd her own.

They strode on. Shanstra needed battle, and she needed to draw sustenance.

Benny and Trinket had taken hasty cover in what used to be one of Banksburgh's best-known night bars, at the edge of Londinium Plaza. Fragments of bottles and the crusted stains of drinks still decorated the scraped, burnt chrome of the elegantly curving bar and its mushroom-like tables. To Bernice it looked like a graveyard of entertainment, somewhere that the ghosts of sodden old drunks came to haunt.

From the mostly intact window, they could see out into the plaza with its golden statues catching the light. And they could see the arrival of the skimmer whose approach Bernice had detected.

The skimmer came gently to rest in the centre of the plaza, the hum of its propulsion unit fading to silence. They saw three figures alight from the vehicle, and move to stand beside it. All three, Bernice could see, wore the simplest grey and brown Spacefleet uniforms, and one of them was a woman, but she could not make out any more details.

She could hear her own breath, and Trinket's.

And there was a familiar whining sound, getting closer.

'What a hellish place this has become.'

Darius Cheynor, hands on hips, gazed across the deserted, rubbish-strewn Londinium Plaza, wondering

116

what it had been like when it was alive, bustling with colonists on their many missions of the day.

Cassie Hogarth, arms folded, was leaning against the skimmer. 'I don't reckon it was ever much of a holiday camp. Do you?' She glowered at the captain with her one visible eye. Cheynor made a noncommittal sound.

Leibniz, his glasses filled with sunlight, did not join in the conversation. He was thinking about the fate of Gadrell Major, and was beginning to wonder if he had been more gullible than he ever imagined he could be.

Like bubbles carried on the wind, four Phracton airborne units floated in from the southern apex of the plaza.

Cheynor and Hogarth straightened up. Leibniz remained at a distance, his fingers pressed into his palms. He didn't like this, and he was not going to pretend that he did. It upset his innate sense of balance and precision.

Hogarth, meanwhile, was filled with a rush of emotion, much of it conflicting. Excitement, awe, fear, but also frustration. She had argued with Captain Cheynor for nearly half an hour, trying to get him to allow her to have a slimline fusion grenade concealed in the sole of her boot. He had refused point-blank. He said he had made a deal with the Phracton Commandant, and that he did not intend to break his word: it was to be the senior officers, alone, unarmed, on a mission of peace. He would not have her jeopardizing that. A mission of peace! She doubted it even now.

Cassie was beginning to wonder about her own audacity. Not only in questioning her captain outright, but in the way she was still burning with resentment now, still thinking he had been wrong.

Still thinking of the anger she would die feeling if those Phracs floated over and blasted them. Defenceless and clueless – what a way to die. It made Cassie want to spit.

The Phractons advanced across Londinium Plaza.

117

12

Alive in the City

'Tell me,' said the Doctor.

Nita Bedi clutched the plastic cup of coffee and let it warm her chilled hands. Her eyes looked up at those of the Doctor across the whitewashed hospital room, her expression hostile and challenging. 'You knew this would happen.'

'No, no,' said the Doctor softly. 'Please. I had no idea. Tell me the story.'

Nita took a deep breath, and began to intone in a dead, flat voice.

'There was a princess called Savitri who reached the age when she should marry. She told her father that she wished to go out into the world before she married, to pray at the temples and to hear the words of the holy men. She knew that this would bring her closer to the Guardian Spirit, and she thought also that destiny would bring her a husband when the time was right . . .'

Trinket had not known whether to trust this woman with her array of alien devices, but right now he was glad of her presence, given the situation out in the plaza.

He saw the Phrac globes hover and settle about twenty metres from the officers, on the other side of the fountain.

Words were being exchanged. The captain, a medium-sized man with a beard, seemed to be doing most of the talking. The other two officers stood one on either side of him, the woman with her arms folded, and the skinny, whitish-blond man looking uncomfortable as if he did not want to be there at all. Trinket's eyesight was excellent – much better than he had ever let Livewire know – but they were still to far away for him to be able to read any expressions.

'Do you know what's going on?' he hissed to Bernice.

She was watching intently, her hand never far from her obviously important canvas satchel. 'Looks like we might have caught them at an awkward moment,' said Bernice.

Trinket had already got used to her saying things like that. He wasn't sure he understood them all, but they were at least better than Livewire's sharp words or Polymer's sneering.

Polymer. He closed his eyes for a second, unable still to believe it.

When he opened them again, he saw the sunlight falling on another distant figure. She was striding out from the buildings on the other side, heading for the group in the centre of the plaza.

He gasped.

It was his half-sister, Livewire.

'And so Savitri went out into the world and did as she said she would, learning, sleeping under the stars. One day in the forest, she met a handsome woodcutter named Satyavan. They fell into conversation, and Satyavan told Savitri of his sorry fate – how he used to be the son of a king, and how the king had been overthrown, had his palace and fortune taken from him. Now the old man was blind and frail and the two of them lived alone in a cottage in the woods.' Nita paused, sipped her coffee.

'Go on. The point of storytelling is to finish, you know.'

'It's going to be all right, isn't it, Doctor?'

The Doctor leaned back. His face was in shadow. He looked sideways at Nita, his gaze unreadable. 'No,' he said. 'Not for the moment.'

She took another gulp of coffee. Her hands were shaking.

119

'Savitri returned to her family and announced that destiny had brought her a husband, as she always said it would . . .'

Trinket felt Bernice's hand pulling him back.

'No! You can't go out there!'

'It's her,' he managed to say.

Bernice swung him round and looked into his eyes. 'Do you feel anything strange? Because I certainly do. It's something I felt on Earth, a kind of tingling like someone running their fingers over my thoughts. It's mind control, Trinket! The Doctor was right!'

Trinket, horrified, broke away from her, and backed into one of the crumbling tables, sending it and its debris toppling into the mirrored wall, shattering their reflections with a crash. It echoed out into the square.

He backed away from the woman Bernice. To think he had almost fallen into her trap, he thought. Not only an off-worlder, but a madwoman too. Didn't she see he had to go to Livewire?'

He judged the distance, and ran.

'Then?' coaxed the Doctor.

'Savitri's marriage was announced. But there was a holy man in her father's palace, a man with the power to see things that others did not. He warned her that she should not marry this man Satyavan, for he was cursed to die, and had only twelve months left to live.

'She was determined, though, and soon the ceremony was arranged. An iron ring was fixed around her wrist, and they walked around the fire seven times while chanting the ancient prayers. And after they were bound together, she went to the woods with him to his poor cottage, to be his wife. She did not tell him what the holy man had foreseen, but she knew it had to be true – Yama, the god of death, never breaks his word.' Nita's voice faltered and she let the coffee cup bounce to the floor, scattering droplets.

'As true as death,' said the Doctor softly. 'Isn't that what you say?'

The rain had stopped and the afternoon sun was seeping in behind the gauze curtains, a sickly yellow. It was too thin, and too late.

Bernice had to think through her options fast. But she knew what she was going to do. Her mind was tingling with the voice of . . . what?

She broke cover. The plaza was before her, unfocused. She swung to the left, saw the smooth globes of the aliens, and then to the right, where the human officers were turning, turning towards her. And there, straight ahead, running right into the danger zone, was the boy with his tangled hair. And his tall half-sister was standing with her feet apart, confidently lifting a large and lethal-looking crossbow.

'Stop!' Bernice Summerfield shouted.

As an opening gambit, she knew it lacked panache. She would never even have tried such a thing had she not seen it work for the Doctor on several occasions.

The Doctor . . .

It was worth a try.

Bernice grabbed the little pyramid from her pocket and hurled it out on to the ground. It clunked as it hit, and sprouted a wisp of light, which metamorphosed with alarming rapidity into the smiling figure of the Doctor.

'Well,' he said, 'what have we here?'

The tall girl dropped to one knee, changing her aim with incredible skill and swiftness.

She fired. The crossbow bolt went right through the hologram and hit the foremost Phracton globe with a resounding crack.

Nita's eyes were glistening. They reflected the earnest, closely listening Doctor. 'The marriage was a happy one. Savitri proved a loyal and loving wife, but each day she was possessed by the thought that the hour of her husband's death was growing nearer, though she said nothing to him about it.

'After twelve months, he came. Death. They were out

121

in the forest one day, walking, and he stepped on to the path in front of them, a dark, robed figure, carrying a noose. He said he had come for the soul of Satyavan, and he took it, leaving the body limp and lifeless there in the forest clearing.

'But when Yama left the clearing with the soul of her one true love, Savitri boldly followed.'

One of the Phractons began to lift up above the square, moving into a decidedly threatening position. Its motor unit whined, sending dust whirling up from within the abandoned fountain.

Bernice, dazed for a moment, scooped up her hologram by snatching at the Doctor's foot. It compacted. He had been standing there watching interestedly, she noted.

She ducked down beside the skimmer, next to the one-eyed woman.

'I told him,' the woman snarled, more to herself than to Benny. 'I told him we should have come armed!'

The captain, indecisive, turned round to glare at her, and Bernice Summerfield found herself looking into a familiar pair of eyes. But she had no time to react, nor even to mouth his name. The Phracton's weapon engaged once, twice, sending shattering bursts into the paving. Chunks of stone fountained and sizzled.

Bernice risked a look over the top of the skimmer. The girl called Livewire was standing there. Just standing there. And now she had dropped the crossbow and was putting her hands to her temples.

Where the hell was Trinket? Bernice had time for that one thought before the tingling in her mind opened out, like vast torrents of water breaking down the final resistance of a dam.

It cascaded through the channels of all her perceptions.

And there was a scream, like the horrifying cry of a child being wrenched from its mother's womb.

'And Savitri spoke to the god of death, looking into his blank eyes, and she asked for the soul of her beloved to

122

be spared. Yama could not do this. He told her she should prepare the obsequies and arrange for the burning of her husband's body in the traditional way. He was impressed by her resolve, though, and said instead he would grant her a wish, to lessen her grief.

'Very well, then, she said, and chose her father-in-law's sight to be returned. Yama told her it was done, and once more turned into the darkness of the forest with her husband's soul. But Savitri followed.'

The Doctor nodded. He had his hand on Nita's warm forehead. He only hoped that his gentle hypnotism would spare her from the absolute terror and pain of what she was soon to know.

It tore through Londinium Plaza, carried by Livewire alone. The force of the pain, the shattering anger – the coruscating power that was Shanstra, the will of Shanstra, the desire of Shanstra.

It slammed like walls of light into the swooping globes of the Phractons.

Bernice had her hands over her ears and her eyes tightly shut.

Cheynor's call to take cover was drowned in a scream of energy that was part human, part alien, the sound of molecules being forced apart. In a matter of just a few seconds, three of the Phractons' multi-bonded casings split and shattered as if they were no more than barley sugar sweets. Down fell rain of charred casing and circuits. The remains of the three globes dropped and smashed like eggs, two into the fountain, the other on to the square.

The fourth Phracton seemed to have been singled out for special attention. Its globe wobbled, then dripped like wax from a candle, falling slowly towards the ground. It sizzled, sprouted strange protuberances that branched off from one another like tributaries. Just a second later, there stood what looked like a glass tree in the centre of the fountain, its twisted, blobby branches made up of deformed bits of Phracton. The creature's stretched body hung suspended in the glassy trunk of the tree-shape.

The remaining three globes bubbled, deflated. The screams of the bluish creatures inside were choked as they were slowly incinerated by their own temperature regulators, flesh frothing out of the broken shells. Tentacles were thrashing helplessly, trying to operate circuits that no longer existed.

With her face forced into a rictus of sadistic delight, Livewire sank to her knees.

Like an ancient memory, the tale was concluded. Nita's gaze never left the Doctor's. 'Savitri followed Yama into a dark, cold place. And Yama, who was astonished that any mortal should defy him so, offered her another wish to lessen her grief. If that is so, said Savitri, then I choose for my father-in-law's kingdom and wealth to be returned.

'Yama told her that it was done. But still she would not leave him. She followed the god of death into a place of rank swamps and swirling mists. Now he was enraged, and told her to leave him at once. Just one more wish, she said. He agreed. She asked to be allowed to have many children and to see them live to a full, old age. The god of death thought this to be a good wish, and granted it.

'Then Savitri said, "You must know that, under Hindu law, a widow cannot remarry." '

'Yama realized that it was so, and that he could not go back on his word – he had been tricked by a mortal. And so he released the soul of Satyavan, and told the cunning Savitri it would be a long time before either of them encountered him again. They went back into the world, where they found all of Savitri's wishes granted, and the couple lived a long and happy life.'

'Good,' said the Doctor. 'Sleep.'

Nita's eyelids came down, and her head slumped forward.

'As true as death.' The Doctor shook his head sadly, placed his hat on his head and left the lounge.

Outside in the corridor, there was a crumpled white coat containing a crumpled white junior doctor.

'I'm very sorry,' the medic said. 'I was just coming to find the, er, next of kin?'

The Doctor pointed silently into the lounge.

'Ah. Well. Thank you.' The medic frowned and looked the Doctor up and down. 'Excuse me, sir, but – you were the one who came in earlier? With the, er, accident?'

'That's right.'

'You were suffering quite badly from shock, as I recall.' The young man unhooked his stethoscope. 'Are you sure you're fit to be up and about? It was only a few hours ago.'

The Doctor sighed, raised his eyes and tapped his umbrella on the floor. 'Let's see,' he said. He grabbed the end of the stethoscope and pressed it to his chest. The young doctor made a surprised but grudgingly accepting face. This turned to puzzlement when the Doctor moved the stethoscope to the other side – and then to astonishment.

'Now, just a minute – ' he began indignantly.

'I can't spare one. Time is precious. It has to be rationed.' The Doctor gave him a brief, centuries-old and weary smile. 'Good day.' He strolled down the corridor, swinging his umbrella.

At 18.38, Tilusha Meswani had looked into the contented face of her new-born son, Sanjay.

At 18.40, she had seen the face of the Doctor for the last time. He was standing on the other side of a sheet of glass, his hands folded on his umbrella, his face showing unfathomable pain, as if he were the guardian of some ancient and secret knowledge. She smiled. Her ordeal was over.

As black clouds descended on the fringes of her vision, she was sure that she saw two small, green eyes glowing in the depths of that new darkness.

At 18.45, the brain of Tilusha Meswani officially ceased to function, and on her home world of Earth, the first stage of the usual bureaucratic process of recording and registering was engaged.

On a wider plane, other ripples spread out from the single event of her death. The next sequence in a huge and ancient battle was initiated. The Doctor knew this, but Tilusha, who had unwittingly been a part of the wider scheme, did not.

And on another plane still, whether her soul went to join the gods or the spirits was a matter for Tilusha Meswani alone.

13

Armageddon Days

'It seems, Professor Summerfield, that you and I are destined to run into war at every turn.'

Bernice lay back against the padded headrest of her chair in the *Phoenix* visitors' lounge, and let her thumb stroke the filigreed patterns on her glass. 'It couldn't be helped. There's some horribly dangerous power at work here, and that's what the Doctor sent me to investigate.'

'Ah, the Doctor.' Cheynor, leaning back in his own chair, sighed deeply and shook his head. 'How we could do with him now.'

Bernice smiled in a gentle, covert way to herself. After she had recognized the face of Darius Cheynor – really only a fleeting acquaintance from over a year ago during the business with the Garvond – she had wondered whether chance could possibly have brought them together again. Knowing the Doctor, she doubted it.

There had not been time for much of a reunion. Attention had rather been focused on the smoking remains of four Phracton units which sizzled in the otherwise silent square. Pillars of smoke jutted upwards into the grey sky. Bernice saw the glutinous, blue remains of the nearest Phracton bubbling out of the burnt casing on to the ground, and quickly turned away.

She caught Trinket's eye. He had been there all the time, about twenty metres away. He was cradling a dazed Livewire in his arms.

127

There had been no option but to return, then, to the *Phoenix*. Darius Cheynor had explained to Bernice, in very sketchy outline, how he had ended up as captain of his own ship and what had brought him to this dismal place. Bernice had decided that he seemed disparaging about Earth Council, and vague as to his own career history, as if he did not want to dwell on it. She had also noticed during the ride back in the skimmer that the officer with the eyepatch, Hogarth, seemed satisfied about something, while the man, Leibniz, wore an air of grim resolution.

A second skimmer had been dispatched with a security team to bring Trinket and Livewire.

All efforts to contact the Phracton ship had met with silence, Cheynor had told her. He had given the impression that he found this more frightening than an answer.

Now, in the visitor lounge, Cheynor gazed past her into the distance. Bernice had the impression that she was a guest of honour on board this ship, presumably thanks to respectful memories of the Doctor's intervention. Despite the Doctor's absence, Bernice had some idea of what was happening, although she did not know how she was going to explain this to Cheynor.

'I've got something to show you,' she said, standing up.

She placed the small pyramid on the table in the centre of the room, and she saw Cheynor's tired eyes trying to focus on it.

'What's this,' he said, 'more conjuring tricks?'

'Better than that,' Bernice assured him.

The Doctor stood in the hospital corridor, amid the bustle of crowds. People passed him: a bald man in a wheelchair, pushed by a blank-faced young woman in a green dress; two junior doctors talking in hushed and urgent tones; a Chinese man on crutches with a resolute expression.

The Doctor made passing guesses about the stories that lay behind them all, but other speculations occupied his mind. Every so often, he would take out his fob-watch

128

and glance at it, raising his eyebrows in what an observer could have seen as either surprise or impatience.

There was the hurried sound of footsteps. The Doctor brightened, putting away his watch, and raised his hat to the bespectacled senior consultant and the ward sister who appeared through the swing-doors to his left. He joined them, and kept pace with them. The consultant was saying, ' – monitor the situation and see – ' As they reached the doors of the lift, he seemed to become aware of the Doctor's presence. He swung round and glared at him. 'Can I help you at all?'

The Doctor tilted his head to one side and frowned. He appeared to be looking at the lapel of the consultant's white coat. 'Is that gravy or blood?' he asked, tapping his finger on the offending lapel.

'I beg your pardon?'

The lift doors swished open. The sister looked uncertainly from the doors to the Doctor and back again. It was not the first time she had seen the strange little man.

'The Meswani case,' she murmured to the consultant.

He sniffed, and adjusted his spectacles with one hand while brushing at the lapel with the other. 'I don't have anything to say at the moment.'

'No,' said the Doctor grimly, 'and if you don't listen to me, you never will have.'

The lift doors closed again, and the indicator light showed that it was moving up once more.

'Do you think that should have happened?' asked the Doctor in a tone of mild interest, as if he were discussing the weather.

The ward sister pressed the lift-call button several times, but it did not light up to indicate a response as it should have done. She frowned.

The doors bulged outwards. They billowed like sails in the wind for a fraction of a second before they shattered into blazing shards, unleashing a torrent of streaming green light.

There was an intense but brief burst of heat. The consultant hit one wall of the corridor, the ward sister the other, their clothes scorching as if exposed to a furnace. A storm seemed to erupt in the corridor, ripping posters from the walls and peeling away chunks of paint and plaster.

The Doctor, who had kept his distance, shaded his eyes with his hat and risked a look into the heart of the chaos. 'Kelzen!' he shouted. 'Stop that now. Stop it at once! I'm here to help you!'

A figure was forming at the centre of the thick, foggy light as the storm seemed to subside a little.

Beside the Doctor, the consultant and the ward sister, dazed, were picking themselves up.

The figure was a child, a boy of maybe seven or eight, wrapped in a sheet. His glossy black hair fluttered in the wind, and the golden-green glow from his eyes cast a sheen over a strong, brown-skinned face. 'My name is Sanjay,' he said, in a rounded voice that carried a note of reproof.

'Congratulations,' said the Doctor, placing his hat back on his head. 'Just an hour ago you were still tied to an umbilical cord.' He stood up gingerly. 'Is this fun, Kelzen? Taking over a human life, a human body? Making it fast-forward through the seven ages of Man as if they were some tedious film?'

Sanjay's body seemed to ripple like water, and before the Doctor's eyes his hair grew longer, his body taller and firmer. The Doctor blinked. In the green haze, he was now looking at what appeared to be a muscular, long-legged youth of about fourteen. 'The boy wants to be a man,' said a voice whose timbre seemed to be fluctuating away from that of Sanjay. 'I sense it in him. And as you know, Doctor, we can make wishes into reality.' It was the voice he had heard in his half-conscious state after the accident, the voice of the Sensopath.

'Kelzen,' said the Doctor urgently, with his hands held up in front of him, palms outward, 'don't do anything without reflecting. I think I know what your problem is. You're still assimilating your powers in this world, wanting

130

to experiment, and his mind is unformed. You have to try to curb yourself. Please!'

There was a choking sound to the Doctor's left. He sighed, turned, saw what he expected to see: the consultant being lifted off the ground by invisible hands grasping his lapels.

'This really won't do, Kelzen,' said the Doctor sternly. 'Do you want me to help you, or not?'

The expression on the boy's smooth face became a scowl for a second, and the Doctor felt a mental twinge directed like a dart at him. The consultant dropped with a gasp to the floor.

'Better,' said the Doctor. 'Concentrate now, Kelzen. You mustn't let your other selves break through. This boy has a malicious spirit, and if you take hold of it there's no telling what it might do.'

The consultant was staggering to his feet, rubbing at his reddened neck. He was helped by the ward sister, who was staring in horror at the figure in front of the lift.

The form, strangely androgynous now, stepped forward, its head tilted, looking curiously at the Doctor, as if to say, 'And why should I trust what you say?' Light seemed to billow in its wake, curling and spiralling like oil in water.

The Doctor looked into the long, brown face and saw changes happening as he watched: the eyes shifting from brown to green and back again, the skin rippling, chameleon-like ... Was it the strong gaze of a young man in front of him now, or the angular face of a pale woman, her eyes and mouth unnaturally large?

The Doctor held out his umbrella like a boat-hook. 'Come with me,' he said. 'You're not safe here.'

The Sensopath hesitated. The hand that reached tentatively for safety was spindly, long, multi-jointed – no, it was human. The Doctor sensed reality warping around him. The clock on the wall above the lift had dribbled down almost to the floor, where it solidified. Senses began to blur in an unwelcome synaesthesia, and the image of the clock jangled like an alarm in the Doctor's mind.

131

There was laughter deep within the bell, laughter, it seemed, from distant shores of time.

'Please,' hissed the Doctor. 'We haven't much time before the TARDIS returns. And there are dangerous people on this world, people who would kill you as soon as look at you.'

The Sensopath gripped the hook of safety. Two eyes of myriad colours met the Doctor's, but he set his expression grimly and gave nothing away.

'Come on, then,' he said.

The pixie-like figure sitting on the table in the visitor lounge of the *Phoenix* was, to all intents and purposes, the Doctor. Cheynor watched, open-mouthed, as the hologram performed that uncanny body language which he didn't realize he had remembered: the restless eyes, the finger tapping on the chin. The coat was brown, Cheynor noticed, and the Doctor appeared to be wearing a loud jumper in contrast to the smart waistcoat he remembered. That, along with a slight blue fizzing around the edges of the figure, was the only difference he perceived. The hologram seemed to be looking around the room without noticing the other occupants.

'The Doctor gave this to me,' Bernice explained. 'It came in useful back there in the plaza, didn't it?'

Cheynor did not want to admit that the bewildering succession of events had left him dazed. He had only been able to see, smell and hear the destruction of the Phractons with whom he had come to negotiate; nothing else seemed to matter. He caught her grin and wondered if it had been worth getting out of bed today. 'A portable Doctor,' he said faintly. 'Whatever next?'

'It can't actually do anything,' Benny continued, 'but it does seem programmed to respond to an infinite number of parameters.'

The hologram-Doctor looked up indignantly. 'Do?' he said. 'What exactly do you want me to do about this mess?'

Cheynor, taken aback, stood up, placing his glass of

cordial down on the table with somewhat unsteady hands. He cleared his throat, and looked at Bernice for inspiration.

She shrugged. 'It's only a glorified computer simulation,' she said. 'Don't let it get above itself.'

'Simulations have rights too!' exclaimed the hologram-Doctor, and hopped down off the table. He stared intently at Bernice. 'But if you cut me, I will not bleed. If I cry . . .' He frowned, then scowled at them both as if he would much rather be elsewhere, doing something more interesting. 'So, what have you come up with?'

'In less than an hour, I imagine the Phractons will attack us,' said Darius Cheynor. His voice carried surprising calmness. 'After all, the way they see it, we massacred their diplomatic party.'

'Only it wasn't us,' said Bernice. 'It was the woman Trinket saw earlier. The one who had a blazing row with a chum of his.' She shuddered.

'Hmm.' The hologram-Doctor appeared to be examining the wood of the table for flaws. 'Well, if I were you I'd hope your opponents have noticed the presence of something more powerful than all of you. Because if they haven't . . .' He straightened and smiled up at the ceiling, before deactivating gently into a four-foot globule of silver light, which rushed back down into the pyramid.

'Oh, great,' Benny said angrily. 'I bet he programmed it like that deliberately, too. No one gets to interrupt him, and he always has the last word.'

The door slid open, and Hogarth strode in. After looking Bernice up and down in a decidedly hostile manner, the communications officer addressed Cheynor. It was not quite the exchange Bernice had been expecting.

'You wouldn't listen, would you?' she said, black-gloved palms flat on the table. Her tone held grim resolution, but also a hint of gloating. 'Give the colony to the Phractons? Peaceful settlement? No, Captain. War is what we came here for, and war is all that's going to happen.'

Cheynor turned away from her in anger. 'So what would

133

you have done, Cassie? Blasted the Phracs the second they appeared under truce?'

'Taken armaments with us. At least we could have defended ourselves against that girl!' Hogarth's visible eye was open wide, unnaturally so, showing stark egg-whiteness.

'And what would that have achieved? Apart from killing an innocent party?' Cheynor's righteous anger gave him new strength as he rounded on Hogarth. Bernice remembered seeing him like this in their previous encounter: a man with something shattered but strangely noble about him.

Hogarth was undeterred. 'That girl is uncanny. That stunt with the Phracs, it was just to gain our confidence. She's like them. Twisted. And in case you'd forgotten, *sir*, she's currently sitting in our medlab, waiting for the moment when she can pull her next trick!'

'No,' said Bernice, stepping forward. 'I don't believe she'll do anything.'

Hogarth barely spared her a glance. 'I don't listen to civilians.'

'That's a shame. Because they often talk sense.' Bernice strode up to the woman, deliberately making herself closer than was comfortable for either of them. She got the impression of something knotted up inside Cassie Hogarth, physically and mentally. 'I don't think for a moment that Trinket's sister is the evil here, and nor did Captain Cheynor. We *know* there's something evil out there, and the girl was just the channel for some...' Bernice shrugged. 'Some force that seemed to tear her apart. You saw her after the Phractons died. As if she'd been burned out too, inside.'

Bernice stopped, aware that her voice was louder than she would have liked and her throat was very dry. She was taking something of a risk; after all, her knowledge of what was happening was based on the Doctor's theories about Tilusha Meswani, and she did not see Hogarth responding favourably to the idea that she had come forward in time to prevent a tragedy.

134

'This woman's talking rubbish, Captain,' Hogarth said coolly, apparently unshaken. 'I just hope you've got that medlab well guarded.' She turned on her heel and strode out of the room – typically, for the *Phoenix* crew, without waiting to be dismissed.

Cheynor looked back at Bernice. 'I'll be needed on the bridge,' he said. 'I've beamed requests for assistance through the comsat, obviously, but I can't see anyone bothering with us in time.' He sighed deeply and, just for a second, closed his eyes against the world. It did not go away. 'That's not the idea, you see. We weren't sent here to win.'

'What do you mean?' Bernice poured them both another glass of the fruit cordial.

'Well, I suppose I have to tell someone. And it can't be Leibniz or Hogarth.' Cheynor sat down, and scratched his beard with one hand while tapping the arm of his chair with the other. 'We were sent here to defend Gadrell Major's porizium deposits. By the time we got here, most of the city was in ruins. Defence became skirmishes, and we got most of the civilians out. And now we're not allowed to leave. It got me wondering, you see, Bernice. Wondering about how valuable this lump of rock really is to Earth Council.'

'I don't see what you're saying.'

Cheynor sighed. 'This conflict is not about porizium or any other mineral deposit. There hasn't been porizium in abundance here since . . .' He shrugged, waved a hand. 'Way back. But the Phracs don't know that, do they?'

Bernice met his gaze. 'And if there's one way to keep your enemies out of your hair . . .'

'Exactly. The largest military deployment ever seen by the Phracton Swarm has been arriving on this planet for weeks now. They're prepared to colonize it once they've destroyed and rebuilt it, and my guess is they're ready to start digging. For a valuable mineral – that doesn't exist.' Cheynor smiled grimly, just on one side of his face. 'And Earth Council sends a disposable ship that's been out on patrol for too long, with a commander who doesn't quite fit in because he hasn't made a great success of anything much. It's all rather neat, isn't it? I imagine the intention is for us all to rot here.'

Benny's mind was racing. If what Cheynor was saying was true, and the whole human–Phracton conflict on Gadrell Major was just a diversion designed to keep the Phracton fleet away from Earth's solar system, then it was the most staggeringly audacious betrayal she had ever known the Earth administration to be capable of.

But, even more importantly for their current situation, it meant that the human and Phracton forces stood a chance of being brought together to fight the true enemy in their midst. An enemy who could burn people to death with a single thought.

Benny's mind drifted back to the Doctor – the real Doctor. What was he doing – or rather, what had he done, five hundred years in the past? (That sort of thinking always set her head reeling, so she preferred to think of their activities as simultaneous. In terms of the timeline she and the Doctor lived on, they were.) If he had contacted the Sensopath inside Tilusha's child, then he would be arriving in the recalled TARDIS at any moment. She just hoped the creaky time machine was being reliable.

'I need to talk to Trinket and Livewire,' Bernice said. 'I think I can be useful there.'

Cheynor nodded.

136

14

Time Out

The Doctor stood at the main console of the TARDIS. The light in the room seemed somehow dimmer than usual. He thought briefly of all the transient lives who had passed through there, and of those who had died in this very room – some of his own previous selves among them.

After he had activated the Stattenheim remote, the police box had popped back into view just where he had left it, at the foot of the City Hall steps. One or two people had given it a double take, as if sensing that it had not been there two seconds ago, but the Doctor had ignored them.

Now, he operated the controls, locking on to a signal which the TARDIS had stored in its data-banks. After nodding in satisfaction, he strolled over to the large wing-chair in the corner of the console room, by the hatstand, and his shadow fell over its impassive occupant.

The body which the Sensopath inhabited had grown at an alarming rate. Sanjay Meswani – for the jet-black eyes that looked up now to meet the Doctor's were his – was now a handsome young man of some twenty years, with high cheekbones and a firm, expressive mouth. His hair fell almost to his shoulders, tucked behind his ear on one side. He had borrowed a baggy, white shirt from the TARDIS wardrobe room – one of the Doctor's old ones, in fact, with tiny symbols, similar to question marks, embroidered on the collar – along with the trousers from a dinner suit which the Doctor vaguely knew he ought to recognize. Sanjay's large, smooth hands rested gently on the arms of the chair and his legs were neatly crossed.

The Doctor peered at him in a troubled way. He knew that these physical characteristics were being controlled by Kelzen to some extent, but he had already seen the physical world showing the mental struggle as Sanjay's own mind tried to assert itself. The mouth, the Doctor thought, was Kelzen's. This seemed to be confirmed when it grew as he watched, filling out with red-blackness and stretching the skin of the face.

'Why did you get involved, Doctor? What advantage is there for you?' The voice was educated, slightly mocking, and could have been that of a young man or a deep-voiced woman.

'None,' said the Doctor. 'I make a habit of sticking my nose in other people's affairs – some would call it philanthropic. I was worried about the child.'

The Sensopath tilted back the head of its new body, and let out a deep, velvety laugh. 'Your concern extends to the unborn, Doctor?'

'My concern is for all life, whatever its form. Of course, for the infant, the division between the self and the external world is nothing like as distinct as for the adult – almost the fusion of the drug addict or the dreamer. I suppose that's what made it such an ideal receptacle for you.' The Sensopath was silent. The Doctor squatted down beside the chair. 'Marvellous thing, birth,' he added. 'More males of the species should know what it's like, though. Do you know about sea horses? No, I suppose you don't. The female sea horse has an appendage, you see, and it transfers the eggs into the male's pouch, where he fertilizes them.' The Doctor beamed. 'And then there's the groove-billed anis bird, another denizen of Earth. Once it has chased off all the other males, its hormone levels adapt, the testosterone level in its body drops and it incubates the eggs itself.'

'You are very well informed, Doctor.'

'Full of useless information. Now try to keep calm,' the

Doctor said urgently. 'The last thing you want to do is create a channel for either of the others. Do you understand?'

'Why not?' The dark irises seemed to grow bigger, filling out the whites of the eyes. 'Isn't that for me to decide? I am a free agent, you know.' Sanjay/Kelzen crossed its legs, and settled back in the chair with a relaxed and superior expression on its unstable features.

'Yes, and you're getting a free ride too!' The Doctor's voice hardened. 'This clash of wills has already caused enough damage in the physical world. It killed Sanjay's mother. Don't let it kill him as well.'

Anger flashed in the dark eyes. 'I do not need a lecture from a Time Lord!'

'Ahhh.' The Doctor leaned back slightly, and his face fell into shadow. He tapped his mouth with his forefinger, nodding like some wise gnome. 'So, you know who I am. And if you know that, then you should appreciate that a lecture is perhaps exactly what you do need.'

'Time Lords are just a legend for our race, Doctor. In the time I come from, whole star systems have been born from chaos and been swallowed by supernovas since the time of Gallifrey. Would *you* listen to a voice from a primitive, ancient race?'

'Yes, actually,' said the Doctor. 'I've met more legends than I'd care to mention, and some of them have been very wise indeed.'

Kelzen/Sanjay made a dismissive sound, and looked away from the Doctor. The skin, rippling under the light, became paler, and the nose took on a more bony and streamlined appearance.

The alien side was still there, fighting with the human.

It burned, the pain of the onslaught. The whole Swarm had felt it. Now, the Phracton web glittered and shook with a thousand scalding, angered impulses, all directed into the Commandant's personal receiver.

At first, he could not believe it. An accident, surely?

139

His four aides had somehow malfunctioned – an error in the programming of their life-support systems?

No, came the answer from his Secondary, spiked like daggers. *The bipeds killed them. The bipeds destroyed our Swarm-brothers. You said we could trust them. You are to blame.*

The Commandant retreated into his thinking-space. He considered detaching himself from the web and undertaking a personal mission to the humans' ship. It would be risking his life, but then here, in the heart of the web, a concerted effort by the caustic Secondary and his followers would be enough to kill him, too, so he had little to lose.

Nothing to risk but another failure.

As soon as he uncloaked from his personal space, the thoughts skewered him, shot with virulence along all strands of the web.

A counter-offensive. Now. Honour demands that our Swarm-brothers be avenged.

Then honour is a fool, riposted the Commandant. *There may be some force on this world of which we have no knowledge, something attempting, for its own evil purposes, to set bipeds and Phractons at one another –*

Honour! Now! The swift, angry thoughts began to stab at his senses like a thousand needles.

And he knew, then, that his command was slipping away from him.

The Doctor said, 'Power brings with it responsibility, Kelzen. Think about that word for a while. Responsibility.'

The Sensopath turned back to the Doctor and smiled. There were large, square teeth behind the broad lips. 'As you do, Doctor?'

The Time Lord turned his head slightly, his eyes flicking down and back up again.

'Yes,' Kelzen/Sanjay went on, 'I have noticed your guilt during our moments of communion. You confronted much of it, some time ago, when an entity called the Timewyrm made you enter your own mind. But since then there has

140

been more. Much, much more. You feel . . . responsible –
to use your word – for a great deal.'

'Perhaps I do. But I don't misuse power.' The Doctor
scurried round so that he was confronting the Sensopath,
and held a hand up, the fingers slightly curved towards
the ceiling. 'Anyone's hand can hold a weapon. To kill, to
maim, to play with the destinies of others for sport. That's
what your sister, your fellow – Shanstra – is like, isn't it?'
The Doctor drew a deep breath and clenched his fingers
slowly into the palm of his hand. 'Anyone can abuse their
abilities. It doesn't take much, and it's not power. I've met
enough dictators to be able to say that for certain, Kelzen.
No.' The Doctor lowered his hand. 'Real power. Imagine
knowing yourself to be capable of killing, of hurting. And
choosing not to. When you make the conscious decision
to be merciful, Kelzen, is when you truly evolve beyond
the stage of saying, "I'm bigger than you, so I'll hurt you."
Mercy – that is power.'

'Time Lord philosophy.' The Sensopath was haughtily
dismissive.

'If you like.' The Doctor shrugged. 'I only got a double
gamma for that at the Academy. My opinions are based
on what I learned myself, long after leaving the Time
Lords to their petty feuds.'

The Sensopath was silent.

'I need to find out more about Shanstra and Jirenal,'
the Doctor said after a moment or two. 'But until I do
know more, it's dangerous for you to attempt communion
with either of them. Which is why we're going to Gadrell
Major.'

The Doctor stood up, walked over to the corner by the
scanner, and counted down a column of roundels until he
reached the one he wanted. He opened it to reveal a
cupboard, from which a cascade of electronic components
fell on to the floor, followed by a couple of fishing floats
and a leather-bound book called *Black Orchid*. He
ignored the clutter, and did not take long to find what he
was looking for: a brass-coloured, circular object like a

141

tiara. The Doctor reached towards his passenger with it in his hand.

The Sensopath recoiled. 'What is that?'

'It's a very basic thought wave damping device. I wish I'd had this when I met the Vardans. Primitive, but it'll have to do.'

'What do I do with it?'

The Doctor beamed. 'You wear it, of course,' he said, and slipped the circlet on to the Sensopath's forehead.

Kelzen/Sanjay closed its eyes. 'I still do not know why I should trust you, Doctor.'

'Don't worry,' said the Doctor. 'Some of my best friends have said the very same thing.'

The TARDIS flew on through the vortex.

Jirenal was feeling restless. He had decided to attempt a simple experiment.

At the end of one of the glittering halls of the Centre, there was an enormous crystal cliff, behind which he could see shapes moving. His guide, Amarill, had respectfully nodded when he had asked to be shown over to the translucent wall.

They walked past Pridka whose robes were orange, denoting less responsibility than Amarill in her green. The tiny fins on their hairless skulls rippled gently as thoughts passed among them. Jirenal had, as yet, found nothing of interest in them, but he was keeping an open mind.

One technique he had perfected, which set him apart from the Pridka, was that of shielding his thoughts. He knew only too well what might happen to him if they were to discover his true nature too soon.

Amarill had an elegant stride, Jirenal had noticed. She had not broken it when, every now and then, she waved her palm over the flat, black square in the crook of her arm to show the visitor some interesting images or statistics. Jirenal looked into the projector with gentlemanly courtesy each time, and nodded intently whenever she explained something to him.

Amarill, for her part, did not find the visitor disconcerting, as the Director had indicated in his subvocal inflexions to her. On the contrary, she thought he was charming, compared with many of the humans who passed this way. He seemed humanoid, if on the tall side, and she thought he was rather elegant and beautiful, with his dark suit, adorned with a clasp at the neck, and his rich, dark hair. His mouth seemed enormous, and very expressive. Whenever he smiled – showing dazzling, square teeth – the mouth seemed to occupy the whole of the lower half of his face.

Amarill exchanged a friendly, encouraging look with the visitor as they stepped on to the pad in front of the Yzashoks' recreation tank. He had his hands behind his back and was looking up at the shimmering blue face of the tank with interest.

'These visitors exist in an amniotic fluid that responds intimately to their brain patterns,' explained Amarill, and beamed a digitized diagram of Yzashok biology on to the projector. Jirenal nodded, but his attention was focused now on the frosted surface of the tank, behind which the swimming, lizard-like shapes of the creatures could be seen. 'The Yzashoks are a race of philosophers,' Amarill continued, 'who consider the confluence between the harmony of the self and communion with others to be the highest achievement of the mind. Many of them come here in order to seek that very harmony.'

'Very noble,' remarked Jirenal. He looked over the edge of the still-rising gravpad, as if he had only just noticed that they had climbed high enough for the Pridka minions below to be mere blobs of orange and blue. 'Could we stop here?' he asked. 'Heights do not really agree with me.'

Amarill nodded respectfully, and the pad bobbed to a halt, some sixty metres above the bustling floor of the hall.

Jirenal looked intently at her. 'You are very kind, to show me around like this.'

'It is my job,' she answered.

143

Jirenal reached out a spindly, flexible hand. 'Neverthe-less,' he said, 'I should like to thank you for your kindness.'

Amarill felt the visitor's finger touch her forehead before she realized what he was doing.

The sensation fell, like a shutter. First, a feeling of calm, enveloping all the extrasensory networks of her highly developed brain. She felt a huge, overwhelming sensation of tranquillity, and as her senses combined, she saw – felt – tasted – the sensations expanding, blossoming like huge red flowers in her mind.

And then the flowers began to burn.

The Pridka were a sedate race, unused to tumult or dis-order. They did not, in general, occupy themselves with mundane tasks like the collection of debris, as an army of robotic drones – silvery spheres with a multitude of flex-ible attachments – fulfilled this necessity. When the drone on duty in Hall 275 saw a black object tumbling from a gravpad anchored halfway up the Yzashok recreation tank, it moved in to sweep up the offending item. The drone registered the black square as a standard infor-mation projector, obviously dropped by the guide on the gravpad. It secured the item away in its storage unit, and moved on.

The kiss is purely of the physical world, It is the first sensation that Amarill dell'katit vo'Pridka has ever felt purely with the basic senses, unenhanced by telepathy. She draws away from Jirenal in shock. She puts a hand over her mouth, tries to stop her body from shaking uncontrollably as she looks at his wide, glistening mouth, his long, white and alien face.

What has happened? She can feel nothing. It is as if all her receptors have been deadened.

And then the beautiful flowers open up again, not just red this time, but burning with a multitude of unsuspected colour, like vandalism and riots in her mind. The colours of passion, the colours of devotion and subjugation to Jirenal.

144

'Excellent,' says his voice, inside and outside her mind. 'The Pridka have earned their reputation.'

'What – what have you done?'

'A simple game,' says Jirenal, standing before her, a strong, dark shadow, his hands clasped behind his back. 'I entered your mind, and adjusted it. A mere test of my powers.' His head swivels slowly to look at the translucent surface of the tank to the side of their gravpad. It stretches above and below them. 'Imagine if I were to attempt such an experiment – ' he glances back at her ' – on a larger scale.'

And she watches, helpless, as he presses his forehead up against the surface of the tank and closes his eyes in concentration. He places his palms flat on the tank too.

For a minute, nothing happens. Then, a shrill beeping sound emits from Amarill's wrist unit. She checks the readings, in horror.

'Stop! Please!' She tries to grab Jirenal's arm. His hands, flat against the crystal blue surface, seem immovable. His expression is one of the utmost concentration. 'The temperature!' Amarill cries desperately. 'You must stop!'

The lizard-like occupants of the great communion of minds, irresistibly attracted to the pull of Jirenal's, are swimming towards him. They are clustering on the other side of the tank like filings attracted to a magnet.

Amarill is pale with horror. Her fins are rippling uselessly, sending out blank messages to her fellow Pridka. No feeling. It is like going blind.

In the tank, the fluid crisps to ice, trapping every one of the Yzashoks like flies in amber. They are silent and still.

Jirenal lets out a long, satisfied breath. He lowers his head, and his hands, and then looks up to smile at Amarill.

15

The Dead in Mind

'So,' said the Doctor, striding through the TARDIS corridors, 'you have reached the stage of civilization where you can expand your minds without the need for drugs. You are the most advanced telepaths I've ever met. And yet you still haven't learnt to be more than children with expensive playthings.'

That is a harsh judgement, Doctor.

The voice, in his head, was definitely that of a woman now. It was the sort of voice that a human being might have found suggestive of a long, hot soak, with a glass of of champagne on a table beside the bath-tub. The Doctor, of course, did not respond to such allure in the same way.

'You grew,' the Doctor said, 'developed as a race . . .' He paused at a four-way junction where the roundels seemed slightly larger and tinged with more grey. He was thinking. 'And became so responsive to telepathic suggestion that you could use it, much as a human would use physical strength, to affect elements in the physical world. You built cities by the power of thought alone.'

It is more than thought, Doctor. Such an inadequate term. In your terminology it is felt as a kind of – A pause. *– music.*

'Hmm,' said the Doctor. He took out a coin from his pocket, tossed it, caught it on the back of his hand with a resounding smack and looked at it. He shrugged, and turned back the way he had come.

You cannot understand what it is like. You are not a Sensopath. To be almost totally cut off from the harmony of communication with my kind – it is worse than being deprived of sight and hearing.

'I realize that.'

The Doctor paused before a section of the wall, tapped on it with his umbrella. It swung open with a creaking sound. Steps led down inside, down into the blue-grey churchlike coolness of the tertiary console room once more.

At the edge of the city of Banksburgh, the rubble was piled high. Twisted metal, like strange plants with leaves of rust. Ton upon ton of stone, forming giant hills of debris. Abandoned canisters and crates.

A wind blew, like the last wind of all time, causing great upheavals of dust that shrouded the wasteland as if in fog. The city could dimly be seen, below in the valley, the pinnacle of the library still jutting above it all.

Out of the gloom came bright beams of green, sweeping across the debris, and behind them, with a purposeful gait, came the predatory figure of Shanstra. She looked around the destruction, and was pleased.

Behind her, following at the hem of her cloak like a faithful hound, was Suzi Palsson, her face tired and drawn, yet unnaturally bright with attention and devotion. She stood several paces behind her mistress as Shanstra, hands on hips, nodded and smiled grimly.

'Good. If this is what they are capable of on their own, then with my power among them there will be even greater sport.' She gestured with a long arm. 'Come.'

They scrambled down a vast slope, a scree formed from the remains of the city suburbs. About halfway down, the remnants of a house poked up like a dead face, its windows yawning emptily across the scree. Rammed up against the wall, covered with a film of dust, was the shell

147

of a Phracton unit, and there was a brittle, half-collapsed human skeleton in the dust beside it.

'Remnants of war,' said Shanstra in fascination. 'These fragments of life and death.'

Rippling blue light washed over the Gothic architecture, but the Doctor went straight for the stone console. 'I'm calibrating the signal from its original source,' he said to the room in general, knowing that the Sensopath would hear the thoughts that accompanied his words. 'With any luck, we ought to materialize very close to where the TARDIS left Bernice.'

Ah. Your . . . companion. I believe she has an interesting mind?

'And she wants it to stay that way!' the Doctor snarled suddenly, glowering up at the vaulted ceiling for want of anywhere better. 'Didn't your mother tell you not to go poking about in people's heads?' He had finished his calibrations, and now he lifted his hands from the console like a triumphant concert pianist. One switch had to be thrown, and they would be locked back on to the correct path.

I contained myself within the child. I believed I had done the right thing.

'Yes,' said the Doctor moodily. 'We'll see.'

He stabbed at the final switch, and the TARDIS lurched.

Bernice was let into the medlab after a few moments' discussion with the guards on duty outside. The conversation was reasonable, and largely detailed the insalubrious duties the two would face being given by Captain Cheynor if they refused access to his special guest.

Livewire was sleeping peacefully, with two electropads attached to her temples. Above her, a number of screens monitored her vital signs. Trinket sat beside her, in fresh clothes but still tense, with shadows of tiredness on his young face. He looked up gratefully as Bernice strode over to join him. She thought he seemed to have got about two years older in the past two hours.

'The medics said,' Trinket ventured, 'that there's nothing actually wrong with her. She did lapse into coma for a while, but now it's just ordinary sleep.'

Benny nodded, sitting down. 'I'd imagine the use of all that mental energy took its toll on her body.'

'You really know what's happening, don't you?' Trinket said accusingly.

'No more than you. Trinket – ' She paused, exasperatedly. ' – Look, I can't go on calling you that. What's your real name?'

He made a dismissive sound, turned away from her to look at the floor. 'I don't use it. If you're my friend, you won't use it either.'

Bernice smiled. 'You remind me of someone I used to know. A friend of mine, and the Doctor's. She used to prefer a name of her own. But she took her real name back, eventually.'

'What happened to her?' Trinket still would not make eye contact, his fringe falling over his eyes.

'Ah, well, she's part of the past. Listen – you're still the only one to have seen at first hand what this Shanstra can do, right?' Trinket nodded resignedly. 'And as for her,' Bernice said, looking at the pale, sleeping girl, 'I wonder if she can remember any of it.' Benny let out a long breath. 'You never know, with these things. There's been a few times when I've woken up, head bouncing off the ceiling, not knowing what *species* I was. Had to do the check-list. Two arms, two legs, warm blood – hey, I must be a mammal.' She clicked her tongue to herself. ' "What am I?" makes a more original impression than "Where am I?" don't you feel?'

Trinket looked up. He had not really been listening. 'You don't think she's been messed about, do you? I mean, permanently?'

Bernice placed a hand on his shoulder. 'Look, let's just wait 'til she comes round. We don't know what she's been

149

through, do we?' She crouched down beside him. 'Are you two very close?'

Trinket drew breath, slumped back in his chair. 'We worked out after a while that we were gonna have to work together, to survive. So we did. But she – she was always on the edge. Going on about how we'd get a gun, then more guns, and get armed, to kill the Phracs.' He shook his head. 'All these great schemes she had. Our leader.'

'What did you mean, you *have* to work together?'

Trinket glared at her for a second, as if she were responsible for all his problems. 'Livewire knows I'm not stupid, so she needs me. But she's never forgiven me for being born. And killing our mother.'

Bernice recoiled from the bluntness, as if from a blow. 'For . . .' She swallowed hard.

'I was a difficult birth,' explained Trinket, disparagingly.

'Ah. I see. And big half-sister blames it on you.'

'They had to choose. Between me and her. There was no one around to make the decision, so the doctors took it for me. They saved me.' He shrugged. 'Suppose I should be grateful. But I've had to live with the knowledge . . . that Livewire secretly wants me dead.'

'She wouldn't,' Bernice said too quickly. 'Trinket, she wouldn't.'

'No,' he said. 'She's all talk. Sure, she had her crossbow and she tried to use it. But she wouldn't have killed the Phracs herself, if she'd been under her own control. She hates them, for what they've done to our city. To our world. She hates them, and that hate became real. You saw it. You saw it!'

'Yes. I saw it.'

Trinket met her eyes now, and she thought she saw some kind of gratitude there, a recognition of her understanding.

Your exploits have certainly had a great deal of variety to them, Doctor.

The Doctor beamed, as he checked readings and

pressed switches here and there. 'Exploits? Oh, yes. The time-space visualizer carries records of them all.'

Not all, it would appear. Are you aware that there are gaps in the earliest data?

'Ah, well.' The Doctor shrugged. 'I did wonder.' His brow creased. 'I always intended to sort that matter out with the Time Lords. It wouldn't surprise me if they hoarded them on the Matrix for their own self-indulgence.' He became aware that a pool of light was forming in the corner of the room, and so, politely, he addressed it. 'And so what have you discovered about me?'

The light took on the aspect of the malleable face of Sanjay/Kelzen, flickering blood-red in the shadows of the cryptlike room. This time, it spoke, the voice echoing off the stonework. 'Oh, many things, Doctor. You seem ... arrogant at times.' The Sensopath smiled. 'You scheme, and manipulate. You are never predictable.'

'Well, I can be. Depends what you predict.' The Doctor grinned and twirled his umbrella nonchalantly. 'Which ones did you see? I'm dying to know.'

And futhermore, continued the silky voice, back inside his head, *one of your favourite ploys is to pretend to be far less intelligent than you are – to give you time to out-think your enemies when they least expect it.*

The Doctor's broad smile was replaced by a scowl.

In the early days of your current body, I observed, you affected a kind of whimsical idiocy, in order to mask your darker side.

The Doctor looked away shiftily. 'I don't have a darker side,' he attested, but without much conviction. 'It was all a fabrication of the Matrix.' He looked up, meeting the huge gaze of the image. 'But enough about me!' he said with evident delight. 'Tell me more about yourself'

Shanstra placed her hand on the curved shell of the Phracton unit and pulled the globe towards her. Dust slithered from it, making Suzi jump back in alarm. There was a cascade of circuitry from the gash in the side of the globe, attached to the remains of several dry and strangely shaped organs, withered like ancient fruit.

'You did not see what the girl achieved in the square, my beloved,' said Shanstra gently as she pulled the Phracton's internal wires from their housing. 'But you felt it. So much hatred. She wanted it to be directed, not to fester inside her like some cancer. I helped her to focus it.' Shanstra seemed to pause for a moment, almost as if she were pondering the implications of her words. 'Just as I have focused your emotions, dear Suzi.'

Suzi was sitting on an upturned crate and gazing into the distance, because she did not particularly want to see what Shanstra was doing with the Phracton remains. But now she turned her head in the alien's direction, and seemed to be thinking about what Shanstra had said. A flicker of recognition animated the blankness on her face, gave it a tiny hint of its old, human colour back.

Shanstra was holding a grapefruit-sized section of a Phracton organ, on which wires were meshed in a complex web pattern. She took it in her hands like a grail, and held it up to the dim light. There was the faintest of glows from within the ball of alien flesh.

Shanstra smiled. 'So. Not quite dead. These are resilient creatures.'

Suzi was standing over her. 'I want to go back to the library.'

'Let me concentrate, Suzi.' Shanstra did not even deign to look at her. 'There is more than one mind here.'

'You've been leading me on by saying you could bring Colm back to me. God, have I been stupid!' Suzi's fringe was fluttering in front of a desperate, angry face, eyes and mouth creased with sadness.

She remembered now. Colm Oswyn was dead.

Colm had left her. The day after she had lost her job, he had gone back to his hypermodel. She'd been making overtures to him via v-mail for months, and Colm had been keeping it all a secret – he didn't want to let Suzi go unless he was absolutely sure of success on the other front.

She had been so angry. He had been her One, she was

sure of it: drunk a little too often, a bit of a know-all, but basically good to her, kind to her. She had never wanted to love anyone more. To love him and kill him.

But she had tried to forget, to enter into her new job with enthusiasm, to begin a new life. There had been gatherings, though, friends' celebrations and parties where they could not avoid one another. The last one being the Tranter wedding on Magellani, where Suzi Palsson had seen Colm downing the green dragon cocktails all night and wondered, briefly, if he might be an unhappy man. And outside, later, when she had seen him slip and lose his footing by the bay, the only witness.

He had called out to her, drowning. As the waters closed over his ridiculously bow-tied neck and then his cropped head, Suzi Palsson had watched with interest. She had made no attempt to save her former lover, for this was the moment that she had been waiting for Fate to bring her, year after year. The moment of glorious Suzi-power, of ego-revenge.

On some worlds – but not Magellani – she had discovered later that allowing death by omission of action was a crime ranked almost with murder. That made her feel good. Warm and strong inside. It had been almost like killing him, but without the mess.

Then came the nightmares.

Then came the nightmares that were real.

This woman had got inside her head, found the guilt and squeezed it out, like poison from a boil – to draw mental strength from the passion, Suzi now realized. Not to help her, poor Suzi.

Reality was a friend of hers again, and she saw: Shanstra kneeling on the dust, her horrible face suffused with that parasitic concentration, her hand supporting a withered ball of organic matter which was connected by fibres and ganglia to the shattered globe of the Phracton's travel unit.

Suzi was shaking and sweating. That feeling had returned. The desire to kill the beloved.

* * *

153

The Doctor was listening.

Our race could have abandoned physical form, but we chose not to. There are certain... pleasures... which a purely spiritual existence does not afford.

The Doctor nodded. He had his eyes closed, but he could still see the face of his passenger floating in that wasteland of the unused mind. A face warping between human male, handsome, with an echo of Tilusha's stubbornness, and the unnaturally long, broad-lipped face of an alien woman.

We were bonded, Doctor, Shanstra, Jirenal and I. You must understand what this means for a race such as ours. Yes, we had separate processes of mind and body, but we were linked together, always responding.

'Telepathic Siamese triplets,' the Doctor said to himself. 'I should have known.'

Yes, Doctor. Yet it is more than that. The nature of the link is such that our thought processes... became integrated. Essentially, Shanstra is me, I am Shanstra and Jirenal is both of us.

There was a deep, resonant sigh, which seemed to the Doctor to echo through all the passageways of the TARDIS before spiralling down to where he stood.

We are One, Doctor. One and the same.

Shanstra was not surprised when she looked up to see the gun pointing between her eyes, and behind it, cold and resolute, the face of Suzi Palsson.

She smiled. She could sense the girl's desperation, her fear, under the shell of her resolve.

'Please, dear Suzi,' said Shanstra gently.

'It's no good. You aren't a goddess, you're just a parasite.' Suzi's voice wavered, but the gun remained firmly in position. 'It's over, Shanstra.'

Something went wrong. The bonding did not work. Because of an incompatibility, perhaps. But by this stage, we were one another. How can a being be incompatible with its own self?

154

'Don't know. Ridiculous idea,' said the Doctor, a little guiltily. An observer might have seen him dart the briefest of glances at the TARDIS console – almost the kind of look a human would give a friend to say, 'Stay out of this, you.'

And so we were declared unsuitable to remain in our society. My relative youth meant that I was unable to control the vast reserves of energy that were now at our service. To tell you the truth, Doctor, I did not know – I still do not know – exactly how we were developing. Jirenal – his uncertainty, I think, leads him to rashness. He is keen to experiment.

'And Shanstra?' asked the Doctor grimly.

She is dangerous. The Sensopath paused. *We were given a choice. Total annihilation, or an existence, outside time. To drift for eternity, with only our unity of mind for companionship. And so we chose the vortex.*

'And something happened,' mused the Doctor. A light was gently pulsing on the grey surface of the console, he noticed. 'You were scattered through history.'

A freak accident.

'Oh, I hardly think so.' The Doctor shook his head. 'I think Shanstra was just beginning to show the extent of her powers.'

Dust billowed across the ashen landscape. Suzi Palsson was conscious of herself and Shanstra, like two figures in some tableau, the grey dust clinging to them and turning them into living statues. One holding a gun to the other.

A thought was growing in her mind. A picture, in wild, angry technicolour. She tried to suppress it, knowing it had been placed there.

'No,' she said firmly. 'No!'

She thought of the shattered library, the wisdom of a colony, a culture, lying in ruins, even if the building was still near intact.

She saw – the images had stabbed into her mind from Shanstra's – the destruction wrought by the huntress in Londinium Plaza. She knew what had happened there:

desire had been made concrete, and for all she knew, it could have destroyed the girl.

She saw the face of Colm Oswyn hovering like the mask of a ghost on the face of the woman in front of him. His hair rippled, soaking wet, and his eyes stared whitely at her.

White light burst outwards from the eyes, engulfing her. She was aware of the gun growing hot in her hands as the face of Shanstra-Colm, its eyes gushing liquid fire, lifted up, hollow and horrible like a Hallowe'en phantom.

The thought had penetrated into reality. And the gun in Suzi's hand sizzled and melted to a stub of metal. She cried out as it burnt her hand, and it dropped, scattering globules of metal.

There was silence.

Shanstra was above her, placing a hand on her quaking shoulder. 'You see?' she said gently. 'Your mind belongs to me now. There is really nothing you can do about it. And when the time comes for the music of the Infinite Requiem, you will hardly notice or care anyway.'

'Infinite...?' Suzi's throat was dry. Her lips felt detached from her body, and she was aware of her limbs succumbing to cramp.

'I have discovered the most powerful mental focus on this world.' Shanstra held up the soft globe of flesh, encased in its mesh of wires leading into the remains of the Phracton. 'These cyborgs exist on a network of minds, a mental grid. Their thought processes will be ideal for the refocusing of all my latent powers. And then I shall be able to reunite, across time, with my other selves.'

Shanstra closed her eyes.

She guided her thoughts like a heat-seeking missile into the web, tearing up node after node of energy. Phracton minds, confused as to what was happening, reached out, but could not grasp the slippery intruder.

Shanstra's mental missile lodged home. It burst, scattering thought-shrapnel, deep inside a cocoon of hatred, anger, xenophobia.

156

Deep in the mind of the Phracton designated 4Z-88* – the Secondary Commandant of the Gadrell Major expeditionary unit.

'Go, my children,' said Shanstra, a whisper, a light but inescapable suggestion in the heart of the web. 'Let your hatred, your anger, emerge. Begin your attack.'

And from the Secondary's mind, it cracked, shattered, spilled. Like one domino, knocking a huge and intricate tree of more dominoes, sending pulses out –

Saying *KILL>>>>KILL>>>>KILL>>>>*

Part Three

MIND CITADEL

Only those who have lived all their lives under the dark clouds of vague, undefined fears can appreciate the joy of a doubting soul suddenly born into the kingdom of reason and free thought. Is the bondage of the priest-ridden less galling than that of the slave, because we do not see the chains, the indelible scars, the festering wounds, the deep degradation of all the powers of the Godlike mind?

Elizabeth Cady Stanton (1860)

16

Media, Messages

The TARDIS did not actually materialize close to its last landing place. It shimmered into view on top of a rocky outcrop, and the Doctor was outside almost immediately with his portable telescope.

The city squatted on the horizon in one direction, hazed by red smoke and dust. The Doctor turned slowly, scanning the bleak, reddish landscape, until –

'Aha,' he said. 'Terran ship, if I'm not mistaken.' The glassy pinnacle, which had looked at first like a spar of rock, jutted up quite clearly now, incongruously technological among the sunset-coloured rocks.

There was a rustle at his shoulder, a shift of molecules like a silk curtain opening into another world.

The Sensopath, over two metres tall, stood at the Doctor's side and towered over him. He looked up from the eyepiece, and did a double take. The alien seemed to have appropriated another of the Doctor's old items of clothing: the electric-blue cloak of mourning which he had worn on his visit to Necros. His old shirt with the questioning lapels hung loosely over an unmistakably feminine body, and lush cascades of hair fell to the waist. The spindly hands had developed still further, and looked full of hidden strength. The Sensopath's eyes were green, but dull, like unpolished stones, beneath the coronet of the thought-wave damper from the TARDIS.

'Well?' the Doctor said grimly.

'Oh, yes, I can sense her.' The mouth moved like blood. 'She is so close.'

'Good. Stay there. No closer.'

'Doctor.' Kelzen's voice was commanding. 'This is me we are dealing with. I will find it difficult to resist communion with what is, essentially, my own mind.'

'I know. But you must.' The Doctor looked up at her, his fingers pressed together in front of his mouth as he spoke. 'I need you here to help me, but above all there must be no communion until I've worked out the best thing to do with you all.'

From high in the sky, there came the growing hum of a drive unit.

'And there, unless I'm mistaken, is my lift,' said the Doctor. 'I suggest you get back in the TARDIS where I showed you – right now.'

Kelzen rounded on him. 'Why?' she asked challengingly.

The Doctor sighed. 'I'm not running auditions for companions here. You'll be falling over and spraining your ankle next. Just do as I say – please!'

Hogarth got the pilot to bring the skimmer in low, following the trace which had just appeared on the ridge in Sector D. It should not have been there, and it did not fit comfortably into Cassie Hogarth's world-view.

As the skimmer contacted with the ground, red dust sprayed up on both sides, and some of it clung to the skimmer's hood like old, rusty bloodstains. Hogarth, priming her weapon, frowned at the strange blue box and the incongruous figure which stood before it. 'All right,' she said to the pilot, 'get this thing open.'

The skimmer's top flipped up, and Hogarth's gun was instantly trained on the intruder, a small man in a crumpled white suit.

'I wouldn't try anything on,' she called out.

'Well, indeed,' said the man, who, as far as Hogarth could see, was busy trying to tuck an old-fashioned viewing instrument into his inside pocket. 'I'd heard this was hardly the centre of sartorial industry. Kolpasha's the place for that, I think you'll find.'

'Get in,' said Cassie Hogarth, motioning with the gun. 'The Phracs will be in this sector in a matter of minutes. And if you get in the way, they'll spread you all over the landscape like butter. Right?'

'How charming,' said the little man, as he came forward. 'Service with a simile.' He raised his hat at her and settled himself in the back seat of the skimmer with his hands behind his head. 'Phractons, eh?' he said in a low voice to the impassive pilot. 'This should be interesting.'

Like a swarm of glass bees, the wave of Phracton air modules undulated over the ruins of Banksburgh. They seemed to cling together, forming a single tornado of light and sound.

Heading towards the *Phoenix*.

In the collective mind – buffeted and buoyed by its strength and hatred – rode the will, the dark side of the Sensopath.

Her body – the physical manifestation which called itself Shanstra – sat bolt upright on her throne at the centre of the ice-rink. Snakes of fire were coruscating around the stadium, bouncing from the vidscreens, leaving brief images like stains of green light; images of screaming mouths, lashing tentacles, the occasional glimpse of the buildings and the ground far below. And at the heart of it all sat the demonic, beautiful alien, her eyes hollow, her mind travelling.

Travelling.

She gripped the neural circuits of the Secondary like an old, experienced horse-rider back in the saddle after years away. A rider who was just beginning once more to remember the power of the wind in her hair, to feel at one with the flanks of the animal, to respond to its impulses and to guide them, direct them.

The Phracton Swarm was vengeful. And angry.

Suzi Palsson, in the streets far below, heard the whining

sound of the Swarm, growing to a thunderous rush like a shuttle booming over her head.

She saw movement in the chink of light between the buildings high above her. Meshed with girders, the channel of brightness revealed a momentary image of the glittering Swarm, hurtling towards destiny. Scraps of waste paper, rags, dust, all lifted from where they lay and seemed to dive-bomb her like a flock of angry birds. Suzi remained impassive, like a statue, staring up into the sky. Doors of old warehouses banged in the gale, and for a moment it was as if the ghosts of the dead had clawed their way back up on to the surface of Banksburgh to investigate the commotion.

Share the beauty of it, Suzi.

There she was, still there in her head. Suzi closed her eyes, felt rather than saw the tumult in the street subside.

She remained gazing at the strip of brightness after the Phracs had passed over.

She closed her eyes. There was a latent sensation of flying, if she concentrated – Shanstra's influence. Shanstra, riding in the sky with the angry horde of alien creatures. She could block it out. It was there, like an image projected on a wall of her mind, but she didn't have to look at it.

She remembered, now, one of the many books she had absorbed during quiet hours in the library. During those lulls when the off-worlders were away and the library had almost become her lover; the dust, the buzzing of the lights, the blink of the vidscreens, all as familiar to her as the outlines of Colm's body, as the feeling of his short, spiky hair beneath her hand.

Suzi walked along the desolate street, remembering the story. A fairy tale, a legend, about a dark goddess from some mythical world, who loved her children so much that she did not allow them even to be born. Somehow they would become absorbed into her body, absorbed back into the hollows of nothingness, trapped forever. Some escaped from the womb, but the monstrous mother

164

would devour them whole so that they descended once more, down into the blackness.

Suzi, without realizing it, had stopped against the cold stone wall of one of the buildings, shaking uncontrollably. She buried her face in her arms.

Still there, in her head. A rushing, hurtling sensation, and a rich, wine-dark laugh, seducing and mocking her.

Shanstra was her goddess, her mother, her all-embracing reason for being. She had swallowed Suzi like one of those children, but Suzi wanted to be a poison. And one of them – Suzi or Shanstra – was going to have to die.

17

Ruined in a Day

'My brain hurts,' said Bernice. 'Otherwise I'm fine. Thanks for asking.'

'I didn't,' answered the Doctor.

'I know.'

'I'm sorry.'

'Should think so.'

The brief exchange took place in an unoccupied corner of the *Phoenix* bridge, now with its crew functioning at full capacity. Benny could hardly believe these were the same listless individuals she had seen earlier; they seemed suddenly to have turned into professionals. The cards had been cleared away, the seats tilted up from a comfortable resting position into upright positions of battle.

The huge screen showed a false-colour density image of the terrain, with computerized blips marking the relative positions of the wave of Phracton attackers and the arrow formation of the *Phoenix* fighter craft.

And, leaning on the rail of the command balcony, watching it all like a hungry hawk, was Darius Cheynor, with Horst Leibniz at his side. Bernice had been quite relieved to see Hogarth heading off to lead the defence force, but felt rather guilty about it and now, belatedly, wished her well.

There had been little time for Cheynor and the Doctor to exchange more than a cursory greeting, as the Phractons' advance had already been picked up on the comsat

166

link by the time the Doctor was brought in. Bernice had watched it all, and had been quite impressed by the sudden shift to efficiency. And now, her presence on the bridge, along with the Doctor's, seemed to be not only tolerated, but required.

She was not going to ask for the finer details of what had happened on Earth. Somehow, she had gathered, Tilusha Meswani's child, which had become a grown man overnight, was now housing a telepathic female alien who might be their ally, and might not. Or was the alien containing the boy? The Doctor had been worryingly ambiguous about that.

'And anyway,' the Doctor went on, quietly, as the hums, clicks and crackled reports from around the bridge gathered intensity, 'the human brain doesn't feel pain. Headache pain is caused by receptors external to the cerebral organs, in the duro-matter. The brain itself is quite numb.'

'That's what I like about you, Doctor,' sighed Bernice, 'always ready with the comforting answer.' She noticed Leibniz detaching himself from Cheynor's shadow and coming over to join them. 'What did you do with our friend, by the way?'

'I left her in the Zero Room. Safest place.'

Bernice looked confused. 'I thought the Zero Room had been jettisoned ages ago?'

'It was,' said the Doctor, with a mischievous look in his eye. 'But that was before I got my old TARDIS back from the Silurian Earth – remember?'

He appeared to give his whole attention to the tracking screen, as Leibniz sidled over, his eyes bright behind his round glasses.

Bernice held her breath, wishing she had more time to tell the Doctor her worries. She had not had particularly good first impressions of either of Cheynor's officers. While Cassie Hogarth had struck her as standoffish and arrogant, these were at least human foibles, and Bernice could understand them even if she did not particularly like them. But she found Lieutenant Leibniz more unsettling. It was something about his eyes.

Leibniz met Bernice's gaze coolly. She looked away. 'I wanted you both to know,' he said, in his quiet but compelling way, 'I am watching you.'

'Thank you,' said the Doctor, in an equally unsettling voice, as he turned round slightly to look at Leibniz. 'I'm glad someone still takes the trouble.' With a sudden movement that startled Bernice, he lifted up his umbrella, pushed Leibniz aside and strode across the command balcony to Cheynor. 'Captain. This is not the most useful place for me to be right now.'

Cheynor frowned. 'What do you mean, Doctor?'

'I have to get to the Sensopath and find out what she's doing here, what she wants. It's the reason I'm here. I need to take a skimmer out and talk to her.'

'Doctor, we are fighting a war!'

'A petty conflict over non-existent mineral deposits?' riposted the Doctor scornfully. He seemed to take a grim satisfaction in Cheynor's reaction – astonishment, followed by panic. 'Oh, yes, I know. And no, Bernice hasn't told me. I just have a slight advantage of perspective, shall we say. And if you get me a skimmer now, I may just be able to save a few lives.'

Cheynor, to his credit, was indecisive only for a moment or two. He nodded. He's improving, Bernice thought. And she also noticed the way that Leibniz silently accompanied the Doctor from the bridge without waiting for Cheynor's order.

Kelzen.

She was startled. One of the primitive beings, sending her a telepathic signal? It could only be the Doctor.

Kelzen's physical body was floating cross-legged in the large-roundelled chamber deep in the TARDIS which the Doctor had called the Zero Room. Her constantly shifting face was showing the strain as she struggled to allow the Doctor's circlet to work in harmony with her own mind, keeping stray impulses at bay.

She reached, carefully. *Yes, Doctor.*

168

Is there any way you can locate Shanstra without her finding and channelling you?

A pause. Kelzen deliberated. *It is possible. I am feeling . . . the strangest splintering of her signals, and yet a unity.*

Keep it at this level, Kelzen. Get into my mind. I need you to direct me and Leibniz to Shanstra's base, and I can't do it without you.

The Sensopath drew a long, shuddering breath. *Very well, Doctor. We need each other's help.*

The Phracton Secondary's module tore through the air of Gadrell Major, gases burning against the surface of the globe.

Deep within his nest of circuits, he shivered with newly boosted power and courage. What was it? Something was driving him onward, secure in the knowledge that the humans would die. And the feeble Commandant, who had remained behind with a monitoring team in the Centre, would be forced to admit the error of his ways, then annihilated. His power was almost at an end anyway.

A wave of Earth fighters banked into view in the clear blue sky.

The Phracton's instructions were as swift and clear as thought. For they *were* thought. Sent through the web, through the Swarm.

Through something else, another being whose laughter kicked like a drug through the electronic and organic brain of the Phracton Secondary.

And only then did he realize there was something there, lurking, controlling his mind. He plunged, not quite prepared, into the battle.

Blip after blip flared against the unreal colours of the screen. They bathed the watching *Phoenix* crew in angry light. Bernice stood beside Cheynor, watching in frustration.

A TechnOp's report came through loud and clear. 'Captain. The Doctor and Leibniz have reached Banksburgh.'

'Good. Keep the trace on them if you can.'

The shifting background on the screen was rotating as the computer compensated to keep the fighters' blips central. It was like a macabre electronic game, Bernice thought in despair. And it could have been avoided. She should have stopped it. If the Doctor had been here earlier – would he have been able to do anything?

Whoever wins today, Bernice thought, Gadrell Major will lose.

Suzi Palsson ran her finger through the dust on what had been her desk.

The reading room of the library was covered in rubble and dust and the remains of computer equipment. It was a ghost, a shadow of the place she had known. She knew she had come back here for something important, but she had forgotten now what it was.

One of the computers was still working. Screen-saver patterns zoomed and flickered at her from the far corner of the room. She remembered how she always used to curse the ancient technology they were given on frontier worlds, but now, it seemed loved, wanted. She reactivated the machine and her own face stared out at her.

Startled, Suzi blinked. She looked again at the revolving pixels of her own head, there on the screen, turning like a vase on a museum plinth. Maybe that was what she was now, a museum piece, the old Suzi gone forever.

She read all the information about herself. It was not hard to work out that someone had been in here, accessing her personal file.

Images jostled for space in her mind. Three kids. Of course, they had known where to find her. There had been the scrawny boy and the huntress with her crossbow. And a charred skeleton floating across the room on a tide of green light, destroyed by –

Suzi closed her eyes, but could not block any of it out.

When patterns started to blossom in the red-blackness, she suddenly remembered what she had come back for.

* * *

The Doctor watched Horst Leibniz as he guided their skimmer through dingy, deserted backstreets. Neither of them spoke, but the Doctor's face was grim and brooding. He was listening to Kelzen. She was sending him an image of something cold, and flat, and white.

The Doctor turned to Leibniz. 'Is there an ice-rink anywhere around here?'

The haggard-looking first officer did not seem surprised by the question. 'It's where we're going.'

'Yes,' said the Doctor thoughtfully. 'So I'd noticed. I wonder how you knew?'

'Do you really believe, Doctor,' said Leibniz in his crisp voice, 'that no humans at all have extrasensory abilities?'

The Doctor, for once, was lost for words.

'It's why I was assigned to this mission,' Leibniz continued. 'I don't work for Cheynor, although he doesn't know it. I work for the Earth Security Council as a resident intuitive.' For a moment he flicked his diamond-bright gaze towards the Doctor. 'I'm a telepath, Doctor.'

'I see.' The Doctor's uneasy eyes looked Leibniz up and down. 'And you just happen to be around when a mind-controlling alien turns up?'

Leibniz smiled grimly. 'I could say the same about you, Doctor. Didn't you come here looking for trouble?'

'I never need to,' muttered the Doctor grouchily. 'Trouble's always right there waiting for me when I get up in the morning.' He glanced at Leibniz. 'Not that I sleep. Properly,' he added.

'I see. Well, I was sent by Adjudicator Hagen. She pulled strings to get me assigned to this mission, as soon as we knew Phractons were involved, so that I could have an advantage in negotiations. They're a mental collective, you see, a kind of swarm – '

'I've read about them,' said the Doctor curtly.

'Hagen found out – don't ask me how – that Earth was sending the *Phoenix* off on a suicide mission. It's all a set-up. They wanted a diversion to keep the Phracs away from Earth's solar system, and we're the cat's-paw. Hagen sent me to see if anything could *really* be done. If I could

171

negotiate, try and commune with the Phracs more closely. And then this spanner gets thrown in the works. I didn't expect anything like it.'

'A diplomatic party's incineration is rather more than an inconvenience,' suggested the Doctor. 'By the way, you do realize you're driving straight towards those glass doors, don't you?'

'I'm fully aware, Doctor.'

'Good, good. Just checking. Had I better, ah, duck down, or cover my eyes, for example?'

'If you like,' said Leibniz, as the vast, black-glass entrance of the Banksburgh Sports Complex loomed in the viewer.

The Doctor slid lower in his seat.

'It won't help, of course,' Leibniz added.

The skimmer hit the doors with a crash and was thrown slightly off centre. Splinters of black glass shot past the windows. The vehicle hit the floor of the foyer, juddering furiously and shaking the Doctor and Leibniz up and down. Then it hit the nearest wall and came to a complete stop.

To the left of her fighter, Cassie Hogarth could see distant mountains and the slim dart of one flanking ship. To her right, the shattered towers of Banksburgh and the other flanker. And dead ahead, a wall of Phrac units.

The enhancer over her left eye showed the landscape in textured detail. It still failed to make more than blobs of the creatures in their shells, the airborne army heading for her and the rest of the squadron.

'Engage them dead centre.' She heard her own voice, robotic, crackling in the speaker inside her helmet. 'Let's show we mean business.'

'Acknowledged,' said her left flanker.

'Acknowledged,' confirmed the right flanker.

Cassie eased her ship down, half seeing, half feeling the others follow her lead.

She remembered other worlds, other battles. The Sontaran whose head had deflated like a balloon when she blew his probic vent open on Titan. The Caxtarid who had kept her prisoner for hours in the dense swamplands of one of their moons, and who had let her escape only when it was obvious that the tanks were raging through the front lines, destroying everything. She remembered the Caxtarid every time she looked in the mirror. Preserved human eyes were highly valued trophies for them. It had been Cassie's price for her life.

Why? Why had these old memories suddenly surged, bringing fury, hatred? There were voices, furiously demanding orders, in her ears. She realized she had missed her optimum mark by two seconds.

'Lock on and fire!' she screamed.

The sky erupted in streams of light.

A Phracton module, spinning towards her, gushed smoke and a trail of something blue before pirouetting groundwards.

Cassie banked and swerved. The *Phoenix* fighters were losing formation. Phracs were returning the fire, and she saw three traces flare and die on her monitor. There was debris. Wheels of flame whirled in the air like angry demons.

Cassie flipped through a full circle, aware that there was now total confusion in her headphones. She snapped several orders, but doubted they got through.

And right in front of her, there was a Phracton unit, so close she could almost see the creature's eyes.

Reflexes kicked in and she fired once, twice, too many times. The creature's casing shattered and her own fighter hit the explosive backlash with an impact that threw her wildly off course, ground becoming sky.

Cassie could hear her own breath in her ears. She tried desperately to regain control of her ship. Banksburgh was coming up fast on the viewer, there were two Phracs on her tail, and she'd lost the squadron.

It was over.

Both of her pursuers opened fire. Her own hand clicked twice on the FIRE control. It was her last action before she died.

173

As Cassie and her ship were incinerated, the thought remained, almost as if it lingered on, somewhere, without her: What was this all for?

On the tracking screen, the formation had splintered into chaos the second they hit the Phracton attack line. They had all seen Hogarth's left flanker go down, but she seemed to have abandoned the other.

'Damn! Hogarth, what are you doing?' Cheynor could not believe his eyes. 'She was late with the initial run. Of all the people to miss the optimum – '

'If they attack the ship,' Bernice asked quietly, 'have we got sufficient defences to keep them back?'

The look which Cheynor gave her was a mixture of pity and despair.

And on the screen, Hogarth's own trace flared and died.

Livewire's eyes opened.

Trinket jumped to his feet, dropping his video game to the floor with a clatter.

She sat up, blinking, and in one sudden, decisive movement she pulled the sensor-pads from her temples. The screens above her couch began to flash and emit a trilling alarm.

'No!' Trinket shouted. He had never been so frightened. 'Nurse! Nurse, quickly!'

'I can hear the sound of death,' said Livewire gently. Her expression was one of bafflement.

'They're fighting.' Trinket was backing away from her slowly.

'Fighting?'

'The Earth ship and the Phracs. They think they're going to battle it out over this lump of rock.' Trinket surprised himself with his vehemence.

Livewire swayed back and forth for a second or two, and then looked up at her brother with a bright, clear gaze.

'Who are you?' she asked.

* * *

174

The Doctor flung open the doors to the arena and was thrown back almost immediately by the harshest wind, like fire and ice combined.

Behind him, Leibniz clung to the door, shielding his eyes as if from light. Through Kelzen, the Doctor could just about feel Leibniz's mind, bobbing like a surfboard on the Sensopath's tidal wave.

There, before them, was Shanstra, the queen of ice and darkness. She stood up from her throne, arms held high, hair rippling behind her in the wind, her eyes bright green with power and desire. Coronas of fire, like spiked whips of green light, flowed from her outstretched fingers as she burnt off the excess energy. Behind her, the huge screens were flashing up the briefest images – of fighters, both human and Phracton, blazing from the sky.

The Doctor, battling fiercely, held on to his hat and staggered forward to the very edge of the ice-rink. He did not dare to meet those terrible eyes.

'Shanstra!' His voice, above the tumult, was that of a drowning man. 'Shanstra, you must stop this. You don't know what chaos your powers are causing in the physical world!'

She threw back her head and laughed. The sound became light, formed swirling patterns in the air above her.

But I do, I do, Time Lord, said her mocking voice as it rifled the filing cabinets of the Doctor's thoughts.

The Doctor closed his eyes and began to picture, one by one, the companions he had gained and lost. He was remembering it had worked with the Haemovores. He hoped it would work again now.

'Doctor!' Leibniz was at his side. 'Doctor, she's got into the Phracton collective. She's somehow managing to guide them, direct their hatred against us – '

'I know!' snarled the Doctor, with his eyes still tightly shut. 'Keep quiet!'

– And last of all he came to the memory of Ace, the girl, the woman, the warrior, now gone for ever – and the

*thought, with all its strength, was lobbed at Shanstra, like
meat to a ferocious dog.*

For a fleeting moment, she was distracted, reaching with
a tentacle of thought to grab this new morsel of emotional
intensity – and her link to the Phracton collective
weakened.

The Doctor pressed the advantage. Something else,
something unusual, pulsed down Shanstra's channel to the
Phracton Swarm.

The Phracton Secondary screamed as channels of fire
coursed through his circuitry.

There was a mind, cutting into his. A sharp, devious
mind skewering that of his new mistress and sending coun-
ter-impulses into the Swarm.

His module banked and swerved, spinning out of control like a ball thrown by an angry child.

The Doctor had taken a risk. He felt her sensing Kelzen's
touch in his mind.

And now, realizing how she had been deceived, she let
out an unearthly shriek and shattered the roof of the
arena. Down it fell, in a torrent of molten glass and metal,
like deadly, slow-motion rain. Fragments began to hit the
ice, destroying it.

'Get out,' the Doctor told Leibniz. 'Now!'

'You're coming too,' he muttered, and grabbed the Doctor's arm.

Life – awakening –
  Life returning.
  With control, with new, fresh power, comes life.

The Phracton Commandant's mind had been riveted
down as securely as a door in a gale. Now, it broke free,
shattered its bonds, smashed through the controlling
influences of the treacherous Secondary and back into the
Swarm.

His mind glittered in the web, touched every Swarm-
brother with the same tendrils of calmness.

176

Stop this madness, it said. *Stop it at once.*

The Battle of Banksburgh, which decided, eventually, the fate of Gadrell Major, was fought entirely in the air and was later reckoned to have lasted approximately sixteen Earth minutes.

At the end of this time, the Phractons – whose attack force leader (Phracton 4Z-88*, Secondary to the Commandant) had been among the casualties – grouped above the city and, at the Commandant's instruction, ceased hostilities. The Swarm, for the most part, remained unclear about how the Commandant had regained control. External influence was suspected.

When the attack was called off, the Phracton Commandant opened a channel from the web to Captain Darius Cheynor of the *Phoenix*, requesting that he personally be allowed to board the Earth ship to negotiate.

At around the same time, Cassie Hogarth's fighter, together with that of the Phracton she had taken with her, hit the river bridge, slicing it in two. Glass, metal and smoke shot upwards in a cocoon of mud and water, echoing through the ruins of Banksburgh.

A kilometre away, in a different but related incident, Banksburgh's sports centre turned into a giant Roman candle, whose dazzling light faded as soon as it had shone.

18

Wake Up, Little Suzi

Suzi Palsson turned the handle of the old-fashioned safe in the library office, thankful that she had recalled the number. Inside its velvet, padded interior there sat the object she had been looking for.

This weapon was nothing like her laser-pistol; in fact she had long thought that it could be purely ornamental. She sniggered to herself as she thought of the irony. The kids had come here, looking for her so they could steal her gun, and there had been one in the safe only a few metres away, had they bothered to look.

It had an ivory handle, cool and smooth, and a jet-black surface that seemed to swallow light. Silver flanges adorned the barrel, inlaid with intricate engravings which had been the work of her great-grandfather. These old-fashioned firearms were familiar to Suzi, who had spent many hundreds of hours at the screen of her reader, both here in the library and at home. She knew how they operated. Gas pressure was generated when the propellant was burnt in a chamber called the breech, at the rear of the gun – rather like the process of an internal combustion engine. The pressure on the projectile base depended on the propellant's properties, the amount burned, and the spatial distribution of the gases.

She checked the chamber: there were two slim, smooth bullets in it. She snapped it shut, wondering how long it would take Shanstra to know about this one, and if it would be possible to shoot her in the back before she realized.

The problem was, Suzi reflected, she did not know if she was capable of killing a being as perfect and beautiful as Shanstra. Suzi still loved. She still believed.

There was someone standing in the doorway.

Suzi gasped and jerked the gun up to cover him. The visitor was a small man with an owlish, intelligent face, in a rather crumpled-looking white suit and paisley tie. He smiled, and raised his hat to reveal dishevelled brown hair, greying slightly at the temples.

'I do hope I'm not disturbing,' he said quietly. 'You see, my friend outside detected your presence. I thought I'd pop in and tell you it's all over.'

'What's all over?' snapped Suzi. She could feel her body beginning to shake. 'And who are you, anyway?'

'Well, you can call me the Doctor. Most people do. I've also been known as Ka Faraq Gatri, Theta Sigma, Merlin, one you'd never be able to pronounce, and, er – ' he smiled fondly, ' –nanoceph. But don't let that bother you. Names are so nominal, in my experience.' He folded his hands behind his back, and smiled. 'The war,' he added, 'to answer your other question. The war is over.'

Suzi's hand faltered and she almost dropped the gun, but when the Doctor came closer, her hands gripped the cool ivory handle more tightly, and her sweaty forefinger stroked the trigger. 'What do you mean?'

'I mean that, although it's been rather messy and bloody, a kind of settlement is being negotiated as we speak. A – conciliation service forced itself into the situation. So why don't you put down that rather antiquated firearm, and come along with me?'

Suzi gave a half-hearted grin. 'Hey,' she said, 'my mother told me not to go off with strange men.'

'Well, I've had seven different bodies, so that must make me very bizarre indeed.' The little man smiled as if at some private joke. 'Mind you, my last one was stranger.'

Suzi suddenly felt rather absurd, standing in her office and aiming another gun that she did not have the conviction to use. She sighed, clicked the safety-catch on and placed the weapon inside her jacket. 'All right,' she said, 'so where are we going to go?'

The answer came from a clipped voice, just outside the door. 'Nowhere, for the moment.'

There was another man behind the Doctor, tall and anaemic-looking, with spiky white hair and a pair of brightly shining eyes behind small round glasses.

Suzi did not break her gaze in time. She felt something brushing delicately across her mind, and saw the man's bright eyes from within, illuminating the caverns of her thoughts. She gasped.

'You're not allowed,' she protested.

The Doctor looked up sternly. 'Did you just do what I think you did? No, don't tell me.'

'It's there,' Leibniz said. 'Traces of what we just felt. Of that alien. It could be hiding in her.'

'Trau Leibniz,' said the Doctor patiently, 'in your years of ESP work with the Earth Security Council, have you ever had to deal with a creature so powerful it can use mental energy to convert desires and fears into terrifying events in the real world?'

Leibniz opened his mouth to answer.

'Don't bother,' snapped the Doctor. 'It's rhetorical.' His expression became calmer, more conciliatory, and he motioned for Suzi to sit down, which she did.

'What are you doing, Doctor?' Leibniz asked. 'If this one's a true perceptive, she's my business.'

The Doctor ignored him. 'Sorry about my ill-mannered friend,' he murmured gently to Suzi. 'Would you mind if I hypnotized you?'

For the first time in many years, there was a Phracton officer on the command deck of an Earth ship.

Two of Cheynor's guards stood in readiness at the doors to the briefing room, which had been made into an impromptu arena for negotiation. Cheynor felt they would probably not be needed.

He had to admit that it was still an intimidating experi-

180

ence, seeing one up this close. And not just any Phracton – the Commandant himself of this expeditionary unit. The globe housing the creature was at least two metres across, and some effect – half shadow, half a kind of frosting – made sure that the being within it remained indistinct. When the Commandant spoke, Cheynor saw, the tentacled form within the globe expanded and contracted like a bellows, and the words from the grille on the globe's central band of black were punctuated by liquid slurping sounds.

'What – I fail – to under-stand – Captain,' ventured the Phracton Commandant, 'is – why – you did not – share – your infor-mation with me – earlier.'

Cheynor sighed. 'I would have,' he said. 'I called your representatives to Londinium Plaza, remember?'

'Yes,' the alien answered thoughtfully. 'There are those – in the – Swarm – who do not – trust you – hu-man. Those who sus-pect you – of trickery.'

'Please! I wanted to make them realize that we're being made to fight this war against our will, and for no purpose other than the peace of mind of Earth Council.'

The Phracton drew what sounded to Cheynor like a deep, shuddering breath, and the interior of the globe was suffused for a second with an opaque blue light. 'That – is not – honourable – of Earth Council,' he said after a pause.

'No,' Cheynor answered wryly. 'I said something similar myself, only less politely.' He sat back in his chair and addressed the Phracton's speaker-grille. 'It would be simple now, for both our forces to get off this world and forget about it. Unfortunately, that can't be done. For one thing, I've got an orbital platform full of civilian refugees looking for a home, and there's a hell of a lot of clearing up to be done.' He paused. 'And secondly, we've both suffered casualties, you know that. I lost one of my best officers up there today. But it hasn't all been strictly you against us. There's something else here, something insidi-ous that threatens both our races, and I want to find out what it is.'

181

'Indeed. And I – am as reluc-tant – to leave this – matter unres-olved – as you.'

Cheynor stood up, walked round the table so that he stood as close as he dared to the Phracton Commandant. He saw that the surface of the globe, although it appeared to be of a material similar to plexiglass, was astonishingly thick, and marked with the lacerations of battle. A gentle fizzing sound emanated from the surface, reminding Cheynor of the electric fences used on some colonies to keep the indigenous animals out. 'I want your word,' he said, 'that when all this is over, your people will help us to make Banksburgh habitable again. We need to pool our technology. There's so much we can teach one another.'

'My – word?'

'Yes. Your bond of honour. I understand that's of the highest value to your race, and – '

'And – is – not – given lightly!' The Phracton seemed to hiss and bubble inside its casing, causing Cheynor to take a step backwards.

All right, he thought. I can see now why I never wanted to join the diplomatic corps.

'I'm sorry,' he said after drawing a deep breath. 'I didn't mean to cause offence. It's just that I've been reading up on the history of your race, and, well, while there are some humans I wouldn't trust even after a sworn state-ment signed in blood, I know that a Phracton's word cannot be broken. That's why I'd accept it as a guarantee from you.' Cheynor looked up hopefully at the giant globe. 'It was meant to be a sort of compliment,' he added lamely.

The blue haze filled the globe again and Cheynor saw the blurred form inside beginning to vibrate, shaking as if in terrible fury. A low hiss began to emerge from the speaking grille, building in volume and pitch, underlaid with a grotesque roar of static.

Only then did Cheynor snap out of his bewilderment and alarm, and realize what was happening.

The Phracton Commandant was shaking with laughter.

* * *

'And Shanstra loves you?' The Doctor's question to the hypnotized Suzi hung suspended in the air, like the dust in the weak sunbeams that were straining through the window. Leibniz sighed in exasperation, but the Doctor ignored him.

Suzi, glassy-eyed, nodded. 'She loves you, too,' she pointed out, staring vacantly past the Doctor's face.

The Doctor, frowning in disapproval, withdrew his face a few centimetres. 'I find that highly unlikely,' he said, 'as I've never met her.'

The thought crossed his mind that he had, in a sense. That the distillation of Shanstra's other side – one that had, possibly, more regard for sentient life – was currently sitting in the Zero Room of the TARDIS. And should Leibniz have any suspicions, he could very easily find out this fact. The Doctor was banking on the hope that his Gallifreyan mental discipline could overcome the primitive probing of a Terran ESP agent.

'Believe in Shanstra,' insisted Suzi. Her face had taken on a glittering, artificial smile, and the Doctor was beginning to wonder if the trance had been such a good idea. 'Only then will you truly understand her.'

'This is getting us nowhere!' Leibniz snapped. 'I could get through to her in half the time.'

'No doubt,' said the Doctor acerbically, without taking his eyes from Suzi's face. 'But the difference, Trau Leibniz, is like that between a bulldozer and an archaeologist. Suzi . . .' He looked into her eyes again. 'Your love for Shanstra is not real, is it? There's something behind it. A darker desire.'

'I . . . She . . .'

'Yes?'

'She used me. By showing me Colm. He used me too, and I let him die when I could have saved him. So now she has to die as well.'

'Hmm.' The Doctor was doubtful. 'We're getting into deep water here. Desire for love and revenge combined. I don't want to harm her.' He leaned thoughtfully on his umbrella. 'Suzi, I want you to concentrate on yourself.

183

Think of all the good things you've done for yourself in life, and give yourself a little pat on the back for them.'

Suzi closed her eyes and seemed to go off into a contented sleep.

The Doctor leaned back. 'A bit of self-esteem never hurt anyone,' he murmured to Leibniz. 'Worth more than the spurious congratulation of an alien deity, at any rate.'

'What's happened to her?' Leibniz asked.

'I thought telepaths didn't ask questions like that?' the Doctor teased. Leibniz opened his mouth, but the Doctor held up a hand to forestall the objection. 'All right, point taken. She's undergone a complex kind of brainwashing. This Shanstra creature has latched on to Suzi's insecurity about herself, to her low self-esteem, her desire to be loved. She's filled the gap with a controlling love, neo-maternal with proto-erotic elements. Essentially, she's been given what she thinks is something to live for.' The Doctor winced and shook his head. 'The pattern of cults all over the universe.'

Leibniz's hair seemed to stand up even further as if it were responding in a kind of empathic surprise. He sat down on the carpet with his arms folded across his knees. 'I suppose it's no use trying to argue it out of her rationally? I mean, if I said I didn't believe in fairies, and you took me down to the bottom of my garden and showed me a few prancing about, I'd have to eat my words. Only the problem with gods and goddesses is that it's meant to be in their nature that they can't be shown and seen in that sort of way. Convenient, eh, Doctor?'

'I'd imagine,' the Doctor said, leaning over Suzi and peering into her ears, 'that Shanstra wouldn't reveal her love and glory to a sceptic like you, Trau Leibniz. Only to one who wants to believe.'

'As I said, very convenient.'

'Yes. And as the Sensopath's power is derived parasitically, the more who believe in her as a goddess, the more powerful she will become. But – ' the Doctor stood up and smiled reassuringly ' – she can't do anything cataclysmic until she reunites with her other selves.'

184

'Other selves?'

'Trust me. I'm a doctor. Come on, let's get Suzi back to the *Phoenix*. And after that, I have an important job for you and Bernice, while I pop into the future for a few millennia. Clear?'

'Clear as Draconian chess, Doctor,' said Leibniz, in weary resignation.

'Really?' The Doctor looked surprised. 'I'd actually meant to baffle you. I'll try harder next time.'

19

Stupid and Contagious

The assembly arena was dark and curved, its glossy walls sweeping upwards into unreachable vaults. At the moment it was being used for a purpose of which the Director of the Dream Centre would not have approved.

Jirenal surveyed the long line of orange-robed Pridka with satisfaction, but also with contempt. A mixture of intimidation and marvel, he thought, that was all it needed to be a god, even in this highly evolved society.

'I shall draw strength from each of you,' he said, as he walked along the line. 'Wherever you go, you will introduce new subjects to my power and my glory. This will be our mission, and your task.' He nodded. 'Go.'

The Pridka bowed once, and dispersed from the vast hall, leaving Jirenal standing alone at the centre with Amarill, her green robe the remaining splash of colour in the dark place.

'I do not think it was right,' she said slowly, signs of strain on her normally serene blue face. 'What you did to the Yzashoks.'

Jirenal grinned, spread his black-gloved hands. 'They are not dead,' he said. 'Merely inactive. It was a demonstration of my abilities.' He shrugged. 'One which, it is true, has left me rather drained, for the moment.' Amarill did not look convinced, but she looked up when he touched her chin. 'Those who come here to be healed,'

186

Jirenal murmured. 'Where is their first port of call, in general?'

Amarill's eyes were open wide, sea-blue. 'The Dreamguide, of course. The Dreamguide is the senior Pridka, carrying the wisdom and knowledge of generations. It controls the Recreational Dream Experience and is specially trained in the healing of fragile minds. It takes visitors through subconscious experiences, some happy, some sad, in order that they may emerge with a greater knowledge of themselves at the end.'

'Ah, yes.' Jirenal smiled, and the open-ended comment seemed to take wing and flutter into the cold heights of the arena. 'The Director did mention such a process.' He straightened his jacket. 'I want you to go to the Dreamguide. I wish to hear what it has to say about me.'

'About you?' Amarill did not understand. 'Why?'

'Child, what did I tell you about questions? You accept. Have faith in Jirenal, faith in the Infinite Requiem to be played at the end of creation.'

'Yes.' Amarill lowered her head.

'We must all have faith. Only by uniting all your powers with mine can I regain the strength needed to reach out to my other selves and bring us together in harmony. Do you understand?'

'Yes.'

The swathe of fins was rippling gently, Jirenal noticed, but he could read her greatest worry like a message telegraphed from a hillside. Still there was that sense of dullness in her mind, of non-reception, concerning her greatly.

Or could it be completion? Jirenal suggested in amusement.

Or could it be – *completion*, she suddenly wondered in awe?

Might it not be, Jirenal suggested, lobbing the thought into her gaping and waiting mind, that now she loved Jirenal and loved the Infinite Requiem, that there was no more to learn? That questioning was useless, and only faith mattered?

Of course, Amarill realized. The reason that there were

187

no more gentle impulses flowing into her brain from the other Pridka was that there was no more to learn. That questioning was useless, and only faith mattered.

Reassured, Amarill followed her master, lover and god from the arena, and on to the nearest gravpad.

Bernice had found Trinket slumped in a chair in the medlab, with his head in his hands.

'Don't tell me – sibling rivalry?' Bernice ventured.

'I told her she was mad,' Trinket muttered, looking up at her in dismay. 'She didn't remember me. She's gone.'

'Oh, brilliant. For a moment, I thought you'd done something intelligent. So where was she heading?' Another thought struck her. 'And why didn't the guards stop her?'

He shrugged. 'She's not a prisoner. They don't have the authority.'

'So where is she?' Bernice demanded.

'She said something about . . .'

'Yes?'

'About needing to talk to a kindred spirit.'

Not every member of the Phracton collective had responded when the order to return to base had come from the Commandant.

Shanstra's mental force – like a caress with a dagger, sometimes drawing blood – had affected every one of them, but most individual Phractons had managed to isolate the affected areas, both hardware and wetware, and shut them off from their main nodes of operation.

There were some for whom the blade had gone deeper.

And these were no longer Swarm-brothers with their fellows. They were Shanstra's pets, extensions of her will.

Shanstra had reduced the sports centre to a circle of blackness spewing viscous smoke, which was clearly visible from her new position on the shattered chequer-board of Londinium Plaza.

One by one, her new servants had come to her, and she

had lain an affectionate hand on each crackling globe, sending her instructions into their receptive cyborg minds.

She was biding her time.

The skimmer containing the Doctor, Leibniz and Suzi Palsson landed in the docking bay without incident, and the Doctor, who seemed to have acquired the respect and obedience of most of the crew, demanded that he and Leibniz be taken to Captain Cheynor. He assured Suzi that she would be in good hands, then grabbed the nearest TechnOp and told her to look after their esteemed guest, Ambassador Palsson from the colony of Bibliotecca, and to give her the best quarters with everything she wanted.

With that, he and Leibniz disappeared into the nearest elevator-tube, leaving the bemused TechnOp staring at Suzi, who tried, with reasonable success, to cultivate a haughty and refined bearing.

The Phracton swivelled with remarkable speed when the arrivals were shown into Cheynor's briefing room. The Doctor gave a cautious smile, but he was aware that Leibniz was staring intently at the alien.

'Stop that,' the Doctor muttered, realizing what was probably happening. 'It's rude.'

Cheynor cleared his throat. 'Doctor. Horst. Glad to see you back safe and well. I've been discussing terms with the Commandant here.'

'Good. Excellent,' muttered the Doctor, in a tone which implied, to Cheynor's annoyance, that he was hardly interested in the aftermath of the war. He strode over to Cheynor's desk, hopped up on to it and lay down, ignoring the disarray of papers. 'We've been looking at this from the wrong angle,' the Doctor said. 'Wouldn't you agree, Commandant?' He turned his head towards the Phracton and raised his eyebrows.

The Commandant's globe swivelled back and forth and a long, shuddering breath sounded from the grille. 'I do not – see – the re-le-vance of your ques-tion.' Cheynor and Leibniz exchanged a glance.

'How many of the warriors in your Swarm fell under the control of Shanstra?' the Doctor asked sternly.

The Commandant's globe pulsed with a soft blue glow before he answered. 'It is – difficult – to say,' he admitted. 'The signals – of the dis-honourable – are blurred. Also – some of – the Swarm – are ma-naging to – iso-late her influence.'

'Are you saying, Doctor,' Cheynor asked urgently, 'that although I've just made peace with the Commandant here, there's no way of telling how many of the Phractons are still loyal to the Swarm?'

'Yes,' said the Doctor. He sat up, and his legs dangled over the edge of the table. 'Interesting, isn't it?' He hopped down. 'I'd imagine Shanstra is planning something, now. I don't think she'll make a move until she's absolutely ready.' Another thought seemed to strike him. 'Where's Bernice?' he asked.

Livewire found Suzi on the gallery on the ship's observation deck. It curved vastly above them, revealing the new skyline, shattered but liberated, of Banksburgh.

'Hello,' the huntress said, quietly.

The archivist did not turn to look at her. 'I don't need her any more,' she said. 'Neither of us needs her.'

A cold bleakness seemed to shroud the body of the huntress, like a mist. 'The hatred,' she said. 'It felt . . .'

Suzi turned on her in anger. 'It felt like what? A fantasy? You're just a stupid girl, a silly little girl with delusions about being big and heroic. There's more to it than that! No wonder Shanstra was able to control you so easily.'

Livewire stared coldly at her. She clenched her fist, braced herself. Then she relaxed and unclenched her fist again. No. Maybe it was not the way.

Suzi smiled.

Livewire tilted her head to one side, and, as if she was learning how to do it for the first time, she smiled as well.

There was a commotion at the entrance by the end of the walkway, and Benny hurried in, followed by a sheep-

190

ish-looking Trinket. 'You're supposed to be lying down,' Bernice told Livewire. 'What are you doing?'

Livewire looked at Suzi, who met her gaze as if to say, 'Up to you, now.'

Livewire looked over Bernice's shoulder at the pale and concerned face of her half-brother. 'Getting myself sorted,' she said. 'Maybe.'

Bernice raised an eyebrow.

Travelling Hopefully

20

Travelling Hopefully

Amarill stood before the Dreamguide.

The projection of the Dreamguide could be found at the gateway to one of the centre's most popular attractions, the Recreational Dream Experience. Against a dark background, framed by the gigantic metal gateway, the Dreamguide's face was huge, sexless, beautiful: a projection input to several senses at once, physical and telepathic.

Amarill, who was far enough advanced to be able to request her private audience, normally felt every caress with keenness and love. Now, she was blank. Receiving nothing. The only sensory input came from her link with her new master Jirenal, as she assumed it always had done. She knew, too, that he was cleverly helping her to emit simulations of thought to the Dreamguide, so that it should not become suspicious of Amarill's lack of response.

The mind-voice which spoke to the Dreamguide had the timbre of Amarill dell'katit vo'Pridka, but the words and thoughts were those of her master, her saviour, Jirenal.

A visitor wishes to meet you. A very special visitor. Can you accommodate him?

The Dreamguide breathed deeply, gathering the wisdom of the Pridka minds which it stored. *All beings are welcome here.*

Amarill bowed. *Thank you. I shall bring him.*

The Dreamguide's mental tendrils pulled her back, momentarily. *I will not allow access without the Director's permission*, it said sternly.

It seemed that it had sensed something – Amarill's hesitancy, maybe, or even a hint of what was concealed in Amarill's mind.

Then I will obtain it, came the reply.

Very well. Amarill dell'katit vo'Pridka, you seem troubled. Do you wish to share anything with me?

A pause.

No, Dreamguide. Nothing.

Nothing.

Deep inside her mind, protected by layer upon layer of thought – which etiquette stopped the Dreamguide from penetrating – the Sensopath laughed.

Millennia away – or just a breath away – the sunset bathed Gadrell Major in wine-coloured light, and burnished the glittering tower of the *Phoenix*.

In the visitor's lounge of the ship, Bernice demonstrated a card trick to two members of the Phracton delegation. Nearby, the Doctor was leaning over the tiny holo-pyramid, a jeweller's eyepiece fixed into his right eye. He was making delicate adjustments with a laseron probe.

'Benny,' he said, lifting his hand.

She excused herself from the two aliens and hurried over. 'What is it?' The Doctor removed his eyepiece and lifted up the pyramid to the light. One side had been opened out like a flap, revealing layer upon layer of glistening silver circuitry. 'I've given our friend here a little reprogramming.'

'Don't tell me. He can quote Shakespeare, juggle and play the spoons.'

'Oh, better than that. It's integrated to some extent with the patterns of the TARDIS's symbiotic nuclei, so that the hologram can be your contact while I'm gone.' He snapped the flap shut, placed the pyramid on the table, then tapped it twice.

The pyramid lost form, became a cloud of light swirling upwards to form a shape in a cream-coloured suit.

'Good evening,' said the h-Doctor, standing on the table. He raised his hat. 'Bernice. Doctor.'

The real Doctor leaned back in his chair and chuckled in delight. 'Glad to see your sartorial taste has improved.'

'I don't think you've quite got my accent right, though,' mused the h-Doctor. 'What do you think?'

Bernice looked from one to the other. 'You'd better switch him off. I'm going to forget which is which.'

'Not just yet, Benny. I have some more instructions to program. And this time, you're going to help me.'

Shanstra arrived at the gates of the former vice-governor's residence with at least a dozen Phractons in tow, bobbing on the energy fields that trailed behind her dark cloak.

She looked appreciatively up and down the house. It was a great, dazzling cube of white, gold-shuttered, with an ornate portico in silver and gold, the cornice displaying the vice-governor's red and gold coat of arms. Beyond the house, jade-green lawns descended in gentle steps to Londinium Plaza. It all seemed largely to have escaped the bombing, for which Shanstra was grateful.

She turned to her minions. 'This will do. Find any who still remain here, and eliminate them.' She drew herself up to her full height, and her eyes shone. 'I shall summon my powers, and unite our minds with the other parts of myself. And then it will be the moment for the Infinite Requiem to begin.'

The Phractons bobbed up the sweeping drive of the house. Without stopping, the leaders of the phalanx blasted the doors open, leaving a shattered, burning surround.

Amused, Shanstra followed them into the house. She stepped into the marble hall with its glittering chandelier, and watched as the Phractons dispersed to the various rooms and corridors.

Framed in the burning doorway, looking out over the

194

ruined city, Shanstra breathed deeply and spread her mind as far and as thinly as she could. Like a web.

Yes, as she had thought, there was something. She was sure there was something, like her name being called from a hubbub of foreign tongues, or a familiar face in a sea of many.

Kelzen's pattern had been strong back in the ice-rink when Shanstra had almost broken through. And then there had been those two interfering idiots who had escaped. The human, an extrasensory, weak by her standards but exceptional in terms of these primitives – and then there had been the other.

The Terrans did not have the capacity to hide Kelzen from her, but if they were being aided by a Time Lord . . .

He had ploughed a swathe through her smooth control of the Secondary, her command of the Swarm, just long enough for the Commandant to regain control over his crazed warriors. It was clever. This creature was evidently something to watch out for.

She gathered in her web, and focused on the intermittent beats of sound echoing through the house. She smiled as she recognized the satisfying noises of weaponry. Her Phracton hunting-dogs were doing their job.

The Doctor strode across the ridge where he had left the TARDIS, followed by a motley assortment of companions.

Immediately behind him was Darius Cheynor, dressed in battle uniform, and following at a couple of paces, trying to keep up, was Suzi Palsson, now bright-eyed, kitted out in fresh clothes from the *Phoenix*: plain coveralls and a long cloak. Her quicksilver hair was glossy and fresh again, and she was looking human, free of the bonds of Shanstra. Bringing up the rear, motor unit humming gently, was the shining globe of the Phracton Commandant.

Outside the rickety blue police box, they stopped, and the Doctor nodded. 'Everything in place?' he asked Cheynor.

The captain nodded. 'Leibniz has his instructions,

195

Doctor. I just hope he and Bernice aren't being sent into danger – '

'Bernice is more than capable. And I think Mr Leibniz can look after himself,' the Doctor said, cryptically. 'All right, Suzi?'

'I think so.' She smiled awkwardly, brushed some dust from her nose. 'Doctor, is it safe taking me with you? I mean, if I'm not free of Shanstra . . .'

'If that's the case, you won't be safe anywhere,' said the Doctor darkly. 'So you may as well come with me.' He unlocked the TARDIS door. 'Shall we go?'

Cheynor had been looking the blue box up and down with some apprehension. 'I saw this thing arrive, once,' he said. 'Didn't believe my eyes at the time.' He swallowed hard. 'Seen a lot since then, of course,' he added with a degree of resolve. He went inside.

Suzi peered at the blue box. 'Is this the lift, Doctor?'

'Well, it is a kind of portal,' said the Doctor. He ushered her inside. 'A narrow one,' he added in concern, looking at the Phracton. 'Wait there, old fellow. Won't be a second.'

The Doctor popped inside the TARDIS. There was a swirl of dust as it faded from the landscape, accompanied by a sound of screeching machinery that made the Phracton oscillate with concern.

Seconds later the TARDIS rematerialized right where the Phracton had been, solidifying for just a second, and then the blue box disappeared from Gadrell Major once more.

The ridge was silent and empty. Far below, fires burned in the streets of Banksburgh, and the windows of the library caught the reflection of the setting sun. The ruined city, bathed in orange, could have looked almost beautiful: not half-destroyed, but rather half-formed, unborn, waiting to rise anew from its own ashes.

In the dimly lit Zero Room, Kelzen's eyes snapped open. She was aware that she had company.

The Doctor hovered in the greyish shadows by the door. 'No one knows you are here, yet, except me,' he said.

The Sensopath's eyes glowed in the semi-darkness. 'And you assume I choose to do it your way.'

'I assume you are sensible enough. Yes.'

Kelzen chuckled to herself. She unfurled her long body, the Doctor's cloak billowing around her, and she strolled over to stand next to him, her two-metre form towering above the small Time Lord.

'You could be playing with fire, Doctor, you know that?'

'Yes,' he answered, his voice charged with menace. 'Just as long as you don't try the same thing.'

'You do not have the power to keep me here by force,' said Kelzen, amused. 'I trust you to find Jirenal, which is why I have done as you suggested so far. That is where we are going now, I take it?'

'Yes. I've brought some important friends along for the ride.'

'Ah, Doctor. Still the chess player, surrounding yourself with pawns?'

'Actually, no,' said the Doctor. 'I started to tire of chess a while ago. These days, I seem to be playing hopscotch.'

'You are amusing, Doctor.'

'You think so?' The Doctor beamed. 'You should have met my fourth incarnation, he was a real hoot.' The smile vanished rapidly. 'Take a friendly warning, Kelzen: some have found me distinctly unfunny in the past.'

The Sensopath's mouth was large and horrible, as she grinned across her malleable face and showed a barricade of perfect, incisive teeth. 'We have a very fragile trust, Doctor. You are protecting me from Shanstra, yet how do I know I do not need protecting from you?'

'You don't. That's what makes it interesting. And as for not having the power to force you to stay here, remember what I said earlier, about power.'

'I recall the conversation,' said Kelzen haughtily, as she closed her eyes and resumed her levitation posture. 'You advocate this "mercy". Having the power, and not using it.'

'Quite. I did so with the Key to Time. And on a number of occasions when I could have killed my mortal enemies.

197

So, you see, by helping you, not entrapping you, I have won your trust.'

'For the moment, Doctor,' said Kelzen, 'for the moment.' And she opened her eyes briefly to look at him again.

For a second or two, they were Sanjay Meswani's eyes, big and deep and dark and sorrowful. His dead mother's eyes. Then the feline gaze of Kelzen returned. 'The boy's body is safe as long as I am, Doctor,' she said. 'Remember that.'

The Doctor gritted his teeth. 'I'll remember,' he snarled.

He stepped out of the Zero Room, sealing the door behind him.

Bernice was beginning to wonder what she had got herself into. She was sitting at the *Phoenix* briefing table with Leibniz – whom she found faintly unnerving, a marked contrast to the affable Cheynor – and several TechnOps. Also present were Trinket and Livewire, both looking rather awkward at the end of the table.

'The Doctor has his plans,' Leibniz was saying, 'which he has discussed with the captain. But, for reasons of safety, he has not confided them fully to any of us. We are dealing, lest we forget, with an immensely powerful telepathic alien. If she were to get an inkling from any of us of what the Doctor hopes to do, then the entire mission could be jeopardized.'

Benny was watching Leibniz carefully, and thought to herself that his body language rather betrayed his discomfort during his last little speech. His pale face became, for a few seconds, slightly pinker, and the incisive eyes behind his glasses avoided meeting the gaze of any single one of them. She bet herself he had sweaty palms.

'She's a kind of telekinetic as well.' All eyes were on Livewire, who had spoken, calmly and emotionlessly. 'Her thoughts, given enough power behind them, can affect the physical world. It's almost as if she can will molecular structures to change.'

Benny nodded, remembering the shattered Phracton

globes and the strange plexiglass tree that now stood in the centre of Londinium Plaza.

'She digs deep into your brain and pulls up the things that are rotting there, things you thought were dead. Your hatred. Your fear. Worst of all, she makes you believe that, all the time, you're the one in control. That you're getting your revenge on those who hurt you.'

'Which is why she made you kill the Phractons,' Bernice said. 'It's what you wanted to do, isn't it? Save Banksburgh single-handed.'

Livewire looked away, sullen now, not speaking. Bernice silently chided herself for having said the wrong thing again, for forgetting that this young woman was no more than a confused adolescent with conflicting voices in her head and heart.

'And what do you think, er . . .' Leibniz gestured vaguely at Trinket.

The boy realized he was being addressed and sat up straight, licking his lips.

Bernice held her breath. Don't say anything belligerent, she thought desperately.

'What I understand is, the Doctor wants us to create a diversion, right?' There was a general murmur of assent. 'We can't play it too rough. She did for Poly. Burned her to a crisp. Just by looking at her. I don't think we can even get too close to this – ' he chose his word carefully ' – creature.'

'On the other hand,' said Leibniz, 'there will be a small army of us, humans and Phractons. And she is only one.'

'But with some rogue Phracs on her side,' Benny put in. 'And you've all seen the damage they can do.'

There was a momentary, charged silence, as the absence of Cassie Hogarth from the briefing was felt. They knew, Benny had been able to gather, that her ship had gone down somewhere in the river, taking a couple of Phrac units with her, but that it had not been recovered.

'All right, then,' Leibniz said calmly. 'We wait for the Doctor's signal.'

And all eyes, at that moment, became fixed on the small

199

silver holo-pyramid, which was sitting on the table in front of Bernice Summerfield.

'You've what?' Darius Cheynor stared at the Doctor across the main console of the TARDIS.

The Doctor met his gaze, his face set grimly. 'Don't agitate yourself, Trau Cheynor. The Zero Room is the safest place for her to be at the moment.'

Cheynor straightened up, shaking his head in astonishment. 'We're dealing with one of the most dangerous extraterrestrials ever encountered by Earth forces, and you've got her – other half, whatever it is – enjoying your hospitality? You could have got us all killed on Gadrell Major!'

The soft glow of the Phracton Commandant's mobile unit flared brighter for a brief moment, and the alien crackled quietly to itself. The movement was rather more of a threat than Cheynor's hectoring.

Suzi, sitting in the wicker chair in the corner of the console room, spoke. 'Darius is right, Doctor. You should have told us.'

The Doctor scowled. 'I can't be expected to inform everyone of everything. The information was on a need-to-know basis. And you – '

'Didn't need to know. Yes, Doctor, it's a familiar story,' said Cheynor wearily. 'That sort of excuse is a favourite of Earth Council, I think you'll find.'

'Are you going to fill us in, Doctor?' Suzi demanded, arms folded. 'Because I don't think I want to cooperate with you if you're keeping anything back from me.'

'So you don't trust me,' the Doctor muttered. 'I should have known.' He began to pace moodily around the console, hands folded behind his back. 'You, Darius, after I distracted Shanstra for you, dislocated her from the Phracton Secondary for long enough for both sides to see sense. And you, Commandant – ' The Doctor squared up to the scarred, pitted globe of the alien, bending low to speak into its grille. ' – if it hadn't been for my telepathic interference, you would never have wrested control of the

200

Swarm back from your late second-in-command.' The Doctor straightened up. The silence in the console room was uncomfortable. 'And Suzi!' he exclaimed, pointing dramatically in her direction. 'It was only my hypnosis – a very dangerous task, given your state of mind at the time, if I may say so – that helped you overcome the influence of Shanstra. Don't forget that.'

'I haven't forgotten, Doctor,' said Suzi sullenly, unable to meet his gaze. 'All right, so you've got her where you want her, on this ship. What's going to happen? Can you guarantee it'll be safe?'

'The Sensopath is going to tune in with her third self for us,' said the Doctor. 'Discreetly, I hope, so as not to attract attention, and before Shanstra manages to do so. That way, we might have some hope of restabilizing them, bringing them back together into one before Shanstra – the evil, rogue side of the personality – has a chance to have free rein.' The Doctor shook his head and gazed into the distance. 'If we fail, the consequences could be incalculable,' he muttered.

The time rotor stopped and the lighting in the TARDIS console room became momentarily brighter.

'Ah,' said the Doctor, and beamed at them all. 'We have arrived.'

'Where, exactly?' Cheynor wanted to know.

'At the edge of civilization, Captain. Millennia after the death of your solar system.'

Cheynor exchanged a look with Suzi. 'Well,' he said, 'I'm going to believe this when I see it.'

Kelzen had felt the music of the TARDIS. Its crescendo and diminuendo as it rode the waves of the Vortex; its soaring symphonies of effortlessly changing keys forming their pictures in the caverns of her mind. Images came and went, like desert sandstorms, like snow hissing under the light of a brace of suns, like those same suns sinking, falling behind hills of blue that billowed and erupted into the atmosphere.

She had never before communed with an entity like the

TARDIS. Time boiled up over it in great clouds of vortex-surf, and she felt it shudder. Portals whizzed by, exits and entrances, as she sensed its control, its discipline. And deep within the entity, she sensed a hint of its owner, a link with the irascible, unpredictable being called the Doctor.

Kelzen concentrated. There was so much within her now. The TARDIS, like a sea of rippling blue grass. The Doctor, like a grim statue on the cliff-top where the grass ended. And the boy Sanjay, running, confused, through the crumbling ruins of a building, first one way, then the other, shadows rising up to block his path.

I am sorry, Kelzen tried to say to him. *I meant you no harm, but I had to place myself somewhere.* She felt his mind. The anguish of being human, but somehow tougher and more shockproof than others. A child conceived in anger and bitterness, in loveless brutality. Loss, longing, love.

Loss, longing, love...

It came back to her, like an echo from the highest caverns. Reflected, enhanced –

From the TARDIS.

The TARDIS, through Kelzen, recognized Sanjay's feelings, could speak of them, know them.

Kelzen backed out, rode the surface instead of the depths of the time machine's consciousness. She did not know why, but she felt she had disturbed something of the relationship between the Doctor and his machine, something that she should have left untouched.

The journey was ended. The solid, physical world came back to Kelzen in the form of the huge, pinkish-grey O-shaped walls of the Zero Room.

She reached to Sanjay. He was still there, sharing her body and mind, and she reassured him. No more outbursts. No more uncontrollable anger and frustration, causing chaos in reality.

For the moment, there was no signal from Shanstra.

She breathed a huge, long sigh.

21

Misguided Tour

Shanstra settled herself into what had been the vice-governor's padded chair. She swivelled in it experimentally, nodded, smiled. It was suitable for her.

The oak-panelled office was covered with portraits of past presidents of Earth. Shanstra found this conceited, so she directed a hard gaze at the painting directly above the gilded double doors until it crumbled into dust. She then went round each of them, replacing one with a colony of moths, the next with a sheet of melting ice, and so on until they were all gone.

Shanstra sighed with contentment and leaned back, placing her hands to her temples. She summoned the mental waves of her loyal Phractons, positioned on guard at strategic points around the house.

This moment was important.

She had sensed something in the Time Lord's mind, and guessed that he now expected her to make another assault on Kelzen. For which he would no doubt be prepared. So it was time to do the unexpected, instead.

Shanstra began to harness her power.

The Pridka drone, clicking and twitching its metal limbs, surveyed the new arrival on Grove Walkway. The object, a blue box slightly larger than a humanoid, was an unregistered vehicle, and had to be dealt with.

An extendable feeler emerged from the drone and stuck

a small, round pad on the door of the box. A light began to flash bright orange on the pad.

Satisfied that its work had been done, the supervision drone bobbed on and upwards through the foliage of the grove. It had other important matters to attend to.

The Doctor was the first to come out of the TARDIS. His gaze took in the enormous, vaulted roof, the gushing foliage festooning the bright helices that spiralled up towards the top of the dome. Walkways spread out in all directions from the TARDIS, like the spokes of an enormous, white wheel.

Along the walkways, the blue-skinned, orange-robed Pridka moved about their tasks, seemingly oblivious to the unofficial arrival. Two of them strolled past, deep in conversation, consulting the black square of a portable information projector. The Doctor smiled and raised his hat, but the Pridka, a single-minded race, passed by without seeming to register his presence. The Doctor shrugged.

Cheynor, on emerging from the TARDIS a few seconds later, found the Doctor with his head tilted back, admiring the architecture.

'Typical of the Pridka's refinement and aesthetic judgement,' the Doctor said to Cheynor. 'I'd never seen their engineering in real life before, but I knew they valued the contours of light and space.' He smiled briefly at the Earth captain. 'Oh, and don't worry if they seem rude. They do have about thirty-six senses, and they often don't acknowledge you in ways you can see or hear.'

Cheynor was gazing up in wonderment. The beauty of the place lay, as the Doctor had said, in the way the walkways, conveyor helices and vaults seemed to have been sculpted out of shades of pure light and darkness. The ornamental plants, pastel green and rose-pink, looked like Impressionist paintings come to life, and there was something crisp but soothing in the air, invigorating like coastal breezes, yet with all the comfort and hygiene of advanced civilization. The overall effect was one of paradoxical beauty: stylized but organic, pure but stimulating.

'Doctor, I'm amazed. And I'm not even going to ask how that – that contraption of yours brought us here.'

'You'd never understand, anyway, Brigadier,' the Doctor muttered absently, as he looked around, seemingly trying to decide on the best direction. Cheynor frowned, but the Doctor, before he could be corrected, went on. 'You see, the Pridka like to keep the physical world restrained, and they like it to approximate as closely as it can to the beauty of the mind. They're a race of the most peaceful telepaths, and their physical existence is really of secondary importance to them.'

Cheynor nodded grimly. 'So we have to find Jirenal as quickly as possible. If he's here – '

'Then his influence could spread with remarkable rapidity, leaving the floodgates open for Shanstra. Correct. But we have Kelzen. Don't forget that.' The Doctor spun round suddenly and looked up at Cheynor, his expression stern and serious. 'I want you and your new friend the Commandant to stay in the TARDIS. It'll see to your needs. Suzi Palsson and I have other things to attend to.'

Cheynor looked slightly taken aback. 'Ah, I see. The Commandant and I are the backup?'

The Doctor sighed and waved his hands in agitation. 'This is not a military operation, Trau Cheynor, please have that clear in your mind! If I get anything right at all, it'll cause barely a ripple. The last thing I want is for anyone to come in with guns blazing.' He tutted to himself, leaned on his umbrella and looked shiftily away for a moment, down at the receding, concentric levels of the dream centre and the dots of its scuttling occupants far below. Then he looked back up at Cheynor. 'But be ready for my call,' he said, scowling as if he did not want to countenance the thought. 'Just in case.'

'Call?' Cheynor frowned.

'Through Kelzen. Don't worry, you'll hear. Are you familiar with the Venusian lullaby "Klokleda partha menin klatch"?'

Cheynor looked blank.

205

'No, I thought not. All right, I'll try and find something a little more modern.'

Behind them, Suzi emerged, and caught her breath.

The Doctor was impatient. 'Come on, then, Suzi,' he said, looking towards the nearest helix. 'Can't hang around, I've got a job for you.'

As they were about to leave, the Doctor noticed the circular pad with its orange flashing light which was affixed to the TARDIS door. He detached it, looked at it disparagingly.

'What is it?' Suzi asked.

'Parking ticket,' the Doctor muttered, turning it over in his hand. His eyebrows shot up. 'I can't afford that much!' he exclaimed, and slipped the object into a pocket. 'Time for that later, I think. Come on.'

The Director of the Pridka Dream Centre was worried. He had been unable to contact many of his key personnel for several hours, and important monitoring of some dream-active races had been left incomplete.

He would think about the problem over his rest-break. Maybe there was a simple explanation.

In his office, the drone bobbed in with a sparkling drink on a tray. The Director's crest of fins shook in anticipation. He noticed that the drone had mellowed the room specially for him, calling up restful plants, fountains, and a well-known symphony on the audio emitters. This was the kind of thing he appreciated during his relaxation period.

Attention lights on his desk, however, were not at all what he appreciated. And there was one, very bright and very irksome.

'What's that?' he asked the drone crossly, leaning forward and peering at it with big, round eyes. 'Get me someone in that hall, now.'

A call-image of an orange-robed minion appeared, a young Pridka with a mere triangle of tiny fins on his forehead. 'Yes, Director?' he said in a rather awed voice.

'What's going on? What's happened to the Yzashoks?'

The young Pridka smiled. 'Ah, I see, you are concerned, Director. Well, you need not worry. Everything is under control.'

'What?' The Director slammed his glass down on to his desk with force enough to break it. 'Are you mad? Investigate the problem!'

There was a shifting of pixels in the image, indicating that the focus was changing. The Director blinked as a familiar figure stepped into his line of vision, smiling benignly. Black-suited. Black-gloved. Long, rich black hair cascading over his shoulders, framing an elongated face that was somehow handsome and grotesque at the same time. The Director, appalled, recognized his earlier visitor.

'Jirenal,' he spluttered, 'what is the meaning of this?'

The alien appeared amused. 'Meaning, Director? Do your brief and puny lives have meaning, now?'

'What is going on?'

'Show him,' commanded Jirenal, to someone out of the line of vision.

The viewer panned up and down the tank that had contained living, breathing, dreaming Yzashoks, communicating unknown, sublime reflections on art and literature through their amniotic fluid. The fluid that now formed a giant iceberg, trapping the creatures. Trapping their mind-bodies and their elevated thoughts.

The Director blinked. He was beginning to get a nasty feeling in at least three of his stomachs.

Jirenal, black-gloved hands folded neatly in front of him, was once more back in the sights of the viewer. Behind him, the Director could see lines of impassive Pridka, young and old, their gazes strangely blank, as if they were awaiting a command.

'I'm glad you got in touch with me, Director,' Jirenal said. 'You see, I would like to be able to have complete control of this centre, rather than just the little army of minds I command at the moment. I want the Dreamguide.'

On the giant screen in front of him, Jirenal could see the enormous, angry face of the Director peering out. He smiled briefly at Amarill and the other Pridka next to him. They all smiled back. In perfect harmony.

'Impossible!' The Director was standing up, glowering at the screen. 'The Dreamguide is the eldest and most highly developed dream therapist of our entire race. No one can share its powers – '

'I can!' Jirenal interrupted. 'You will do as I say.' He turned to the Pridka who had first answered the transmission. 'You will demonstrate to your Director,' he instructed, 'one of the many imaginative methods by which the Pridka will die, if my demands are not met.'

The controlled Pridka minion nodded obediently to Jirenal.

The Sensopath lifted his hands to his temples and dragged the thought, screaming, from the Pridka's mind, up into the physical world.

The minion stood perfectly still for several seconds. Then the small, developing crest on his forehead peeled elegantly back and curled over on itself, emitting wisps of blue smoke. From the top of his head, other folds of skin began to unpeel and crinkle, then, in the space of just two seconds, the top of the Pridka's head blossomed into a flower of skin and bone, opening the brain to the air.

The Sensopath's eyes glowed. The Pridka's fellows turned their heads as one, and saw a beautiful, white dove flutter from the young minion's skull and soar high up into the vaults of the chamber, out of reach. The Pridka's head, totally emptied of all organic material, was now a dried, cracked-open pod of blue flesh. The body, drained of any controlling influence and now just so much meat and water, fell to its knees, then keeled over on to the floor.

The glow in Jirenal's eyes faded.

The Director's face was frozen with horror on the viewer.

Jirenal spread his hands. 'Apologies, Director. I like to encourage young people to keep an open mind.' He placed his hands on his hips and glowered up at the Director's image. 'Now – shall we talk business?'

* * *

The Doctor had accepted one of the black info-projectors from a passing drone, and activated it as he and Suzi ascended the helix on their pad. Visitors passed them, and Suzi looked curiously at the mix of races. There were humanoids, reptilians in purple cloaks, and many in pressure suits of varying shapes and sizes. Indeed, a whole group floated past them wearing wedge-shaped helmets the size of boulders, with spindly bodies quivering underneath.

'The Borsii,' said the Doctor casually. 'Conquered a whole galaxy a few millennia ago. Got rather big-headed about it.'

The projector was obviously intended to be interactive with their conveyance, as a smiling, blue-skinned face, the size of a shuttlecraft, appeared in the rushing light above them, like a face reflected in a pool. It travelled with them, speaking calmly and reassuringly. 'Welcome to the Pridka Dream Centre, in geostationary orbit around the second world of the Taprid System. A full programme of facilities and special events is available.'

'An appointment with the Dreamguide,' said the Doctor. 'For my young friend here.'

Suzi looked up sharply. 'Are you not coming with me?'

'I have to find someone, remember. The Dreamguide is one of the most experienced dream-healers in the cosmos – according to the TARDIS databanks, anyway – and it can finish what I started with you.' The Doctor's face creased with one of his rare and radiant smiles. 'Your recovery.'

'And can it see me straight away?'

'I should imagine so,' the Doctor said. 'There's room for more than one guest in the consulting rooms of the mind.'

'I don't like it,' said Darius Cheynor. 'Sharing the Doctor's ship with that thing.'

He gestured towards the scanner, which showed a constant image of the blue-cloaked Kelzen, bobbing on air in the Zero Room. Her legs were crossed, her eyes were closed and her long, bony face was tranquil. The Doctor's thought-wave damper, combined with the effects of the Zero Room, seemed to be doing the trick.

The Phracton Commandant hissed quietly to himself in the corner of the console room. 'The creature – is not – in a threat-ening posi-tion,' was his verdict.

Cheynor was not happy. 'The Doctor's had contact with the other, with Shanstra. I mean, she – it – is an empathic being, after all.' He sighed, slumped into the basket-chair. 'The Doctor's taking a bit of a risk, isn't he? If the creature probes deep enough, it might sense his deception.'

'A – fallacy,' stated the Phracton.

Cheynor raised his eyebrows. 'What's that you say?'

'The Doc-tor – is more cun-ning – than you allow.' There was a throaty gurgle from the speaker-grille, and the translucent globe hovered up over the console, bobbing above the time rotor. 'Decep-tion – Trau Cheynor – is not – some-thing felt. It is some-thing done. It is pos-sible – for all kinds – of emo-tions to be – exper-ienced – during decep-tion.'

Cheynor had to admit to himself that he hadn't thought of it quite like that before. This uneasy alliance with the Phractons was giving him new perspectives on life rather earlier than he had expected.

'Well, I only hope you're right, old chap,' he said. A thought occurred to him. 'What can you sense, now? In the rest of the Swarm?'

The Phracton gave a deep, shuddering breath like the release of steam. 'My link – is not as strong – as it was. There are – breaches. There – is – faint-ness from some quar-ters. I feel – '

There was an unbearable pause. It seemed to Cheynor that even the TARDIS held its breath, the constant hum becoming no more than the hint of sound.

' – disss-sent,' the Phracton exhaled. It seemed to shud-der, the lump of dark-blue flesh inside the globe wobbling like jelly.

Cheynor frowned. 'What sort of dissent?'

'The Swarm is – no longer – a uni-ty. There – have

always been – ele-ments – within us – speaking – of rebel-lion. The mes-sages – grow stronger – a-cross the web – as I speak – to you.'

Cheynor folded his arms, leaned back in his chair. 'You have an intricate society. The fact that you don't all agree is a healthy sign, surely?'

There was a long silence.

'Perhaps,' said the Phracton Commandant, and turned away from Cheynor to watch the scanner.

Jirenal stepped through the interface between the Director's office and the foyer, and light meshing closed again behind him. He seemed to cast shadows in many directions, to the corners of the pastel-hued office. And on to the terrified face of the Director himself.

'How pleasant to see you again, Director,' said the alien. 'We are going to see the Dreamguide, you and I.'

'Why, exactly, may I ask?'

'I wish to introduce the Dreamguide to some new and interesting concepts,' said Jirenal with a smile, and spread his hands.

The Director stood up, trembling, his face a vivid shade of royal blue. Pridka body temperature tended to lower when they became angry or upset, and indeed the first signs of a sheen of frost had begun to form on the Director's cheeks.

'You cannot do this,' he said. 'For macrocycles we have been here, renowned throughout the cosmos, the dream centre attracting visitors from all solar systems – '

'Macrocycles! You speak as if such things mattered,' said Jirenal dismissively, and snapped his fingers.

The Director felt himself forced back into his chair, pinned there by invisible bonds.

'Now, please, Director. Do as I say. Otherwise I will have to resort to violence again, which is so . . . shabby, don't you think?'

Part Four

DARK TRINITY ASCENDANT

Whatever is fitted in any sort to excite the ideas of
pain, that is to say, whatever is in any sort terrible . . .
is a source of the sublime.

Burke, *Philosophical Enquiry*

Remember me when I am gone away,
Gone far away into the silent land.

Christina Rossetti, *Remember*

22

Dreaming of Me

The gate to the Dreamguide was easily found. It seemed to be at the hub and heart of the Dream Centre, in one of the echoing, light-filled halls that were its trademark. Suzi saw a great isosceles triangle, framed with a metal so white that, from a distance, she thought it to be pure light. Around the chamber, high above them, gravpads waited, inert, defying gravity. A senior-looking Pridka, clad in red robes with gold trim, stood at a globe-shaped console, dwarfed by the huge gateway. Presumably he/she (Suzi did not know quite how to cope with the Pridka concept of gender) was communing with the Dreamguide through some sort of interface.

Suzi had decided that she trusted the Doctor instinctively. She admired his easy charm as he strolled up to the Pridka monitor, introduced them with the utmost politeness. He then exchanged a meaningful look with the Pridka, after which they bowed slowly to one another. Suzi was annoyed – something had passed between the Doctor and the alien of which she was not aware. But hadn't she just decided that she trusted him?

The Doctor touched her arm, gently. 'I have a mission to complete, and you have to restore your self-esteem,' he was saying. 'You see, part of the effect of the transition from mind to matter, which the Sensopaths have been perfecting, is the effacing of the limit between subject and

215

object. Hopefully, the Dreamguide will give you back your sense of self.'

'Is it dangerous?' Suzi asked, shivering as she looked up in awe at the huge, triangular gateway.

'It's therapeutic. The Pridka have been doing this sort of thing for centuries, in your terms.' The Doctor smiled. 'My own assignment, on the other hand, is probably very dangerous indeed. Which is why I want you all out of the way while I decide what to do with the Sensopaths.'

'Supposing Kelzen won't cooperate with you?' Suzi demanded. 'And what if Leibniz and Bernice don't succeed in keeping Shanstra occupied?'

The Doctor shrugged. 'I shouldn't worry about it. If that happens, none of us will have the freedom of thought even to feel resentment, let alone object.'

Suzi, puzzled, opened her mouth for another question, but the Pridka was making agitated movements.

'Please,' it said, with its big, glistening eyes open wide and staring at Suzi. 'The Dreamguide is ready for you. Please enter the interface.'

Suzi gathered her cloak around her, and started to ascend the ramp. She looked back at the Doctor, who waved and smiled, then she walked forward into the blackness.

Welcome to the Dream Experience. Do not be alarmed by anything you appear to see or feel. The purpose of the Experience is one of transformation: of the negative into the positive, of the unsettling into the everyday.

The voice caressed the innermost mind, like a hand smoothing silken sheets. Suzi felt her healing consolidate itself, and finally let her body relax, immerse itself in the energy fields. In her mind, the dust and fire and chaos of Gadrell Major were but a bad memory.

She let herself dream.

As soon as Suzi had entered the gateway, the Doctor's face had fallen, and the reassuring smile had slipped,

216

freeing the wrinkles of cosmic angst on his ageless face once more.

His expression grim, the Doctor turned on his heel, nodding briefly to the Pridka. 'If I don't come back, get her out,' he said, and strode from the chamber, stiffly, as if containing some dark emotion that dared not be released.

She was in a bare room, covered with dust, shimmering with water light as if at the bottom of a swimming-pool. She looked around, uncertain as to where she should be.

Then, oblong segments of the floor began to slide upwards, revealing themselves as bookcases stacked with ancient tomes, bound in leather of maroon and red and ivy green. All books, Suzi knew, which she had not read. New knowledge.

The library desk was a gigantic, hexagonal console, surmounted by a cylinder that moved up and down like a breathing creature. It rotated gently in the rippling light.

The bookcases grew, looming over her. High up above her, bats screeched and fluttered between the summits of the towering bookshelves. But it was strangely calming for Suzi to be there, in her second home. She looked up, smiling. The library ceiling could just about be seen; it was a disc, no, a dome, rippling like water.

Books detached themselves from the shelves and floated down in front of her, with smiling, cherubic faces. 'Take me,' they said. 'Love me.'

Suzi flung her arms out wide, caught the books, and embraced the dazzling sunshine pouring through the dome of water above her.

The Doctor had been carried upwards through spiralling columns of light, and now he strolled through the foyer of the administrative globe. Everything was a curve, a globe, or a circle, and every surface was suffused with gentle light.

He entered a large, circular space and was immediately greeted by two attendant Pridka with highly developed crests of fins, one in a green robe, the other in orange. They seemed to appear there in the centre of the floor, like images activated by the Doctor's presence.

'May we help you?' said the green-robed Pridka.

'I was wondering if I could see the Director of the centre?' said the Doctor hopefully. 'Tell him the Doctor – a Time Lord – would like to speak to him.'

The Pridka looked at one another, and something unheard by the Doctor passed between them. 'Is it a matter of some urgency?' asked the Pridka in green, with an attempt at a smile. 'The Director has a full schedule of appointments for this cycle.'

The Doctor shrugged, looked slightly bashful. 'Well, I don't like to shout about these things, but actually it's to do with the fundamental stability of the cosmos. Could you manage to squeeze me in today?'

'It really isn't on,' said Cheynor moodily. 'Not on at all.' He unholstered his sidearm and checked the charges for the third time in five minutes.

The Phracton Commandant buzzed quietly to himself, his floating globe casting an egg-shaped shadow across the roundels. 'The Sens-o-path – is commun-icating,' he announced.

Cheynor hurriedly snapped his gun closed again and leapt to his feet. 'What?'

'My sens-ory input – is vastly – more refined – than that of a Ter-ran. I can hear – a com-munication.'

Cheynor glanced up at the screen to check on Kelzen, and was startled to see that the image had broken up. Instead, the monitor was displaying coloured flashes, like the lights of an exotic ballroom, twisting and dancing. Were they forming pictures? Resonances, in the back of Darius Cheynor's head?

With sudden, startling clarity he saw *the face of his dead brother, Simeon, the boy destined for success, for academia, for the mud of a battlefield – and they hauled him out, the man with no face –*

The Phracton was crackling. Smoke was pouring from

the casing, while blue sparks danced like demons in the dimness, strobing on Cheynor and the alien. Horrified, Cheynor covered his eyes.

A sound – the rending of metal and the bawling of a baby, fused cybernetically into a grisly whole – burst outwards from the Phracton's grille, enveloping the console room.

The noise was unbearable. Cheynor dropped to his knees, his hands clamped over his ears. There was a tingling in his mind. It was urgent, like a hand in the wilderness of noise tapping on his shoulder to show him a way out. But he dared not look. What if it was the dead hand of his brother?

Darius Cheynor. Sound became solid, tore like curtains to reveal more sound, an angrier mob of noise, behind it.

He was aware – in a dimmer, thinner physical world like a mere ghost of itself – that the Phracton Commandant's casing shattered, that the limp form within it slopped to the TARDIS floor like a dead baby, twitching and writhing –

Darius Cheynor! I cannot hold her any more. Shanstra is breaking through to Jirenal!

His eyes were clamped so tightly shut that they throbbed with pain. The thought crackled like burning plastic in his mind –

What do you want me to do?

Stop the Dreamguide.

It was the voice of Kelzen.

Stop the Dream. Stop Suzi Palsson or she will die!

The noise in Cheynor's head seemed to become a mere din, rather than the brain-throttling cacophony it had been. He unclamped his hands from his ears, staggered to his feet, blinking.

And stepped in the Phracton.

Horrified, he lifted his boot from the mess on the TARDIS floor. It came away unwillingly, like cheese from a pizza, and there was a pungent smell, ammonia maybe. Something fizzed in Cheynor's mouth and nostrils, as he drew breath to gasp in horror. The pool of sticky flesh oozed from the ball of wrecked circuitry, as if something had slipped in through the crack in the casing and pummelled the creature to death with pure sound.

He backed away, bile rising in his stomach.

The irrational, wild thought bounced around in his head that they were going to think he did it, that the enmity had flared up again and he had killed his new ally in a burst of xenophobia.

Find her, Darius Cheynor. Stop the Dream.

With Kelzen's words like an alarm bell in his head, he operated the door control and dashed from the TARDIS.

The books fluttered around Suzi Palsson, cooing gently. She saw the Dreamguide, its giant Pridka face floating like a sunset above a meadow of blue flowers. The Pridka were noble and beautiful, Suzi decided, with their skins of damselfly blue, their soft, expressive features, and that elegant crest of receptor fins on the forehead. Noble and beautiful. Suzi giggled. She must be getting sentimental. The Dream Experience seemed to be having the same effect on her as alcohol.

She remembered a party: on one of the Earth stations, with mostly Colm's friends, no one she knew, really. At the start she had been restrained, demure even, and after several hours of nervously knocking back the home-made punch, she had been embracing these strangers and telling them how lovely they were.

You have suffered, child, said the Dreamguide gently. *Arrangements have been made for you.*

'Arrangements?' Suzi, perplexed, heard her own query as if it were spoken by someone else.

Your credit has been validated by an independent agent. You are now ready to receive the Dreamguide's ministrations.

The Doctor, thought Suzi with a smile. He must have really wanted me to go through with this. 'So, what do I do?' she asked, leaning her back against the cool trunk of a tree, and letting golden-green light caress her body.

You merely have to remember. It will not seem painful.

220

The past will truly become the past, the present the future. Your life, after you have spoken to the Dreamguide, will have meaning once more. Meaning that you, yourself, have given it, not us. That is the Pridka way.

'Sounds cool,' said Suzi. 'Could I have a vodka and lime while you're at it, please?'

She thought she was joking, but a cocktail shaker appeared, on a small picnic table at her side. Reality shifted once again, and to her astonishment, there was a young man in a waiter's tuxedo, smiling as he shook her drink for her. He had a friendly, lopsided grin that creased his face, and a black fringe falling over his eyes.

We hope you find this image pleasing. The memory is summoned from a favourite Terran entertainment archive of yours.

'You extracted that rather niftily,' Suzi said with a smile. 'Plenty of ice, please.'

He is named Hugh.

Suzi couldn't help laughing. 'Yes, I know.' She took her glass. 'Thanks.'

The young man's hand, as he gave her the drink, brushed Suzi's.

It was a pale, mottled hand, the flesh flaking from it like steamed fish.

Startled, she looked up into his face. It was no longer the face of her favourite vid-actor. She saw –

Empty, white eyes –

A putrefying skull, rippling as if immersed in unquiet water –

Suzi leapt to her feet and tried to scream.

On the horizon, the face of the Dreamguide shimmered and blurred, splintering into a thousand howling Pridka faces. Ten thousand.

'Hello, Suzi,' said the dead Colm Oswyn, reaching out a rotting hand to her. 'I thought we would meet again soon.'

When the Doctor entered the sculpture of pastel light which represented the office of the Pridka Dream Centre

Director, the V-shaped chair was turned away from him. 'May I see you for a moment?'

'Of course, Doctor.'

The Doctor's surprise did not really have time to register. The chair swivelled, and the imposing figure of the Director of the centre sat there. The Doctor took in the salient details of the face: the proud crest of fins, the sheen of his blue skin. His eyes were open wide, his hands were folded neatly in his lap and he was smiling in a benign, welcoming manner.

He did not move at all, due to the fact that his head had been neatly severed from his body and was fixed to the back of the chair, about twenty centimetres above the neck, by a thick bolt of steel.

The Doctor was repelled, but he leaned across the desk and examined the incision. It was a clean cut, which seemed to have severed all of the nerves and muscles at once.

The door sealed itself behind the Doctor. Out of the shadows, a dark, languid figure unfurled itself. Without turning round, the Doctor straightened up, alert, listening, like a hunting cat. Only when he was fully ready did he turn around and face the other occupant of the room.

He knew who it was – what it was – immediately. The mane of black hair, the oval face with its staring, round eyes and impressive dual sweep of cheekbone.

Jirenal folded his arms, tilted his head to one side and unleashed his hideous clown's smile. 'Welcome, Doctor,' he said. 'You requested an audience with me. What can I do for you?'

222

23

You Win Some

Livewire stood at the curved window. In her white clothes, with her bow slung at her waist, she was like a statue of some ancient hunting goddess. They'd let her have the bow back because she had screamed until she got it. Unloaded, of course. That was the compromise.

A shadow fell across her, but she did not look around. She knew her brother's footfall. 'I can feel it growing,' she said. 'The pool of hatred.'

'Look,' Trinket said anxiously, 'do you think you've rested properly?'

Livewire turned to face him now. She could tell by the fear in his expression that he had noticed her bright, feverish eyes. Well, that was good. They were still afraid of her. 'I don't want rest,' she said. 'I won't rest until Banksburgh is our home again.'

Trinket ran a hand through his hair. 'Look, I've been asking a few questions. The relief ship's due shortly to take people off the orbital. I don't think anyone's going to be living here any more.'

'I will,' she said. 'I want to.' He looked perplexed, but then, she thought, he never had understood her. 'When the Phracs came,' she murmured, stroking her forefinger down his smooth face, 'we wanted to get them. To hit back. And now it turns out the war was all a con anyway, and this, this creature turns up. Takes over my mind, kills

Poly. Well, I tell you this. I'm not sharing Banksburgh with any alien. Not any sort.'

'What are you going to do?' Trinket asked. It was a reasonable question, but there was that very slight wavering, the undercurrent of fear. 'They won't let you go with them. Bernice and Cheynor said – '

She moved closer to him, her eyes glinting. 'I don't care what they said.' She held something up. It was the size of a credit card, and inlaid with circuitry. She was pleased by the way Trinket frowned.

'What is it?' he asked.

'Security key to a skimmer.'

Trinket paled. 'You're not – fragging hell, Livewire, how did you get that?'

A momentary expression of disgust crossed her features. 'This TechnOp took a fancy to me. Tzidirov, he was called. It only took me half an hour, and a bit of pride.' She patted his cheek. 'Don't try and stop me.'

'You're not armed. Your crossbow – '

'I'm going to improvise,' she said sharply.

She was by the door.

'You can't – ' he began.

'I mean it, little brother. Follow me and the first arrow is yours.'

Her parting smile left him looking chilled, alone, lost.

Bernice Summerfield stood in the observation gallery of the *Phoenix* and stared out over the higgledy-piggledy ruins of Banksburgh.

She reached into her pocket, then frowned, shook her head. Too easy. But a moment later she put her hand back in her pocket and took out the small holo-pyramid. Bernice stroked it, placed it on the walkway at her feet, and the image of the Doctor blossomed upward.

He was looking askance at her and leaning on his umbrella. 'You can't expect this program to solve all your problems, you know,' said the familiar voice. 'After all, if it could, there'd be two of me running around the Universe without even violating the laws of time.' The h-Doctor appeared thoughtful for a moment.

Benny smiled wearily. She was just starting to realize how recent events had taken their toll on her. 'There were times when it would have been very useful for you to be in two places at once. Like when I was left in India. And on the Vampires' planet.'

'Wait for the signal, Bernice.' The h-Doctor tapped the side of his nose. 'Would you like me to entertain you?' he asked hopefully. 'Now that I've tuned myself into the TARDIS circuits, I can offer you a reasonable range of – '

'No. No, thank you,' she said hurriedly, holding up a hand. She remembered the time that an all too convincing virtuality of Heaven, her home-world, had been set up inside the TARDIS.

'So,' said the h-Doctor. 'Tell me what's on your mind and I'll – ' Suddenly, without warning, he began to flicker in and out of phase. He shimmered into ghostly transparency through which Bernice could see the observation dome, then back into a kind of solidity, and back again.

'Doctor?' she said urgently. 'Doctor!' She sighed in exasperation, hands on hips. 'This is futile, Summerfield. And you're talking to yourself again, you realize that? Yes, I know – '

'Not quite,' said Horst Leibniz, as he strode along the walkway to meet her. He circled the flickering hologram, looking it up and down in a manner that suggested he had not had breakfast properly.

Bernice had been startled, but managed to compose herself with remarkable swiftness. 'The Doctor's gone all two-dimensional on me,' she said in exasperation.

Leibniz, thoughtfully, passed a hand through the hologram. 'Or suddenly acquired greater depth,' he murmured to himself. 'The signal, remember?'

'That's not a signal. The Doctor said we'd be sure, and I know the Doctor better than that.'

The hologram snapped off and the pyramid clunked to the floor. Leibniz lunged for it, but Bernice was there first, and hung on determinedly to the little object.

'Oh, no, you don't, Mr Know-all. I'm not entirely sure if I trust you.'

Leibniz smiled placatingly, and spread his hands. 'Well, I may not be exactly what I seem,' he said, 'but then that's true of a lot of people, *Professor* Summerfield.'

Bernice went cold. 'What do you mean?'

'I had a poke around in your mind. While you weren't looking. It's rude, I know, but no more so than other kinds of search that private agents are forced to make.'

It dawned on Bernice that her gut feeling about Leibniz had not been wrong. 'Agents,' she said with a rueful smile. 'Who employs you, Trau Leibniz?'

'Earth Security Council. The Doctor knows.'

'The Doctor . . . ?' Bernice opened her mouth, closed it again, thought: stop it, you look like a goldfish. 'Well, doubtless he'll fill me in,' she said through gritted teeth. 'So, does Cheynor know about this?'

'Cheynor's a fool. His command of this ship is non-existent, his mission a front for neatly killing two birds with one stone.' Leibniz leaned against the rail, raised his eyebrows impudently at her. 'Now don't tell me you didn't know that, either.'

'Actually, I did.' Bernice folded her arms and glowered at him. 'You're very cold about everything, aren't you?'

Horst Leibniz did not blink, but his eyes, momentarily, seemed to lose their penetrating stare. 'Most people find me that way. When my wife was murdered, all my feeling for the human race seemed to die with her. Compassion ceased to have any meaning for me.'

His calm collected tone made Bernice even more uncomfortable than reproof would have done. She flushed with embarrassment.

'All I could do,' Leibniz murmured, 'was share in her pain. That was about six years ago, and that was when I first began to suspect I might be empathic.'

'I'm sorry,' she said. 'You must think I like the taste of my own toes or something.'

'Not to worry,' said Leibniz, but he had turned away from her, and she could not see his expression.

226

His communicator buzzed. It was one of the TechnOps on the bridge. 'Scans here, sir. We've got her.'

'Mobilize all units,' said Leibniz crisply, 'according to the captain's instructions.' He exchanged a glance with Bernice. 'And I want the Phracs to know what they're doing, too.'

'Shouldn't we wait for the signal?' Benny demanded.

'Don't worry. We will.'

He ushered her into the elevator, but the doors were already opening, and Trinket stood there, his face flushed, looking agitatedly from one to the other. 'It's Livewire,' he said. 'She's going to get us all killed. You've got to stop her!'

Light flowed from Shanstra like glacial water. She gripped the arms of the chair, felt her hair blowing in the hurricane of her own mental power.

'The puny ones are gathering,' she said, in surprise. 'Strengthen your defences, my warriors. I must concentrate on my link to Jirenal.'

She saw her brother, herself, now, and his eyes stared at hers as if out of a mirror of time. Across the wastes of eternity.

With his mind, there oscillated those of thousands of others: a word formed in Shanstra's conscious mind, forcing itself in like a boot kicking a door open, like a baby screaming for its breath as it entered the world.

Pridka. The minds were Pridka.

Shanstra, delighted, felt their strength. It was beautiful, honey-sweet, a wash of emotion and love and faith, with the kick of a drug, the pungency and intensity of sex. The Infinite Requiem was beginning.

Strengthen your defences, my warriors.

A score of Phracton globes bobbed, like bubbles on the wind, outside the white and gold house. Some stationed themselves on the lawn, overlooking the silent city. Once, in another life, some of the minds remembered that they

227

had fought for that city, fought for another cause in the name of something called the Swarm.

That was long ago. There was no Swarm any more. The cause was history; the city was a mere protrusion in three dimensions, a detail of the physical world. They served a greater mistress now.

Excited, hyper-mental chatter passed between the Phracton renegades, their globes pulsing with irregular illumination like mountain lightning. Clicking, twittering sounds echoed out across the green lawns of the house.

Inside, their mistress was preparing, and they had to protect her. To ward off the imminent puny attacks of the humans, and also others of their own kind, those who had joined the humans in their treachery.

This was to be no ordinary battle. This was to be a battle where the weapons were not arrows, or bullets, or plasma bolts. The weapons were the misguided attackers themselves.

The Pridka minion now monitoring the gate to the Dreamguide sensed a commotion at the back of the hall. An angry, uniformed human strode in, accompanied by an ineffectual escort of two drones and an agitated senior Pridka. Voices were being raised as they hurried across the hall, and that sort of thing was never permitted here.

The monitor bobbed nervously as the deputation strode up to him.

'Who's in there?' the angry human demanded. 'Tell me who's in there!' The young monitor looked nervously to his senior for advice.

Tell Trau Cheynor what he wishes to know, came the wary instruction. *He appears unnecessarily agitated.*

The young Pridka cleared his throat and tried to speak. As he had done little but train his mental faculties in communion with the senior Pridka for several cycles now, the voice was rusty with disuse. 'The Dreamguide ... is at present occupied with three visitors, sir.' The young Pridka consulted his info-projector, and data glowed in the air above the black square. 'A Miss Suzanne Palsson from the Terran Empire, and the Director's assistant, Amarill dell'katit vo'Pridka. She is leading a proxy session with the third visitor.'

'A proxy session?' The human, Cheynor, seemed confused, and the elder Pridka stepped in to explain.

'Our best-trained healers can arrange for a link to the Dreamguide in special circumstances. It is like an, ah, account, if you like.'

'And so who is it for?'

'For a Mr Jirenal. On whom I have – ' the monitor frowned ' – no data.' Something nagged in the back of his mind. There was a reason for the lack of data on the third visitor. There had to be.

The human was aghast. 'Stop this session! You must stop it, now!'

The Doctor gritted his teeth and tried hard to keep his voice level. 'You barbaric animal,' he muttered eventually.

Jirenal raised an eyebrow. 'The thing about advanced telepathy,' he said, strolling over to the desk and helping himself to a crystallized fruit, 'is that you really need to have the head for it.' He munched, offered the dish to the Doctor, who responded with an icy stare.

'This was not necessary,' the Doctor said. He met Jirenal's dark gaze, held it. 'How can you say this was necessary?'

Jirenal shrugged his enormous shoulders. 'There was no other way I could have become director of this centre,' he explained, as if the Doctor were missing something reasonable and obvious. 'Where I come from, it is considered noble and just to rise in power by eliminating the contenders.'

'What did you hope to gain from this butchery?'

'Minds, Doctor. Minds. Only the Director's mind-imprint could allow me access to the Dreamguide's world. He would not give it willingly, so I took it by force, and disposed of the, er . . .' Jirenal waved a vague hand at the Director's body. '. . . container. Part of my consciousness

229

is now with the Dreamguide, arranging things to my satisfaction.'

The Doctor's face was shadowed, watching, as alert as an owl at night. 'You don't know what you're doing – what Shanstra is doing,' he muttered, his voice low and threatening. It became a growl. 'You must stop this, now.'

'And through the Dreamguide,' continued Jirenal, as if the Doctor had not spoken, 'it is possible to infiltrate all the Pridka's thoughts. The centre becomes me. With all that mental power behind it, all the minds become us.'

'And in comparison to this, control of the Phracton Swarm was a mere rehearsal,' said the Doctor bitterly.

Jirenal gave a dazzling, horrible smile. 'Why, Doctor, I do believe you're using your intelligence. I'm glad you've started. You see, Shanstra's signals are becoming ever stronger in my mind. When she failed to communicate with Kelzen – largely due to your interference in her booster link with the Phractons – she gathered her strength again, to try and break through to me.'

'Harder, I'd imagine. The signal so weak, the distance so great ...' The Doctor nodded slowly. 'But possible. I was unprepared, I should have seen. How do you communicate?'

'Oh, Doctor, we are bonded, we have a unity that transcends time. Our race has access to the vortex, and Time Lords are but a distant legend.'

'I know that. Through Kelzen.'

'Kelzen. Yes. There is that small matter.'

Jirenal strode up to the Doctor and, smiling, gripped his lapels. He hoisted him up so that the diminutive Time Lord, legs flailing, was eye to eye with him. The Sensopath's eyes were like spheres of polished jet, reflecting the depths of another world. 'You could choose to deliver Kelzen to me, or I could extract her whereabouts from your mind. It is a simple choice.'

The Doctor, red-faced and choking, managed to meet Jirenal's gaze with defiance. 'She ... trusts me, Jirenal ... I ... helped to save her. She won't ... come willingly, even if I do tell you – '

Jirenal's fingers radiated like sudden sunbeams. The Doctor crashed to the floor, his shoulder burning with old, revitalized pain.

The Sensopath kicked him, forcing him over on to his back, and then, suddenly, it was as if the pastel light of every surface in the room became an unbearable, cartoon brightness. At the centre of it all was the ghastly face of the Sensopath, pinning him to the floor with a bar of solid thought.

I will break you down, Doctor. I will smash the dungeons of your mind to yield their secrets. Give me Kelzen!

And the thought returned, uncompromising, bright and ancient like a supernova from the dawn of time, shattering the Doctor's fragile thoughts as if they were coconut shells.

Jirenal burned his mind. Blazing with a fire of determination.

The Sensopath crashed in, ram-raiding the Doctor's consciousness.

24

Pretty Occupied

The security network around the *Phoenix* skimmer bays was totally automated. It took Livewire no more than the stolen key to get through to the airlock of bay three, and then she was faced with a simple combination lock.

She dropped to one knee, forced the keypad away from its housing, and took a small, circular object from her pocket. Ancient technology – 22nd century, she was sure. It had been one of the first things she'd liberated when the looting began in earnest. Its display began to interact with the circuitry in the lock, showing each combination on its tiny LCD screen as it was tested.

Livewire held her breath.

The combination began to appear, digit by digit.

'You must get them out,' Cheynor pleaded. 'Something very, very wrong is happening here!'

He did not understand what was going on, but he had been consumed with the urge to do something. Weeks, months of hanging around waiting for the next move of the enemy: it had helped to galvanize Darius Cheynor into action. To be part of something important, something morally right. Kelzen had somehow communicated to him what he had to do, and although Cheynor did not trust Kelzen, he had faith in the Doctor, and he seemed to trust Kelzen. On top of that, there was the urge to respond to the horror of seeing his Phracton friend reduced to a pulp. Cheynor had just enough of his old, almost prim restraint left to realize, deep down, how dangerous that made him now.

The Pridka exchanged the briefest of glances, and then, apparently responding to instructions, the younger one turned back to the globe-console, ready to place his hands on it and to send a request.

As he did so, the gateway blazed.

Cheynor saw a tall, mainly female Pridka step out on to the ramp, her emerald-green robes glittering in the light, and her face commanding and serenely beautiful. 'I am Amarill,' she said haughtily. 'I forbid you to interfere with what is to happen.'

'Who's she?' Cheynor snapped.

The senior Pridka looked shocked. 'That is Amarill dell'katit vo'Pridka, Primary Healer and assistant to the Director.'

'The Director is dead.' The voice that emerged from Amarill's mouth was almost robotic, as if something were using her vocal cords without prior experience of how they worked.

Cheynor felt a chill spreading through him, and in that same instant he saw Amarill lift one blue hand, palm outwards.

There was a scream, which lasted only a few seconds, because after that time, the young Pridka's mouth became a beak. His head warped, pushed out on both sides and twisted upwards, blossoming into giant wings. At the same time his body was shrinking conversely and his limbs were curving, forming giant, serrated talons.

A shape larger than a fighter shuttle began to lift itself up from the floor. Cheynor, aghast, drew his sidearm, but the senior Pridka knocked it away. 'No! Something is interfering with reality. You will not injure a Pridka!'

Deep, rich laughter echoed from Amarill's mouth, and Cheynor, as he desperately ducked for safety under the console, knew that the voice could not be her own. Damn you, Doctor, he thought. Where the hell are you?

A huge shadow, falling, blotted out the light from the gateway.

The office of the director became a palimpsest, a bridge to another layer of existence. A realm where colours screamed, where sounds stabbed at the Doctor's brain cells and shook the pupils of his eyes.

He recognized, vaguely, the reddish-black void in which he had communed with Kelzen. A place between life and death, where the mind never normally went.

I've communed with both of your other selves, Jirenal. You're making a big mistake.

Jirenal laughed. The sound travelled, hurtling towards the Doctor like an oncoming train in a close-fitting tunnel.

'This is not the way, Jirenal!' the Doctor shouted, and it echoed as if in the real world. He summoned his defences to meet Jirenal's assault.

Come, Doctor, do not resist. I merely want to know you. To help you.

'All right, know me, then!' he snarled. He thought of words, commonplaces. Blocking the way to the higher centres of his mind. 'I'm a mysterious traveller in time and space known only as the Doctor – '

Mysterious? You are as transparent as water!

'I travel in the time vortex in the TARDIS, which means Time and Relative Dimension in Space – '

And we have never come across one another before.

'Disguised as a London police box from twentieth-century Earth – ' *Deliberately –*

' – And it's dimensionally transcendental, which means it's bigger on the inside than on the outside, although of course terms such as inside and outside are purely relative when it comes to dimensional engineering. Which is where the confusion arises!'

And with his last word, the Doctor found himself back in the real world, kneeling on the floor of the director's office, with the dead eyes of the Pridka himself staring at him from the chair.

A huge, flickering pillar of darkness, outlined in tendrils

of light, framed Jirenal. The Sensopath's face was huge, swollen with pleasure and concentration.

The reality around the pillar, where the tendrils touched it, began to warp subtly. Two paperweights mated angrily on the desk and burst into smithereens. The director's desk began to sprout broad red leaves and small buds.

The Doctor nodded grimly. He had temporarily managed to block Jirenal out of his mind. 'Too much else to do,' he muttered, breathless but satisfied. 'So many minds in his new collective. Like finding a needle in a box of needles.'

Keeping a wary eye on the Sensopath, he grabbed his umbrella, checked it over for impurities, and with a grim nod he slid through the wall and on to the gravpad.

'To the Dreamguide,' he said. 'Urgently.'

On the way down, with light rushing in torrents on either side of him, he lifted his hands to his temples and felt Kelzen quiver inside his mind, like a player backstage, billowing the curtain.

Send it, said the Doctor.

The Sensopath's answer came back, jolting, like a hit of adrenalin. *Shanstra will intercept.*

I know. Send it anyway!

And something rippled in the strange mental synthesis, linked by the TARDIS's telepathic circuits. Through the uncanny alliance of the Doctor's symbiotic nuclei, the alien in the Zero Room and the small pyramid in the pocket of Professor Bernice Summerfield.

'You abandoned me, Suzi. You left me to die.'

They walked, half floating, beside the lake of the dream. Mist curled like curious wraiths from its surface, coalescing into clouds that surrounded Suzi and the half-dissolved skeletal body of her lover.

She was not frightened of him.

Suzi scowled. 'Abandoned? I could say exactly the same of you. I became a victim thanks to you. A nobody. You prodded and poked me with your rejection for as long as I could stand it. If you hadn't died when you did, I might

235

have ended up killing you.' Her eyes shone with anger. 'I don't regret it. I feel good about it! So you can't use it against me as guilt any more!'

The bloated white face registered surprise. 'But Suzi – I never meant to hurt you.'

'No,' she said disparagingly. 'That's what they all say.' She put her hands on her hips and shouted into the mist. 'This is you, isn't it? Rummaging into my memories and trying to frighten me? Well, it isn't going to work!' She reached out to the nearest tree and snapped off a branch. It was fungus-encrusted, and came away from the tree as if made of toffee. 'He doesn't frighten me any more!' Suzi yelled, and, swinging the branch back as far as she could, she dealt the Colm-zombie a hefty blow right in the middle of its face. Chunks of flesh burst outwards, off-white globules like soft wax. The faceless image disappeared.

Suzi let the branch fall from her hands, heard her own breath in her ears.

'Cancel,' she ordered. 'Get me out of here!'

There were times when Cheynor considered giving it all up and going into something less perilous: intergalactic marketing, maybe, or the leisure business. Times when he had wondered what the point of his life was. Times like now.

The giant eagle – which, a few seconds ago, had been a Pridka – flapped its wings at the top of the gateway and wheeled, beginning to descend.

Cheynor contemplated the tactics of his withdrawal under the console, and wondered whether it might have appeared cowardly. Certainly, there was a marked contrast with the elderly Pridka, who just stood there, fingers pressed together, looking up into the vaults with an expression of slight concern.

'Frightened, Trau Cheynor?' Again, that voice – from Amarill's lips, but hollow.

He aimed his sidearm, tried to get a clear sighting on the eagle. It was circling him, alarmingly low, its wings

236

like giant sails and its beak a great skewer that looked as if it could quite comfortably take his head off.

'The eagle is not the enemy. You misunderstand the enemy, Trau Cheynor.'

'Perhaps,' he shouted back. 'I like to shoot at what I can see.'

'That was always your problem, was it not? You misunderstood the Phractons, and your own Earth Council, who found you disposable.'

'Mind-reading might be a clever party piece,' said a familiar voice from the doorway, 'but when you've seen it once, it does pall a little.'

Cheynor saw the Doctor, who was leaning on his umbrella in the doorway, raise his hat to Amarill.

'Now,' he said, raising his eyebrows, 'why don't we stop this nonsense, right away?'

Leibniz flicked the switches above his head, powering up the skimmer, running all the tests. Bernice, in the copilot's seat, watched his hands playing over the keyboard with intricate skill. He nodded to Bernice, and the two of them pulled protective goggles down over their eyes.

'Leader to Blue Unit,' snapped Leibniz into his comlink. 'Initiate launch.'

The force – the last, desperate hope of soaking up Shanstra's attention, her deadly energy – might be a suicide squad. Of that, Bernice was painfully aware. But after what she had seen happening in Tilusha's flat in 1997, and to the Phractons in Londinium Plaza, she wanted to be part of it. She wanted to be there at the heart of the action, because in her experience it was those who just sat back and did nothing who got hurt.

And she wanted to be there for Livewire. She had promised Trinket as much.

The girl's trace had been picked up, about five minutes after the unauthorized launch of a skimmer from bay three had been reported. She was just two klicks outside Banksburgh, and Leibniz intended to catch her up. But there was one thing he was not going to have, and that was

Trinket cluttering up the team. So he had made Bernice promise to do the boy's job for him, and bring his sister back.

The signal had come an instant later. It had taken the form of the h-Doctor in 25th-century battle dress, brandishing his umbrella and reciting a famous speech from Osterling's *The Good Soldier*.

Bernice had raised an eyebrow, but she had been in no doubt. 'That's it,' she said. 'We'd better go, or he'll do it once more, with feeling.'

The force was to be composed of two prongs. First, a ground unit of six armed skimmers, and several of the silver Phracton tanks that Benny had heard the humans calling flamers. She had not forgotten her nightmare pursuit through the streets of Banksburgh, and still shuddered when she saw the machines. The second prong was the air support from the *Phoenix* fighters – as many as could be mustered after the Battle of Banksburgh – and the Phractons.

'You realize, when we get there,' Bernice said, 'that there'll be no way of telling our Phracs from hers?'

'Yeah,' answered Leibniz. 'I'd thought of that.'

'And do you have a solution?'

'No,' he said, and smiled briefly.

The skimmer powered up, and shot out of its launch tube, on to the reddish-brown surface of the planet. Others followed.

The final battle for Gadrell Major had begun.

25

Connected

'I see you have a greater imagination than this creature,' said the voice from Amarill's mouth.

The eagle stopped circling in the vaults, became, in the blink of an eye, a silk parachute, which floated slowly down towards them.

The Doctor ran over to Cheynor, grabbed him and pulled him out from under the console. 'Come on, man. We've got to confront it! Not run away!' The Doctor swivelled round, beckoned the senior Pridka over. 'Try and get this thing stopped! Please!'

'I . . . will try. But the Dreamguide alone should have the authority – '

'Please!' The Doctor's expression was imploring. His uneasy eyes took in the glowing gateway – the green-robed Amarill – the parachute, descending, with something attached to it. He licked his lips. 'The Dreamguide, as you know her, no longer exists. Her mental cells – the Pridka minds themselves – have been invaded by a hideous parasite. Can't you feel it in your own mind?'

The Pridka hesitated. He looked up at the gateway, and what he saw must have convinced him for, after a reverential bow, no doubt out of habit, he placed his hands on the globe and began to operate unseen controls, in symbiosis of mind and flesh.

Cheynor grabbed the Doctor's arm. 'Doctor, look!'

Amarill, totally freed from the field of the gateway,

239

staggered forward on to the ramp and slumped, as if the strings controlling her had been cut.

The senior Pridka looked up from the console. 'I can't discontinue the process. It's become autonomous!'

'I rather feared as much,' said the Doctor quietly.

There was a sound from the gateway, like a scream of triumph mixed with the roar of a furnace. Light poured out, for a second illuminating the entire chamber, from the steel floor to the high vaults and inert gravpads. Then, it gathered itself into a bright image of the cleanest bone-white and the darkest black – a face, forming in the triangle of the gateway. It blazed with hotter, brighter power than ever before.

'Oh, dear,' said the Doctor worriedly. 'Now we really are in trouble.' He gripped Cheynor's arms and looked him in the eye. 'What were you thinking of when the eagle attacked you?'

He looked momentarily confused. 'Conflict. War. The futility of my entire career.'

'I see, looking on the bright side,' muttered the Doctor. 'That wasn't an eagle, it was the assimilation of your fears and hatreds, just as that canister descending on the parachute is – ' and the Doctor looked up, staring hard at it ' – not a plasma bomb, but a nectarine.'

He was just in time, and his conviction must have been total, for at that very second the parachute smacked to the floor, scattering chunks of soft yellow fruit. 'Look after Amarill,' the Doctor said. 'I'm going to get Suzi.' He handed his umbrella to the senior Pridka, and his hat to Cheynor.

In the gateway, the elongated face was beginning to form, shimmering as if made up of smaller globules. The huge stripe of a smile, the deep, intoxicating eyes, the cascade of hair, all were present and clear.

It could have been Jirenal. It could have been Kelzen. It could have been Shanstra. It was feeding off the mental force of the strongest gathering of minds in the universe, and it was growing stronger.

240

'Doctor,' said Cheynor worriedly, 'let me come with you.'

'No. Stay here and help our friend here monitor the controls.'

'Doctor – '

'Yes, it's foolhardy and terribly dangerous.'

Cheynor looked astonished. 'But that's what I was going to say!'

'I know.' The Doctor steeled himself. 'Now you see why I have the advantage over you.' He rubbed his hands together like an athlete preparing for a run. 'I didn't get where I am today,' he muttered, 'by being sensible and safe.'

He ran up the ramp, took a flying jump, and leapt into the heart of the incandescent gateway.

Come, then.

Shanstra's whirlpool of light tore through the house, shredding the paintings to canvas, shattering vases with explosive retorts, with fountains of burnt earth. She embraced it, feeling her mind swelling with the power.

'Everything harmonizing. Everything as nothing. As colours blend into white, sounds into the ultimate tone, so existence moves towards a single, cohesive whole. The Infinite Requiem.'

She could do it, if she wanted to.

She could cross over, if she wanted to.

She could reunite with Kelzen and Jirenal, if she wanted to.

She didn't.

'Five hundred to battle source. Hold steady.'

The ground rushed past under Bernice Summerfield.

Banksburgh would become one of those ghost cities now, she thought, a city of wreckage and skeletons, metal bones and human bones, testimony to lives fought for, won and lost. A place where the memories were etched into the surface, waiting for the archaeologists like herself to come along and uncover its secret history.

241

The rushing red earth gave way to crumbling perimeter walls. Liebniz took the skimmer up and the city opened out beneath them, tilted like a 3-D map.

'Follow my mark,' he instructed into his comlink. 'And remember, we want to cause the maximum disturbance. You won't do that by getting yourselves killed.'

Livewire slammed the skimmer controls into full throttle, then leapt out, hit the bank, rolled on to her shoulder. She went over and over and over, conscious of the undergrowth lashing at her face. She slithered in the mud, down into the ditch that protected the house. As soon as she dared – a matter of seconds – she looked up.

The skimmer hurtled forward, churned the gravel surface of the drive. It hit the big iron gates, smashing them open, scattering fragments of metal and glass across the drive, and within a second, three of Shanstra's controlled Phractons converged on it.

They blasted the skimmer without a moment's hesitation. It glowed in the aura of three beams for an instant and then lost form and substance in a billowing cloud of flame and smoke.

Livewire buried her head in the mud. When she lifted it a few seconds later, and peered through the cover of the thick undergrowth, the skimmer was still burning, like a pyre. Like her anger.

She wriggled back into the hollow of the ditch, and started looking for a good strong piece of flint.

'There it is,' Leibniz murmured, as the sparkling gold roof of the vice-governor's residence came into view. 'We're going to come in on Durorvernum Square,' he said to Bernice. 'It's the best landing site nearby.'

She nodded.

Leibniz activated the comlink again, as the ground rushed closer, details coming into view. 'Blue leader to all units. Engage.'

The bombardment began.

* * *

242

Shanstra stood up, the house shaking around her. A crack, like a map of a river and its tributaries, formed across the ancient plaster ceiling above her. She laughed, her mouth wide open to catch the dust as it cascaded down upon her. She let it fall, caressing her body, making grey rivulets across her black one-piece suit, her cloak, her hair.

She felt the rushing wind, saw the brightness of the burning skimmer at the end of the drive. Closing her eyes, Shanstra concentrated more. She recreated the picture through the Phractons' sensory inputs: the splash of water in the three ornamental fountains on the front lawn, the dark, wistful green of cypress trees. She went further, heading for the burning skimmer, and concentrated on it until she could smell the strangely natural aroma of the burning grass, the industrial stink of incinerated metal and plastic. Something else burned in the driveway. Like a streak of pure hatred, pure pain.

Shanstra frowned, tried to focus the mental image. A mind, launching itself at great speed towards the house.

The huntress has changed her prey.

Shanstra laughed delightedly. More sport! The humans had seen fit, in their limited wisdom, to give her a new plaything. She gathered a shaft of thought and launched it, like a javelin, from the house.

Livewire stood in the driveway, the wreck of the skimmer still belching smoke. There were a dozen Phractons converging on her like antibodies swimming towards an infection, ready to eliminate it without a moment's hesitation.

Livewire smiled.

Behind the Phractons, the three ornamental fountains suddenly exploded, spouting flame and stone in place of water.

There were figures now, emerging from the smoke, shadowy, scattering to cover a wide range. Bright beams began to slice the air.

She hit the ground, praying and counting.

'Suzi!'

She heard the voice. She knew she ought to remember it from somewhere. The spectre of Colm Oswyn had receded, but the cold mist was gathering in a whirlpool, whipping up weirdly shaped plants and thorns in the water.

The Doctor's hand was on her wrist. He had a surprisingly strong grip for such a small man, she noticed. 'Come on,' he said. 'I'm having it deactivated.'

For a moment, she was dazed. She smiled at him, saw him through a haze of salt water. 'I did it, Doctor,' she said. 'I forgave myself. They tried to use Colm against me, but it didn't work.'

'Good,' he murmured, but it did not sound at all good the way he said it.

'Aren't you proud of me?' she asked desperately.

The Doctor glowered. 'Forgave yourself, you say? You haven't even admitted responsibility yet. You left a man to die, and all you've found yourself doing is feeling better about it! That's not redemption, Suzi.'

The jungle was darkening around them, shapes shifting into blackness, merging with one another.

'What's happening?' Suzi asked, scowling.

'Nothing of any importance.'

'I may be a mere Earthling, but I'm not stupid, Doctor. Don't patronize me.'

He smiled briefly. 'You remind me of Sarah Jane. The Dreamguide has effectively been taken over by Jirenal. He is the Dreamguide, the Pridka's minds: the blood and nervous system of the centre. I'd imagine that the environment is reverting to its natural, default appearance now that it's no longer feeding on your mind.' The Doctor looked up, raised his voice. 'Isn't that right, Jirenal?'

The Sensopath stepped out of the shadows in front of them, and Suzi had to catch her breath.

It might have been Shanstra – the rich, dark hair and the high-boned face were hers. But there was something heavier and more aggressive about the features, less refined and noble than Shanstra had appeared to Suzi. She kept her distance. Physically and mentally.

244

'Yes, Doctor,' Jirenal purred. 'You are, as ever, correct.'

There was one small pool of light left, and it contained the Doctor, Suzi and the Sensopath.

'Should we be getting out?' Suzi asked.

'Unfortunately not,' said the Doctor, a little guiltily. 'You see, I intended this to happen. And now that I'm here, in the realm of the Dreamguide, I don't want to miss the opportunity to put my plans into effect.' He smiled at her.

Suzi did not smile back. 'You ... sent me in here, Doctor.' A terrible suspicion was growing in her mind.

'Yes,' he said.

'Go on, Doctor.' The Sensopath's tone was mocking as he circled them in the pool of light. 'Tell the young lady what you intended to do.'

The Doctor did not look at Suzi. 'I needed some way of making Shanstra show her hand. Of drawing her out. Your mind has been closer to her than anyone's.' Suzi saw him risk a brief look at her now, but she made sure her face gave nothing away. 'I'm afraid,' he said, 'that my attempt at hypnotherapy simply put a block on your link to the Sensopath. I couldn't eliminate her influence totally from you, even if I'd wanted to. I needed to know whose side Jirenal was on. And so I provided you as a point of reference. I knew that Shanstra would make her move ... as soon as your mind could be accessed by the Dreamguide.'

Suzi just stared at him in disgust.

'And, of course,' said Jirenal in tones of quiet confidence, 'I am the Dreamguide now. Every creature, every humanoid or other species who comes to this centre will experience the same treatment as they have been getting for centuries, just as the Pridka have now experienced it themselves.' He smiled, a flash of white in the darkness. 'A feeling of utter contentment. Of peace with the world. And all because they will have been absorbed into our universal mind.'

The Doctor's voice was quiet and threatening. 'Shanstra

245

may have convinced you, but she hasn't convinced Kelzen. I know that much for certain.'

Jirenal spread his hands. 'It does not matter, Doctor. Kelzen is but a part of me, a part of Shanstra.' He smiled, tapped the side of his nose. 'Oh, I'd like to book myself a little more mental communion with you, Doctor. Just to extract Kelzen's location from you. You understand, of course, that your consent is requested, but – ' he spread his hands ' – regrettably not a prerequisite.'

The Doctor smiled humourlessly.

'Our power will grow,' Jirenal said, 'with each successive mind. Soon, there will be millions of cells making up our Unity. Then billions. Eventually, when we have the power, we can expand from this Centre into other sectors of the Galaxy. There will, eventually, be no cosmos. Only the mind, the music of harmonious minds. Only the Infinite Requiem being played for all eternity.'

'But what for?' gasped Suzi in horror. 'What possible purpose could you have for wanting to do this?'

Jirenal opened his eyes wide in innocent delight.

'Why,' he said, 'because it is beautiful.'

Livewire was alive. She breathed deeply several times, listened to her heart pummelling her body, and peeped out from behind the remains of the fountain. The lawn of the house was like one of the circles of hell, filled with the screams of the dying.

Now, there came the noise of the fighters returning for another strafe. Louder and louder.

Livewire pressed herself up against the stone and caressed the new arrow which she had made in her place of hiding. It was not as good as the last one, for she had not had time to hone it, but the flint was sharp and the shaft, of the smoothest turstati wood, was firm.

The fighters screamed over the crenellated rooftops. She heard plasma bolts cut through the air, and a shattering explosion which sounded as if it had torn out a sizeable portion of the house.

She risked a look. The whole of the western wing was

246

ablaze, a torrent of orange and black pouring from the broken windows.

Two *Phoenix* troopers had dropped for cover behind the remains of a stone wall, and were engaging a single member of Shanstra's Phractons in combat. Livewire saw pulse after pulse raking the surface of the Phracton globe, ensnaring it in jittery crackles of energy, like living creatures.

She loaded her crossbow.

If this was war, she wasn't intending to miss out on it.

Bernice ran.

She was following Leibniz and two troopers, and expecting at any moment to be cut down by a volley of shots from the distant Phractons. But, she reasoned, they could be just as confused as she was; the fire and smoke on the grand lawn had given it a haze of total chaos.

Unbearable heat seemed to be coming from all sides. She saw Leibniz stop, rap out instructions into his comlink.

Something stirred in the billowing smoke by the entrance to the house: something round, glistening and moving.

'Leibniz!' Bernice yelled.

For a moment, the two of them stood there, immobile on the battlefield, watching the Phracton motor unit float out of the smoke with its laser-tube extended.

Leibniz's gun swung to cover the Phracton.

Bernice felt as if time had stopped. She could hear the roaring of the flames in the background, but she did not want her mind to linger on the sound, knowing all too well what it brought back for her.

Then the speaker-grille buzzed: 'Re-group – your forces – Trau Leib-niz. We will de-fend – here.'

Benny felt relief rush through her, and saw Leibniz relax too.

'Don't do things like that,' he said to the Phracton, lowering his pistol. 'I was about to kill you.'

247

26

The Quality of Mercy

'I had hopes for you. I came here thinking I could reason with you, the last of the Sensopaths.' The Doctor made no attempt to veil his disgust. 'Instead, I find you steeping yourself in acts of barbarism to rival Shanstra's own.'

The two of them were circling one another, like dogs squaring up for a fight.

'I see,' Jirenal murmured, amused. 'You had hoped to appeal to what you would call my "better nature"?'

'Don't you find it strange? That such an advanced race should have nothing better to occupy itself with than a complex form of bullying?'

'And what right do these other . . . animal races have to the existence you would afford them, Doctor?' For the first time, Jirenal sounded truly angered. 'Do you realize how little their shallow, one-dimensional existences mean to us? Even those who call themselves telepaths, telekinetics, parapsychics. Just children, playing games for which they will never know the rules!'

'The Pridka know the rules. They are noble, proud, beautiful. Amarill was, once, before you destroyed her! And humanity – they may not be perfect, but they have rules too! This is humanity! Look!' And he pointed to Suzi Palsson. 'A human being. A complete person whose existence, no, whose life has been made worthwhile because she stopped being frightened of the past. And when she's accepted some guilt for her actions – ' the

Doctor met Suzi's gaze ' – her life will be ready to start again!' The Doctor lifted his chin and stared Jirenal in the eye. 'Little triumphs, little tragedies. Learning to live with loss, and redemption. It's part of being individual, Jirenal.'

Suzi swallowed. 'Don't push him too far, Doctor – '

'It's all right,' he whispered. 'I know what I'm doing.'

The Sensopath made a dismissive sound, a sneer on his long, white face. 'How many times have you trodden a caterpillar underfoot? Or watched a wasp try to escape from a glass, struggling feebly until it runs out of air?' Jirenal's huge grin swept across his face in a tide of red and white, cartoon-huge, horrible. 'These beings are all wasps, and caterpillars.'

'What hideous arrogance,' the Doctor muttered. 'Your new-found existence hasn't given you any concept of individual freedom.'

'Which means, Doctor?' Jirenal spread his hands.

'Which means that you're not keen to retain your existence as Jirenal, as a whole being. You want to be reunited with Shanstra. Strange. Very strange.' The Doctor lowered his voice to a mere whisper. 'Now, I wonder what Kelzen thinks about that?'

Horst Leibniz had seen Karin dying several times over already.

His wife's eyes seemed to rise from a sea of glutinous mass in his mind – before his eyes –

In another world – one which might have been called real by another Horst Leibniz, one of flesh and blood – he was *kicking in a door, bursting through into a marble hall, his boots crunching on glass.*

Karin's eyes were those shards of broken glass, the emotions of pain pouring out into him from her plague-wracked body. Into his own mind. Only she didn't know that was happening, she had never known what she'd married.

The toxin was of Draconian origin, swift and efficient. The assassin – not even a name to her former employer –

249

*had launched the dart from a pistol, among the crowds that
afternoon in the Experience Park on Magellani.*

*And Karin had slipped, falling in Horst Leibniz's arms,
the life slipping out of her as the escalator carried them down.*

He lifted his goggles, motioning the squad of troopers
to take up positions in the hall.

With the screams of her death in his mind.

The glass was a shattered chandelier, spread across the
marble floor like a carpet of ice.

Bernice, next to him, drew breath. Leibniz looked up.
He saw a big, winding staircase of red, strewn with dust
and rubble, the carpet torn and burned in patches. And
standing at the top of the stairs, lounging on the banister
and watching them like a hungry lioness, was Shanstra.

Bernice had not been at all sure about the wisdom of
actually confronting Shanstra, but the Doctor had been
adamant about this. He had told her not to worry, saying
he would be dealing with the most difficult and dangerous
task when the time came.

This was not reassuring. It sounded to Benny as if it
came from *101 Ways to Pacify a Companion*.

She hardly dared even breathe. She had to have faith
in the Doctor, now, the Doctor who was thousands of
light years and millennia away. But still, she reflected, by
the usual paradoxes, they were linked to the Doctor
through the gateway of this creature.

She – it – was approaching them. Benny's heart was
beating fast, her fear stronger than the taste of smoke in
her mouth and the ringing of battle in her ears. That, she
thought, had been one of the differences between her and
Ace. Benny liked to admit her fears, but Ace had always
been one for pretending she didn't really have any.

Well, Summerfield, she thought, this is another fine
mess the Doctor's got us into. And I don't think he's sure
how we're meant to get out of it, this time.

'Have you come to play?' purred the Sensopath, as she
slinked down the stairs towards them like some celluloid
goddess. 'How nice. I have so very few diversions.'

* * *

250

'Now, Kelzen!' cried the Doctor.

There was a flickering in the darkness of the Dream-guide's domain, like an inquisitive ghost. Suzi saw Jirenal's arm suddenly flung out as if he were being pinned to the darkness, and his body rippling like an unsteady reflection.

The blue-cloaked form of Kelzen was taking shape around him. The faces merged into one, the hair, glossy and even longer than before, seeming to coil around itself and tangle in all directions.

'What's happening?' Suzi gasped.

'The inevitable,' said the Doctor.

Leibniz and Bernice exchanged glances. 'If you'll give us a few minutes of your time,' Bernice ventured, 'we'd like to talk.'

And why bother lying? she thought in desperation. All she has to do is –

Too late. She had done it.

Reality warped in the house. The floor in front of Bernice shattered open in five different places, scattering shards of chandelier and marble.

Her feet flew from under her. Tentacles had sprung from nowhere, were slithering across the floor. One of them had grabbed her firmly by the ankle, biting, while others were reaching out for her wrists.

'Worried about going under, *Professor* Summerfield?' said the echoing voice of Shanstra. 'They were always there, you know. Always just about to find you out.'

Benny, gasping, grabbed a table leg. The tentacles continued to pull her into the gaping cracks in the floor. She realized that Leibniz and the troopers had fallen to their knees, and had their hands clamped over their ears.

Her hands were sweaty on the table-leg.

Shanstra's laughter echoed around the house.

Livewire ran across the flat roof, screened from below by a wall of fire. She launched herself at the nearest latticed window in a ferocious jump-kick, sending most of the window's structure scattering inside the house.

251

Her head was aching. She could sense herself coming close to the woman who had made Livewire kill her enemies.

Livewire leapt in through the smashed window, landing neatly on all fours like a cat, ignoring the lacerations to her arms and legs. Her eyes were bright with hatred as the battle raged outside, sounds ebbing and flowing like a sea of shouts, explosions and plasma bolts.

Livewire liked to know who her enemies were. Her true enemies. Now, she knew.

She loaded her crossbow with the new arrow, and began to move stealthily along the corridor. The irony of having finally, after all this time, got inside the residence of the vice-governor, did not really concern her. Unlike her parents, Livewire had never aspired to do any such thing.

She wanted to kill. She had always wanted to kill.

'What do you mean, "inevitable"?' Suzi asked.

'You haven't worked it out? Kelzen has.' The Doctor nodded. 'She obviously absorbed most of the truly cognitive processes of the Trinity.'

The two forms of the Sensopath were twisting together like plaited strands of hair. They twirled in a bright pillar of fire, dancing a macabre mental-physical two-step.

'So Kelzen's on our side?'

'I certainly hope so.' The Doctor raised his voice, addressed it to the agonized, nebulous form of the Sensopaths. 'Jirenal, look inside Kelzen! Look there, and see what you find! There is the presence of a human. A sentient being call Sanjay Meswani, who will live because Kelzen has chosen not to destroy him.'

Suzi was looking curiously at the Doctor. 'You know a hell of a lot about these creatures, don't you?'

'Enough. Kelzen had a talk from me earlier about the power of being merciful. And now, if I'm right, then the dream centre should have a consciousness strong enough to deny Shanstra access.' He turned to face her, looked into her eyes. 'Now,' he said, 'we leave.'

* * *

Livewire saw the dark figure, a shadow, turn momentarily to face her. Then she lifted the crossbow and fired.

And Bernice felt the grip on her arms and legs slacken. It seemed to stop. Shanstra's mind had broken away from her.

Benny risked a look upwards.

Shanstra was staring at an arrow that had buried itself deep into her body. There was a ring of blood around the shaft where it sat, right in the middle of her chest. Shanstra gripped the shaft of the arrow with both hands, her eyes blazing green with anger, her mouth locked in a silent and furious scream.

Benny sensed Leibniz and the others struggling to their feet beside her. 'She's controlling it,' Benny breathed. 'She's using her mental force to contain the impact of the arrow.'

Shanstra, her eyes and mouth open in pain, stepped on to the next stair down, and then the next.

The house shook to the impact of another explosion. Somewhere Bernice heard a scream. She found her hand sliding into her pocket then, and touching the small pyramid.

All they had to do was break her concentration.

'Here!' Bernice shouted. 'Fetch!'

She hurled the pyramid in Shanstra's direction. Halfway up the stairs, it bounced, clattered, resolved itself into a startlingly lifelike image of the Doctor hurrying clumsily to his feet.

The hologram whirled around to face Shanstra.

'Good day,' said the h-Doctor, raising its hat. 'Can we talk?'

For a second the image was outlined in a bright, angry burst of fire. Then it faded, and a charred lump of metal and circuitry bounced down the stairs and shattered into thousands of pieces like fragments of burnt toast.

Benny blinked. Shanstra continued to advance.

There was a horde of telepathic voices in Shanstra's head,

253

clamouring for attention. And now, she could not enter where her mind was. Something was stopping her.

Kelzen.

Shanstra realized, in a bright, loud millisecond, what had happened. She loosened her hold on the physical world and tried to let her mind, her powerful mind, leap through the shrinking gap.

In order to do so, she had to relinquish control, momentarily, over the flint embedded in her chest.

And when she did so, Shanstra died.

Leibniz saw the image of his lost and beautiful Karin fading in his mind. It was as if she were being put into a drawer again, where he could choose to take her out as and when he wanted.

He heard Bernice say something and only then did he become aware of the way his uniform was clinging to a sweat-drenched body, of the grime and blood on his hands, of the wreck of a house in which they stood.

On the bright red stairs, the Sensopath's long legs were sagging now, unable to support her weight. She fell to her knees, then pitched forward on to her face, and was still.

It was as if the last three seconds had happened within the space of an hour.

Above the Sensopath, on the stairs, Leibniz saw the tall, crisp figure of Livewire smiling sadly to herself. She lowered her crossbow.

For a moment, nobody moved. Then Leibniz, wiping his eyes, staggered towards the prone body of the Sensopath at the foot of the stairs. She was as pale in death as she had been in life, alabaster-white, strangely calm and beautiful.

He heard Bernice come running up behind him. 'Careful,' she said. 'I've seen this old vid called *Fatal Attraction*. Just when you think it's all over, the baddie comes up out of the water and tries to throttle the hero.'

Leibniz shot her a withering look. He extended a booted foot, nudged Shanstra's body. It did not move.

* * *

Within the Dreamguide's domain, darkness was closing in on itself. The whirling confusion of bodies seemed to shimmer like rain under neon, and then, momentarily, to pulse more brightly, as if something else had joined them.

You betrayed us, Kelzen.

The voice reverberated in the domain, whispering yet thunderous. An answer came, like part of the same voice, the wind of eternity sighing through every syllable.

No, Shanstra. It was you. You did it all yourself. Now, I have to leave the human boy to his own life. For now we die.

In the funnel of light, something flashed and glowed like igniting magnesium, and then, there was one body left alone in the darkness.

Amarill dell'katit vo'Pridka was sitting at the feet of the Pridka elder, hunched into her green robe, weeping quietly to herself.

Darius Cheynor, embarrassed, turned away. At that very moment, the gateway blazed with new light, and the figures of the Doctor and Suzi Palsson, hand in hand, shimmered out of the domain.

'Well,' Cheynor said to himself, 'wonders will never cease.'

The Doctor, his every movement twitchy and agitated, ushered Suzi down from the ramp and followed her. He took his hat and umbrella back, nodding his thanks to the Pridka and to Cheynor.

'Well?' Cheynor wanted to know. He was still reeling from the events of the past hour, and he had no idea what had gone on inside the gateway.

The Doctor, placing his hat back on his head, drew a long breath. 'Kelzen has made her choice,' he said in grim satisfaction.

The giant face in the gateway seemed to stabilize, its clouds of darkness coagulating against the background of white light, forming a shape. Cheynor watched it in concern. 'You did something terribly clever, I assume,' he said worriedly. 'Didn't he?' He addressed the question to Suzi, who shrugged.

The Doctor's face was impassive. 'She knows Shanstra. She knew that the evil side of her wanted to absorb all minds to exist as a sole, independent being.'

Suzi's mouth fell open. 'So she never wanted to reunite across time with her other selves?'

'If that was all she wanted, she had the power to do that a long time ago. No, she wanted to absorb them.' The Doctor sighed. 'I realized, after I traced her with Leibniz, when she destroyed the sports centre on Gadrell Major.' The Doctor tapped his forehead. 'The thing about opening up a mind-channel,' he said, 'is that it's like a catflap. Things can go through either way. That's how I was able to weaken her link to the Phracton Swarm. But I also managed to convince her it was Kelzen I was interested in protecting. As if I'd forgotten about the third Senso-path. She tried to unite with Jirenal, and played right into my hands.' He brushed a speck of dust from his lapel.

Cheynor thought he understood, but he still had a question. He raised a finger, like a nervous schoolboy. 'And if she'd carried on trying to break through to Kelzen . . .'

'We'd all be dead, Trau Cheynor. Kelzen had been sitting quietly, gaining power too. She wasn't too happy that her sister's plans for universal absorption included herself and Jirenal. When the time came for the transfer, Kelzen was in control. She weakened the link, and stopped it.'

There was a silence in the great hall, punctuated only by the soft weeping of Amarill.

'I hate having to prompt,' said the Doctor, tilting his head slightly, with a hint of a smile, 'but I think it's time for someone to say, "Doctor, you took a terrible risk." '

Suzi Palsson stepped forward, blushing slightly. 'No,' she said. 'I owe you something more than that.'

The Doctor blinked.

In the space of time that it took to do so, Suzi's fist had achieved the desired velocity. The punch took him totally unawares, sending him sprawling on the floor with a loud thump.

Cheynor and the senior Pridka wore expressions of utter horror. Suzi, her hair glinting like armour, strode over to the Doctor, who was struggling to sit up, clutching a broken and bleeding lip. Hands on hips, she looked down at him and chuckled. 'For using me,' she said. 'Just so you never forget.'

Then, though, she leaned down and planted the gentlest, kindest kiss on the top of his head. 'But that,' she said, 'was for saving us.'

27

Redemption

Two days.

It has been two whole days since the loss of our self, our mind-sister. We are preparing for death.

I am not whole again, nor am I quite splintered as before. It presents a strange feeling of . . . calmness.

Our race would learn much from the one known as the Doctor. We – I – became cast into the void for the crime of being too dangerous to live with. For being too far advanced for my own race. That same crime must now lead me away from this world, away from the humans, the Phractons, the Time Lord.

Maybe, one day, I shall return.

The option is there.

But soon, I die. And the thoughts, the memories, all die with me.

That morning, two days after calm returned to the Pridka Dream Centre, the Doctor had several appointments. His first port of call was the restitution network.

The green-robed Pridka in charge greeted him. As they strolled over to Amarill's cubicle, the healer confided in the Doctor that they had already made considerable progress with the subject. The burnt magna-synapses, the fractured interfaces, could all be restored over time, just as a bone could be reset by human technology. The Doctor nodded gravely.

Amarill was seated in a bell-shaped glass dome, surrounded by six white-robed, silent Pridka, their fins rippling gently as they continued the painstaking operation of restoring her.

'Of course,' the Doctor ventured, 'those who do have physical injuries repaired sometimes never walk again.'

The Pridka caught the modulation of his vocal inflexions, and nodded. 'She may never be as strong as she was. It was thought that, one day, maybe, she would be ready to be absorbed into the gateway, to become the Dreamguide. Now, we will be content for her to share her thoughts with us in the smallest way.'

The Doctor sent a genuine smile of affection to Amarill. She would not see it, he knew, but maybe someone, later on, would tell her that he had looked in on her.

She had recovered herself remarkably quickly, he thought. It was not every day, after all, that you had to face sudden, wrenching distance from what you perceived as your god.

'And the Phracton Commandant?' the Doctor ventured.

The Pridka's eyes were downcast. 'We attempted emergency healing, Doctor, after the body was found in your ship. But he was isolated from his cyborg unit for too long. I am afraid life functions ceased during the last micro-cycle.'

The Doctor's next appointment took him upwards, on a gravpad. An info-projector told him that the election of the new Dreamguide from senior Pridka candidates would be taking place in this micro-cycle, and that the rematch between the Rakkhins and the Rills would be staged in hall seven this afternoon. Non-ammonia-breathers who wished to watch from the gallery were requested to make special arrangements.

He reached his destination, the projection halls, and hopped off.

A handsome young human with smooth brown skin and lustrous black hair was sitting alone in one of the halls. Its screens were dark, and all the other seats were unoccupied. He was obviously deep in thought.

'Hello, Sanjay,' said the Doctor affably, from two rows behind him.

Sanjay Meswani jumped. It seemed he had not heard the Doctor's approach. He blinked, several times, opened his mouth and shut it again. He was thinking carefully of the right words to use, for speech was still a novelty to him. 'I . . . have so much to learn,' he said in wonderment.

The Doctor nodded. 'Don't worry. You're in good hands with the Pridka.' He rested his chin on his umbrella, seeming to lapse into deep thought for a moment.

The boy was troubled. 'It was like . . . being imprisoned, but loved at the same time. My body was only half in the real world. Kelzen . . . took over for me. She made everything so easy.'

The Doctor nodded solemnly. 'That is their way. Don't worry, you weren't to blame for any of it.'

'And now . . . for me to stay here is surely . . . wrong, somehow?'

'I suppose I might get into terrible trouble with the Time Lords. Ah, well. I can always come back for you one day, deposit you back in 1997. When you're ready.' He nodded to himself.

'My mother . . .' Sanjay began, hesitantly, his eyes big and dark, still, in many ways, the eyes of a baby. Perhaps it was just as well for him that he had accepted marvels from the day he was born, or this vast distance, in time and space, from his home might have unhinged him.

'Yes?' asked the Doctor.

'Was she a good woman?'

The Doctor smiled. 'She was kind, yes.'

The answer seemed to satisfy the young man, and the Doctor left him there, staring into the dark.

The Doctor's final visit was to the preservation unit.

Here lay the bodies of those whose minds had been temporarily suspended from life. Minds that were exploring higher existences, freeing themselves from the physical, or which simply did not wish to be encumbered – for hours, days on end – with the everyday work of controlling flesh.

It was a new discipline, and only open to certain races. There were many Pridka who found the concept to be too far removed from what they considered their work to be.

A chamber was set aside for the body which had been recovered from the domain of the Dreamguide. Inside the chamber, which was softly lit in olive green, and attended by a single Pridka at a globe-console, there was an egg-shaped, upright hollow, containing the huge and inert body of the Sensopath – the one body that two of them now inhabited. The skin was like old wax, now, and the hair, though still long and full of darkness, had lost its shine. The Pridka had dressed the Sensopath in one of their plain white tunics, the Doctor's cloak and other clothes having been returned to him.

Suzi Palsson and Darius Cheynor were standing in front of the inert, waxen body, watching it with half their attention, while talking in low, urgent voices. They looked like visitors to some macabre museum, admiring an exhibit's form while cagily not quite admitting to one another that they were unsure of its true meaning.

The Doctor nodded respectfully to the attendant Pridka, and bobbed up behind Suzi and Cheynor, who seemed oblivious to him. He tried the other side, leaning around them, but the low and urgent conversation continued. Eventually, the Doctor cleared his throat, and Suzi and Cheynor jumped apart as if a grenade had been hurled to the floor between them.

'Good morning,' said the Doctor, with a disarming smile.

'Doctor,' Cheynor said, scratching his ear. 'We were just, er, wondering . . .'

'What happens to them now? I can't tell you that. They're a race unknown to me as well, you know.'

'But Shanstra is dead,' Suzi said.

'Yes,' the Doctor answered, and for some reason, with that one, drawn-out syllable of his, creaking like an old door, it was as if the winds of ancient memory cut briefly through the room, sending detritus skittering through their minds.

'And so . . .?' Cheynor ventured.

'And so nothing!' The Doctor's face creased in irritation. 'And so the cow jumped over the moon. The princess lived happily ever after and everyone went up the wooden stairs to Bedfordshire.' He sat down on the floor, staring moodily up at the body of the Sensopath. 'Why do people always expect me to have all the answers?' he grumbled. 'It's never that simple. Never.'

Cheynor looked at Suzi, who seemed rather shocked by the Doctor's outburst.

'It . . . doesn't seem to surprise you as much as other people, Doctor,' she ventured, with a desperate look at Cheynor. 'That's all.'

'Surprise me? Hmmph. I've fought the Daleks, the Cybermen and Sutekh the Destroyer. I've made a bargain with a creature of antimatter, visited universes like parodies of this one. I'm rarely surprised now. Sickened, saddened, angered by the things the peoples of the cosmos seek to do to one another. But not surprised.'

There was an awkward silence.

Cheynor cleared his throat. 'Well, Doctor, I think before long we ought to be getting back to Gadrell Major. If we're going to put things back on course, I have a peace treaty with the Phractons to negotiate.'

'All in good time, Darius. All in good time.'

Cheynor nodded. He turned to leave. 'I'll, er, be back in my rooms,' he said, and for a brief and meaningful second his eyes met Suzi's. She nodded softly, and indicated with the tiniest of glances that she wanted to talk to the Doctor for a while.

'Darius – ' the Doctor began.

'Yes?' He turned back for a second.

The Doctor shook his head. 'No. Never mind. I couldn't tell you, even if I wanted to.'

Looking slightly puzzled, Cheynor left.

When he had gone, Suzi sat down next to the Doctor.

'I'm . . . sorry I hit you,' she said. 'I suppose I don't learn. I can still do it, still cause pain.'

'It goes towards making you human,' said the Doctor. 'And it proved to me that you weren't a victim any more.'

Suzi's hands were restless in her lap. 'I've been thinking about what you said,' she ventured. 'About my not really accepting my guilt.'

'And?'

'And, well . . .' She sighed, tapped the knuckles of her right hand against her left palm in a gesture of embarrassment, awkwardness. 'I suppose it was wrong. Leaving Colm to die like that, just out of revenge. But there's nothing I can do about it, to make it better, is there? I mean, it's not as if I killed him or anything.'

The Doctor turned to her and gave her a brief, intense stare. She sighed.

'All right,' she said. 'I'll live with it. At least I can do that, now.'

'You know,' said the Doctor. 'I often think the emotional violence humans can do to one another is the worst thing of all, worse than any of the planet-conquering madmen I've dealt with in my time. It's the most insidious, the saddest. But sometimes, just sometimes, one or two make a new start, and that's all that matters.' It was doubtful whether his words made complete sense to Suzi Palsson, at least not in the way that the Doctor intended them to.

'What a creature,' the Doctor said, looking up at the Sensopath. 'What an impressive creature.' He stood up, offered Suzi his hand to lift her from the floor, and seemed to snap back into the real world. 'You need a good rest, and then a good library to work in. I know the perfect place, actually. Shame it's about five centuries too early for you.'

She laughed, and strolled out on to the walkway, holding on to the Doctor's arm.

On the third day, Kelzen/Jirenal were pronounced clinically dead.

The Sensopath passed into what was judged, by Pridka science and by the Doctor, to be a coma. As the Senso-path's physical and mental constitution remained a mystery, it was impossible to be sure exactly what had happened. All that the Pridka healers could tell was that the vital signs had slipped away.

Autonomous life functions could have been artificially preserved, but the order came from the new director of the centre that they should be suspended.

28

No Other Way

Horst Leibniz stood before the wreckage of Banksburgh and nodded in grim resignation. All around him, the clean-up operation, comprising both *Phoenix* crew members and the relief team from the *Darwin*, picked over the rubble, putting anything of note or of use into plastic containers.

There was a clattering sound from the foot of the hill of rubble, and through the dust, Leibniz saw Bernice Summerfield and the Doctor climbing up to join him on his cairn.

Bernice noticed that the Doctor had been strangely reluctant to talk about the events in the dream centre ever since he had returned with Suzi and Cheynor. He seemed to have become even more moody and grumpy than usual, and as they made the trip from Banksburgh, he had hardly spoken, choosing instead to gaze out at the desolation, occasionally muttering a few syllables to himself.

Bernice tried not to look at the landscape herself. She'd had enough of the stark red rocks of the wilderness, the shattered spires and the bombed-out buildings of this phantom city.

Now, she stood amongst the remnants of homes, with a grandstand view of the torn chessboard of Londinium Plaza, as the icy winds stabbed her body. Benny felt a hollowness, a kind of intuition that none of this would ever be cared about, that Gadrell Major would never live again.

She thought of the burning rooftops of Paris, which she had watched not that long ago. Somehow, this was more desolate still. She had thought there was hope for Gadrell Major.

Leibniz seemed to confirm her fears. 'No,' he said, pouring a hot caffedeine for them both from his flask. 'No, Banksburgh's not going to be rebuilt. It seems the Colonial Office has other plans. There's an unclassed asteroid in the Magellani system – almost a planet – which they think is just ripe for terraforming, and the funds are going there.' He shivered, gripping his cup with both hands.

'Progress,' said the Doctor, hanging on to his hat with one hand while he sipped his drink. He offered no further comment on the word, and left an uncomfortable silence in its wake.

Bernice felt her fringe kicked adrift by the insistent wind, and pushed it back. 'So it'll be left as it is?' she asked. 'In memory of an empty war, for a non-existent purpose?'

Leibniz smiled. 'Well, not quite. There's going to be a forest planted, and some of the trees are going to bear plaques for the dead. It's a colonial tradition, going back to the Mars days.'

Bernice nodded. She knew her Martian history, probably better than Leibniz realized. 'So,' she said, with a fake jauntiness, 'how's the life of a parapsychic these days?'

He grinned. It was a bleak, stark grin, like bones left out to bleach in the sun. 'Mindless,' he quipped. 'I'm not sure I want to work for the Security Council again.'

'Then don't,' answered the Doctor, without looking round.

'Just ignore him,' Bernice murmured. 'He's had a hard century.'

The Doctor pivoted on one heel, came over to Leibniz and looked him up and down. 'It's not easy, is it?' he said. 'Lying to your superior officer. Caught between a rock and a hard place, between the devil and the deep blue

266

sea.' He sighed. In the distance, the crew members, picking over the rubble like grey vultures, were receding, as they moved on to a new quadrant of the city. 'Empirical presumption will always be a source of mistrust,' he told Leibniz. 'Even though Hooke believed in it, and Newton, and many twentieth-century scientists. And Jahn was ostracized for his work with the random event generator.'

'Yes,' answered Leibniz, 'I know.'

'Still, at least you're allowed to live. It could be worse.' The Doctor shouldered his umbrella. 'Best of luck, Trau Leibniz. You'll need it. Come on, Bernice.'

Benny, a little taken aback by the way the Doctor had started to stride off down the slope again, shrugged and smiled.

'Goodbye,' she said.

She wondered briefly what the Doctor had meant when he had said to Leibniz, 'At least you're allowed to live.'

Livewire looked around the shelter where she had made her first arrow. Memories painted themselves across her mind, lurid and dripping.

She shook her head. No more. This place had to be left behind. She was going with the *Darwin* to Space Station R8, and Trinket would be there too. There was a lot of catching up to be done.

She knew she had seen a slice of an internal life which she never suspected, a taste of the power to create and to destroy. It did not feel particularly pleasant. Now, she was ready to face life on her own terms, even willing to accept that Trinket existed, without bearing him a grudge. The two of them had work to do. There would be a colony somewhere with room for a couple of slightly jaded idealists.

Livewire went to the door. She breathed the musty air of the shelter for one last time, and then left.

Bernice found Trinket sitting in the wrecked Londinium Plaza, at the foot of the glassy, twisted tree which used to be a Phracton. Around the square, *Phoenix* crew members were clearing up, and largely ignoring him.

'Strange kind of shrine,' Benny said. 'Don't you think?'

Trinket nodded, while chewing something. He was holding his ShockWave game in his hand, the screen dark. 'It's broken,' he explained. 'Looks like I won't be killing any more aliens.'

'Just as well.'

'Yeah. Maybe.'

There was silence between them. The square rang to the sounds of shouts from crew members and the clunk of wreckage being piled into hoppers.

'You never did really agree with Livewire, did you?' Bernice asked gently. 'About rebellion. Making your own rules.'

He shrugged. 'Problem then is that you have to keep them. And it's your fault if they turn out to be bad rules. At least if they're someone else's, you can blame someone else if things go wrong.'

Impeccable logic, thought Bernice, although not really what she'd hoped for. She wondered what thoughts were going through his young mind, and what would be the best thing to say to him now.

'Don't go soft in your old age,' she said eventually. 'Whether rules are good or bad depends very much on who's making them. Don't end up being worse than them, by trying to be better. But don't ever let yourself be trodden on, either. I'd read *Animal Farm* if I were you.'

Trinket shrugged again. 'I don't bother much with books,' he said.

'Maybe you should. There's a whole library here going to waste. Pack a few before you leave.'

Trinket looked up at her, and saw her impish smile. 'You mean loot them?'

'No,' said Bernice, 'no one else will be using them. I've got it on good authority that this colony's being officially closed.' She held up a handful of disks. 'And besides, I got them for you. Indefinite loan from the archivist. It beats killing aliens, any day.'

268

Trinket grinned.

'Got to go,' said Bernice. 'The Doctor's waiting.'

Cheynor had spent the morning in neutral territory – the remains of Banksburgh's Guildhall, one of the few buildings still to have four walls – with senior Phracton officers, working out the best approach for taking their relations on to a new diplomatic footing.

There had been much twittering and buzzing in the Phracton ranks, and Cheynor wished he'd had the Doctor there to translate the parts which were not meant for human ears.

The main problem was the existence – as the late Commandant had been only too aware – of a strong undercurrent in the Swarm, a faction or pressure group, who were totally opposed to any deal with human beings. Naturally, everything possible was being done to arrive at an amicable Swarm consensus, but all views had to be taken into account.

Cheynor had told them not to worry, saying he thought the Phractons had much in common with humanity.

There was a new purpose, a new fire in Darius Cheynor as he left the Guildhall with his pilot and his bodyguard. For once, he was doing something positive, something that would make him more than an also-ran as far as Earth's authorities were concerned.

He strode down the ramp of the Guildhall to his skimmer, and told his pilot and bodyguard to travel with the remainder of the entourage, as he had promised he would give someone a lift.

Suzi Palsson, with a spring in her step, joined him in the skimmer five minutes later. 'At the controls yourself, Captain?' she said.

Cheynor grinned. 'Well, I sent them all on. I wanted to talk to you about where you want to go.'

She shrugged. 'I'm not staying here with my books and disks for company, living to a ripe old age till I die a well-educated fossil, if that's what you mean.'

'Good.' Cheynor set the skimmer controls, and began

to lift it gently on to its cushion of air. 'So, tell me. What *do* you want to do?'

Suzi smiled. 'I wouldn't mind a lift to Station R8.'

'How lucky,' Cheynor answered, deadpan. 'That's where the *Phoenix* is going.'

The Doctor placed his hat on the time rotor again, and rolled up his sleeves, ready to program the TARDIS for a new destination.

Bernice strolled in from her room, having changed from her borrowed *Phoenix* uniform into her former attire of waistcoat, baggy silk blouse, white trousers, and black boots. She settled herself into the wicker chair with a sigh of contentment. 'So,' she said, 'back in the main console room, then?'

'Yes. The others do have their uses, though. I expect we'll need them again.'

He sounded tired and grumpy, she thought. 'Anything wrong, Doctor?' she asked.

'Hmm? No, I was just thinking about Kelzen.'

'Ah.'

'When Shanstra died, you know, Kelzen could have given her the extra energy she required to overcome the wound. But she knew what it would mean for her, and the rest of the cosmos.'

'Becoming a lump of pineapple in Shanstra's mental trifle,' agreed Bernice.

'Far less. A single grain in a sprinkling of hundreds and thousands.' The Doctor sighed, leaning on the console, and closed his eyes. 'So she let herself die. She let them all die, because she finally learnt what it meant to have a responsibility. And through that they achieved a kind of grace.' The Doctor's eyes opened. 'Perhaps we might learn something from that.' He threw the dematerialization switch, and the TARDIS passed from Gadrell Major into the vortex.

'What about Suzi?' Bernice asked. 'Shanstra got into her mind in a pretty serious way. I know I wouldn't want

270

anyone rummaging like that in my mental underwear drawer.'

'Suzi could have been a problem,' said the Doctor. 'I must admit, I didn't really know what to do about her.'

Benny noticed he was leaning over a monitor screen on the console, and memory came back of the way she had seen him in the tertiary console room after all that time, silently contemplating something.

'Do you know,' she said, 'after all that, I've forgotten totally – what was it you were looking up when the TARDIS intercepted that distress signal?'

'Earth military records,' said the Doctor moodily. The time rotor rose and fell. He looked up. 'Do you want to see?'

'Cheynor to *Phoenix*. Estimate three minutes to arrival.'

The skimmer was heading out into the wilderness now, out to where the *Phoenix* stood like a beacon, like a sanctuary, ready to welcome them.

Suzi Palsson turned to look at Darius Cheynor, and for the first time in many years, she thought she saw something new in the face of a man, something she could understand, which she could respect.

'Coming in for ground run,' Cheynor said. 'Activating retro-thrusters now.'

Bernice, stunned, looked up from the scrolling information on the console monitor screen.

'You're not going to do anything about this, are you?' she said, her face pale in the reflection from the screen.

The Doctor's eyes flicked back and forth. 'You know I would, if I could.'

'But it's not as if it's history!'

'I'm afraid it is.'

'Doctor!'

'There was never any way of stopping it from happening. If it hadn't been then, it would have been some other time, with even more innocents caught up.' He looked up, his face shadowed with sadness. 'And at least we know, now, that Shanstra's influence could not have survived.'

She looked into his eyes and realized he meant it.

And what was most shocking of all to her was that really, she knew. She understood why it had to be.

The fireball was visible for several kilometres. It lit up the dunes and gullies of Gadrell Major's wasteland. Smoke poured into the air, carrying with it a torrent of twisted metal and shattered plexiglass.

The burnt-out shell of Cheynor's skimmer pirouetted upwards, turning in slow motion. It crashed, bounced, scattering flames and sparks as it tumbled down the length of a slope and came to rest on the end of a trail of fire.

Silence reigned.

Epilogue

And Study War No More

EXTRACT FROM PERSONAL LOG, LIEUTENANT-COMMANDER HOLST LEIBNIZ ACTING CAPTAIN, EARTH SPACEFLEET VESSEL PHOENIX, *29TH MAY, 2387*
The obvious theory is that the Phracton infiltrators somehow planted the bomb after Captain Cheynor's return to Gadrell Major. There were rumours of something like this, of course: a breakaway group who still held Cheynor responsible for what they saw as an ambush in Londinium Plaza. Just shows how little they understood of what's happened here on Gadrell Major.

I am at a loss to understand how they feel their cause can be advanced by the elimination of lives in this way.

This sharp, angry coda to all our struggles is made all the more bitter by the loss of a civilian life. I, as acting captain of the *Phoenix* and officer responsible for the evacuation of Gadrell Major, have the task now of locating Suzanne Palsson's family and informing them.

Whatever I say, it will be inadequate, almost counterfeit. It must not mention the Doctor, Bernice, the Sensopaths, all of the strands that meshed together to bring Suzi and my captain together into that fateful vehicle. I must be reductive, I must be simplistic.

The Doctor. Yes. He said something very strange to me as we parted. He told me that at least I had been allowed to stay alive.

273

As if he knew. And yet, despite knowing, could do nothing.

What the Doctor gave us, I thought, was hope. A real hope, not the kind of false dependency with which Shanstra ensnared her followers to absorb their minds. The Doctor tried to bring hope through repentance, through the knowledge that it was never too late to make a fresh start – not for the sake of any spurious deity, but for yourself, and for your fellow human beings.

There may, now, be hope. Cheynor's death is a watershed. The new Phracton Commandant's view is this: if the Phracton extremists really did think that Cheynor was responsible, that he betrayed the Swarm, then they now feel that honour has been satisfied, that justice has been done. The Commandant feels that he is in a position to do business with the extremists, if I can help him.

Of course, this puts me in a difficult moral position. To go into negotiations with a clean slate is for me to say yes, I agree, it was right to kill Captain Cheynor. And yes, it did not matter that you killed Suzanne Palsson. I can tell them that yes, this was war, and there are casualties in war.

So easy.

SUPPLEMENTAL ENTRY

I wasn't going to add anything to this, but it's late at night now and we are on course for the space station.

The funny thing is, I can conjure up Darius Cheynor as clear as anything if I close my eyes, and let my mind wander into that special place it's not supposed to have. A small part of me, maybe, trying to feel like him. Trying to finish what he started. Kind of . . . being him.

Something is not quite right in my head, I know that much. My blessing is a curse, it always has been, but this time it is more as if . . . something is there.

Watching.

LOG ENTRY ENDS

CAT'S CRADLE: WARHEAD
Andrew Cartmel

The place is Earth. The time is the near future – all too near. As environmental destruction reaches the point of no return, multinational corporations scheme to buy immortality in a poisoned world. If Earth is to survive, somebody has to stop them.

ISBN 0 426 20367 4

CAT'S CRADLE: WITCH MARK
Andrew Hunt

A small village in Wales is visited by creatures of myth. Nearby, a coach crashes on the M40, killing all its passengers. Police can find no record of their existence. The Doctor and Ace arrive, searching for a cure for the TARDIS, and uncover a gateway to another world.

ISBN 0 426 20368 2

NIGHTSHADE
Mark Gatiss

When the Doctor brings Ace to the village of Crook Marsham in 1968, he seems unwilling to recognize that something sinister is going on. But the villagers are being killed, one by one, and everyone's past is coming back to haunt them – including the Doctor's.

ISBN 0 426 20376 3

LOVE AND WAR
Paul Cornell

Heaven: a planet rich in history where the Doctor comes to meet a new friend, and betray an old one; a place where people come to die, but where the dead don't always rest in peace. On Heaven, the Doctor finally loses Ace, but finds archaeologist Bernice Summerfield, a new companion whose destiny is inextricably linked with his.

ISBN 0 426 20385 2

TRANSIT
Ben Aaronovitch

It's the ultimate mass transit system, binding the planets of the solar system together. But something is living in the network, chewing its way to the very heart of the system and leaving a trail of death and mutation behind. Once again, the Doctor is all that stands between humanity and its own mistakes.

ISBN 0 426 20384 4

THE HIGHEST SCIENCE
Gareth Roberts

The Highest Science – a technology so dangerous it destroyed its creators. Many people have searched for it, but now Sheldukher, the most wanted criminal in the galaxy, believes he has found it. The Doctor and Bernice must battle to stop him on a planet where chance and coincidence have become far too powerful.

ISBN 0 426 20377 1

THE PIT
Neil Penswick

One of the Seven Planets is a nameless giant, quarantined against all intruders. But when the TARDIS materializes, it becomes clear that the planet is far from empty – and the Doctor begins to realize that the planet hides a terrible secret from the Time Lords' past.

ISBN 0 426 20378 X

DECEIT
Peter Darvill-Evans

Ace – three years older, wiser and tougher – is back. She is part of a group of Irregular Auxiliaries on an expedition to the planet Arcadia. They think they are hunting Daleks, but the Doctor knows better. He knows that the paradise planet hides a being far more powerful than the Daleks – and much more dangerous.

ISBN 0 426 20362 3

LUCIFER RISING
Jim Mortimore & Andy Lane

Reunited, the Doctor, Ace and Bernice travel to Lucifer, the site of a scientific expedition that they know will shortly cease to exist. Discovering why involves them in sabotage, murder and the resurrection of eons-old alien powers. Are there Angels on Lucifer? And what does it all have to do with Ace?

ISBN 0 426 20338 7

WHITE DARKNESS
David McIntee

The TARDIS crew, hoping for a rest, come to Haiti in 1915. But they find that the island is far from peaceful: revolution is brewing in the city; the dead are walking from the cemeteries; and, far underground, the ancient rulers of the galaxy are stirring in their sleep.

ISBN 0 426 20395 X

SHADOWMIND
Christopher Bulis

On the colony world of Arden, something dangerous is growing stronger. Something that steals minds and memories. Something that can reach out to another planet, Tairgire, where the newest exhibit in the sculpture park is a blue box surmounted by a flashing light.

ISBN 0 426 20394 1

BIRTHRIGHT
Nigel Robinson

Stranded in Edwardian London with a dying TARDIS, Bernice investigates a series of grisly murders. In the far future, Ace leads a group of guerrillas against their insect-like, alien oppressors. Why has the Doctor left them, just when they need him most?

ISBN 0 426 20393 3

ICEBERG
David Banks

In 2006, an ecological disaster threatens the Earth; only the FLIPback team, working in an Antarctic base, can avert the catastrophe. But hidden beneath the ice, sinister forces have gathered to sabotage humanity's last hope. The Cybermen have returned and the Doctor must face them alone.

ISBN 0 426 20392 5

BLOOD HEAT
Jim Mortimore

The TARDIS is attacked by an alien force; Bernice is flung into the Vortex; and the Doctor and Ace crash-land on Earth. There they find dinosaurs roaming the derelict London streets, and Brigadier Lethbridge-Stewart leading the remnants of UNIT in a desperate fight against the Silurians who have taken over and changed his world.

ISBN 0 426 20399 2

THE DIMENSION RIDERS
Daniel Blythe

A holiday in Oxford is cut short when the Doctor is summoned to Space Station Q4, where ghostly soldiers from the future watch from the shadows among the dead. Soon, the Doctor is trapped in the past, Ace is accused of treason and Bernice is uncovering deceit among the college cloisters.

ISBN 0 426 20397 6

THE LEFT-HANDED HUMMINGBIRD
Kate Orman
Someone has been playing with time. The Doctor, Ace and Bernice must travel to the Aztec Empire in 1487, to London in the Swinging Sixties and to the sinking of the *Titanic* as they attempt to rectify the temporal faults – and survive the attacks of the living god Huitzilin.

ISBN 0 426 20404 2

CONUNDRUM
Steve Lyons
A killer is stalking the streets of the village of Arandale. The victims are found each day, drained of blood. Someone has interfered with the Doctor's past again, and he's landed in a place he knows he once destroyed, from which it seems there can be no escape.

ISBN 0 426 20408 5

NO FUTURE
Paul Cornell
At last the Doctor comes face-to-face with the enemy who has been threatening him, leading him on a chase that has brought the TARDIS to London in 1976. There he finds that reality has been subtly changed and the country he once knew is rapidly descending into anarchy as an alien invasion force prepares to land . . .

ISBN 0 426 20409 3

TRAGEDY DAY
Gareth Roberts
When the TARDIS crew arrive on Olleril, they soon realise that all is not well. Assassins arrive to carry out a killing that may endanger the entire universe. A being known as the Supreme One tests horrific weapons. And a secret order of monks observes the growing chaos.

ISBN 0 426 20410 7

LEGACY
Gary Russell
The Doctor returns to Peladon, on the trail of a master criminal. Ace pursues intergalactic mercenaries who have stolen the galaxy's most evil artifact while Bernice strikes up a dangerous friendship with a Martian Ice Lord. The players are making the final moves in a devious and lethal plan – but for once it isn't the Doctor's.

ISBN 0 426 20412 3

THEATRE OF WAR
Justin Richards
Menaxus is a barren world on the front line of an interstellar war, home to a ruined theatre which hides sinister secrets. When the TARDIS crew land on the planet, they find themselves trapped in a deadly re-enactment of an ancient theatrical tragedy.

ISBN 0 426 20414 X

ALL-CONSUMING FIRE
Andy Lane
The secret library of St John the Beheaded has been robbed. The thief has taken forbidden books which tell of gateways to other worlds. Only one team can be trusted to solve the crime: Sherlock Holmes, Doctor Watson – and a mysterious stranger who claims he travels in time and space.

ISBN 0 426 20415 8

BLOOD HARVEST
Terrance Dicks
While the Doctor and Ace are selling illegal booze in a town full of murderous gangsters, Bernice has been abandoned on a vampire-infested planet outside normal space. This story sets in motion events which are continued in *Goth Opera*, the first in a new series of Missing Adventures.

ISBN 0 426 20417 4

STRANGE ENGLAND
Simon Messingham
In the idyllic gardens of a Victorian country house, the TARDIS crew discover a young girl whose body has been possessed by a beautiful but lethal insect. And they find that the rural paradise is turning into a world of nightmare ruled by the sinister Quack.

ISBN 0 426 20419 0

FIRST FRONTIER
David A. McIntee
When Bernice asks to see the dawn of the space age, the Doctor takes the TARDIS to Cold War America, which is facing a threat far more deadly than Communist Russia. The militaristic Tzun Confederacy have made Earth their next target for conquest – and the aliens have already landed.

ISBN 0 426 20421 2

ST ANTHONY's FIRE
Mark Gatiss

The TARDIS crew visit Betrushia, a planet in terrible turmoil. A vicious, genocidal war is raging between the lizard-like natives. With time running out, the Doctor must save the people of Betrushia from their own legacy before St Anthony's fire consumes them all.

ISBN 0 426 20423 9

FALLS THE SHADOW
Daniel O'Mahony

The TARDIS is imprisoned in a house called Shadowfell, where a man is ready to commence the next phase of an experiment that will remake the world. But deep within the house, something evil lingers, observing and influencing events, waiting to take on flesh and emerge.

ISBN 0 426 20427 1

PARASITE
Jim Mortimore

The TARDIS has arrived in the Elysium system, lost colony of distant Earth and site of the Artifact: a world turned inside out, home to a bizarre ecosystem. But now the Artifact appears to be decaying, transforming the humans trapped within into something new and strange.

ISBN 0 426 20425 5